Praise for *Three Envelopes*

"This book has a clever plot and plays upon the fear that there are hidden persons out there prepared to do us harm for obscure reasons… There are passages that make you gasp in horror."
Crime Review

"Hezroni's superior thriller debut will send chills up the spines of even jaded genre fans."
Publishers Weekly

"With crisp writing, a claustrophobic atmosphere and plenty of twists and turns along the way, *Three Envelopes* marks Nir Hezroni as a talent to be watched."
Mark Dawson, author of the *John Milton* series

"What a ride! An intelligence world of cracked mirrors, weird echoes and haunting dreams. The story is stunning. It will bend your mind six ways to Sunday and then some. The writing, precise as a laser, runs circles around what you thought you knew was real."
James Church, author of the *Inspector O* series

"Nir Hezroni's *Three Envelopes* isn't your average thriller. Imaginative, fast-paced and originally strange. It reads like a spy-thriller gone mad or out of control."
D. A. Mishani, author of *The Missing File*

THREE
ENVELOPES

NIR HEZRONI

TRANSLATED FROM THE HEBREW BY STEVEN COHEN

A Point Blank Book

First published in Great Britain and Australia by Point Blank,
an imprint of Oneworld Publications, 2017
This mass market paperback edition published 2018

First published in 2014 in Israel by Keter Books

Copyright © Nir Hezroni 2017
English translation © Steven Cohen 2017

The moral right of Nir Hezroni to be identified as the Author of this work has been asserted by
him in accordance with the Copyright, Designs, and Patents Act 1988

ISBN 978-1-78607-379-2
ISBN 978-1-78607-010-4 (eBook)

Printed and bound in Great Britain by Clays Ltd, St Ives plc

Oneworld Publications
10 Bloomsbury Street
London WC1B 3SR
England

Stay up to date with the latest books,
special offers, and exclusive content from
Oneworld with our newsletter

Sign up on our website
oneworld-publications.com

MIX
Paper from
responsible sources
FSC® C018072

To Etty, Noam, and Yuval

NIGHT. AUGUST 1989

Something terrible is about to happen.

It's exactly 1:30 a.m.

I don't need a watch to know.

I wake every night at this time to make sure they don't kill us all.

First I check that the chain is still around my neck.

Hanging from the chain is a small plastic bottle I once found.

Inside the bottle there's a note.

The note tells you how to find this notebook.

That way you'll know what happened when you find my body.

I open the small bottle and check that the note is still inside.

The note says:

> The closet in the children's room:
> open the far right shoe drawer all
> the way and lift up its front edge. The
> notebook is on the floor under the
> drawer. It explains everything.

I put the note back into the small bottle and close it.

I get out of bed and walk quietly from my room to the entrance-way. I walk in my socks so no one hears my steps. Dad's keys are hanging from the lock. Still, they may have forgotten to lock the door.

I push down very slowly on the handle so as not to make a sound and then I gently pull on the door.

It doesn't open.

It's locked.

I push down very slowly again on the handle and again pull on the door.

And again.

A little quicker now but still quietly, 7 times:

Click

Click

Click

Click

Click

Click

Click

The door doesn't open.

I walk back to my room and pass by Dad and Mom's room. They're asleep. Their breathing is peaceful and deep. They don't breathe quickly like I do.

Back in my room.

I remove a ruler from my pencil case.

I take quiet steps back to the kitchen.

No one hears me.

Stuck on the fridge door is a magnetic calendar with pictures of wildflowers. Every month, you tear off a page and the picture changes. This month there's a picture of a red-black flower with the words Coastal Iris written underneath. Above, in bigger letters it says August, and higher up it says 1989, and that means I'm already 10.5-years old because I was born in 1978, which is a number that divides by 2 without a remainder but not by 3 or 4 or 5 or 6 or 7 or 8 or 9. Only by 2.

I open the fridge door. The light from inside floods the kitchen. I wait for a minute to make sure I haven't woken Dad or Mom. If they wake up, I'll say I was thirsty and got up to get cold water from the fridge.

I take the ruler and measure the level of water in all the bottles in the fridge. In one there's 20 centimeters and 7 millimeters and in the other there's exactly 15 centimeters. I don't use a pencil to mark the level of the water on the bottles because Mom tells Dad that's not appropriate behavior for a child my age or any child at all actually, and it worries her.

I'll check the level of water in the morning again. That way I'll know that no one added poison or some other material to the bottles.

I check the level of the water again.

One last time and I slowly close the door.

I peer through the crack in the door to make sure the light in the fridge goes out just before the door closes completely. It's important.

I go into Mom and Dad's room and stand in front of their bed. They're asleep.

I watch them for a few more minutes.

They don't know how dangerous it is.

If I tell them they'll die.

I need to protect us all.

I go to my room and put the ruler back in the pencil case and the pencil case back in my schoolbag. In just a minute I'll put the notebook back in its place under the drawer.

Mom says I should keep a journal.

That's what the school counselor told her.

"It'll help him," she said.

December 3rd 2016

It was 11 in the evening, and an old Land Rover headed down a dirt road under the light of the moon, leaving a whitish cloud of dust in its wake. The nearby town was fast asleep, and apart from the chirping of a variety of insects, the only sound that could be heard was the crunching of gravel under the Land Rover's wheels and the quiet hum of its engine.

The Jeep passed through an open steel gate and continued on for a few dozen meters before coming to a stop outside a small house, then the engine went silent. The dust cloud momentarily enveloped the vehicle, and then drifted back down to the ground. The car's lights went out and the driver's door opened. An elderly man, his hair white and short, stepped out of the Jeep and turned toward the house, striding briskly.

The door to the house opened, and in the dim light the silhouette of a second elderly man was visible. He welcomed his guest with a warm embrace.

"Amiram. It's been a while since we last met."

"A long while, Avner. And I know I'm not supposed to be here. Thanks for agreeing to see me on such short notice."

Avner poured two cups of Turkish coffee and the two men sat at a round kitchen table. The light from a naked fluorescent bulb on the ceiling cast their shadows on the kitchen wall. Avner sipped his coffee. He waited for his visitor to begin the conversation.

Amiram paused for a moment, then placed a thick manila envelope on the table. From it, he removed a large lined notebook, swollen with extra pages that had been stuck inside.

4

"I don't know what to do with it."

"Where did you get it from?"

"It arrived by messenger from the Aharoni-Shamir law firm. I checked them out. He went to see them ten years ago, in 2006, gave them the notebook in a manila envelope bearing my name and address, and paid them $15,000 in cash to hold it for ten years and send it to me today. They haven't seen him since."

"And they're positive it's him?"

"I showed them a picture, and two employees identified him."

"And what if you'd moved in the meantime? Then no one would have found you. It's not like we're listed in the telephone directory."

Amiram sighed. "He left them with detailed instructions in case they weren't able to find me. They had the names and addresses of Shaul Adler, Ronen Agami, Michael Azran, and Motti Keidar, with instructions to approach them one after the other; and if none of the four authorized the handover, the instructions were to deliver it to the Israeli ambassador in London in person; and if he refused to meet—then to the foreign minister's bureau in Jerusalem; and if the minister wouldn't take personal delivery of the package, then to hand deliver three copies to the *Yedioth Ahronoth, Haaretz,* and *The Jerusalem Post* newspapers."

"Suits him."

"He's a psychopath," Amiram said in a deep voice. "Read the first few pages about how as a child he was convinced someone wanted to murder his family. And that's just the beginning. It gets a lot worse."

The two men sat in silence for a moment. Amiram lit a cigarette and inhaled deeply. "It's a bombshell," he said. "It ties us to the mass murder in Canada in 2006. It explains disappearances that the operators division has been investigating until now. He outlines work methods he invented. It's a fucking record of everything he did since he was ten—plain and simple. Everything's documented. I'm retiring in two years and he comes back now to haunt me from the grave."

Avner blew on his coffee, sending a small cloud of steam skyward, took another sip, and remained quiet. Amiram took one last puff from his cigarette and stubbed it out in the ashtray on the table. The only sound was from the insects outside.

After a long moment of silence, Avner glanced over at the kitchen window and then fixed his gaze on the notebook on the table. "Go home, Amiram," he said. "This notebook doesn't exist. This meeting never took place. Move to a different house. Your grandson could be the one to open the next package, and it'll blow up in his face."

Amiram nodded. He stood up from the table and left the house without looking back.

Thick and heavy black clouds filled the night sky and the moon peeked down from between them. Tomorrow would bring rain.

Avner looked again at the notebook on the table. The sound of the Land Rover's engine faded in the distance and then the house went quiet. Avner stood and picked up the ashtray. He emptied its contents into the trashcan, washed it under the tap in the kitchen and placed it on the windowsill. He dried his hands on a small kitchen towel, returned to the table, sat down in front of the notebook again, and sipped his coffee. He was tempted momentarily to burn the notebook and wash the ashes down the drain in the kitchen sink.

Instead, he picked up the notebook and started reading.

NIGHT. SEPTEMBER 1990

I run fast along the sidewalk. I'm on the way to school. My steps are a i r y. The trees flash by quickly. The running doesn't tire me.

I pick up speed and dive to the ground. My body's horizontal, my arms spread out on either side.

My body doesn't hit the sidewalk.

Instead, I hover in the air, approaching the ground faster and faster.

The street is empty and no one sees me.

I move upward, away from the sidewalk.

Higher and higher.

Skyward.

I wake up at 1:30 and go check the door and the bottles in the fridge. I used to have to set my alarm to do so. I'd place it under my pillow. But not anymore.

The calendar on the fridge door says it's the Blue Lupine month of September 1990, and I'll be in middle school next year. 6th grade is boring. I don't get why we need a whole lesson to learn 3 pages from a math workbook. I read the entire book in the first class and solve all the exercises.

At the end of the lesson I approach the teacher and give her the workbook. She looks at me with eyes that move quickly and asks if I did it with Mom or Dad.

"Mom and Dad are very busy," I say to her. "They don't have time to help me with my homework."

The teacher smiles at me and says she'll check the workbook

at home and that if I got everything right, I can sit in the class and read through a middle school math book.

"Everything's been solved correctly," I say to her.

Time turns differently for me. I don't smile and I don't laugh. Not even in my dreams. I don't understand what makes others smile or laugh. I don't even try to understand. Most of the time I protect my family, read a book, or write in my notebook. I create programs on the computer that take mathematic models and display them graphically, like for example the dispersion of a shockwave or a constructive interference. I try to listen to music but it doesn't interest me in particular, other than helping me to identify repetitive sound patterns.

NIGHT. OCTOBER 1991

The sun is shining. The train left Tel Aviv just a few minutes ago on its way up north, and I place the book I'm reading on my knees for a moment and look around. I look at the passenger sitting opposite me. It's like looking into a mirror. The same face, the same hair, even the same small scar on his chin.

He looks astounded.

"You look like my twin brother," he says.

Another boy looks at us from across the aisle. He looks exactly the same, too.

A commotion erupts in the passenger car as more and more sets of identical twins and triplets and quadruplets and quintuplets discover one another.

"Where are your parents?" asks the boy who looks just like me.

I look around. They're not there.

"Leave me alone." I say to him.

I get up and go to the door that connects the cars. I'm in the last car and only one door connects it to the one in front of it via a sleeve.

The door is locked. I push down hard on the handle again and again. Nothing happens.

The commotion in the car continues as everyone tries to figure out the strange resemblances of their lost brothers and sisters. No one is looking outside, except for me. What I see outside is no less strange than what is happening inside.

Everything that flashes by is replicated several times. There are no solitary trees, for example, they're always in groups of 3 or 4—absolutely identical. The same with the electricity poles and the houses.

I feel nauseous.

I open the window to breathe in some air but only feel worse. When I stick my head out the window, everything seems normal. The replicated trees are solitary once more, and the foursomes of electricity poles become single poles again. I draw my head back inside, and everything outside appears multiplied again.

A boy shouts next to me, "We're five, you're the fifth in our quintet. We've overtaken everyone, the rest here are threesomes and foursomes."

I ignore him and try again to open the door and move to the next car. The door doesn't open and the car in front of us moves off quietly into the distance. Someone has disconnected the last car and we're gradually losing speed.

"What's going on?" one woman yells.

"Why have we stopped?" someone else shouts.

"Try to open the doors."

"What's this darkness?"

"Mommy!"

I wake up at 1:30, take out my notebook and go to check the front door and the bottles in the fridge. On the way back to my room I stop briefly in the bathroom and check my chin. There's no scar.

I don't have friends and I get bored being with other children. They're all stupid.

I refuse to go to after-school activities or to Scouts.

Dad tells Mom that it worries him.

"Why don't you go outside for a while to play with Eyal?" he says to me. "He's in your class at school, right?"

On Saturday he sends me out to play with some children who live in the same building. We go to a demonstration that's taking place a few blocks from the building where I live. People are shouting and blocking the road, and the police are trying to disperse them.

The police bring a big truck. There's a structure like the turret of a tank with a steel pipe sticking out of it on its roof.

The truck starts to spray the protesters with blue dye. I stand to the side and watch everyone run away. A little girl in a floral dress with a long black braid in her hair runs and trips over someone's leg. She looks about 6. She loses her balance and falls.

Freeze frame.

In front of the girl there's a fence that separates the road from the sidewalk.

In just a moment the girl is going to crash into the pole of the iron fence in front of her.

Her hands start to move forward to break the fall, but she won't be able to stop herself. The fence is too close.

She realizes she's not going to be able to prevent the fall. A look of fear in her eyes. I absorb it.

Release frame.

The girl's face slams into the iron pole and she sits down quietly next to the fence. She doesn't cry.

You can't see her face.

It's covered in blood.

The blood runs down her face and over her chin, coloring the flowers on her dress red.

Someone picks her up and runs toward the police officers. "Call an ambulance," he yells.

I wait for the commotion to die down and approach the fence.

Under the fence there's a bloodstain and a few small bits of gravel.

I pick up a small stone and examine it.

It's not a stone.

It's a tooth.

My fingers are covered in blood.

I taste it.

It's less salty than mine.

I open the small bottle on the chain around my neck and put the tooth inside together with the note.

December 3rd 2016

Silence and darkness all around.

Amiram wasn't in a hurry. He rolled down the window of the Land Rover and allowed the cool early-December wind to rush in and fill the interior of the car with the smells of winter.

It was good to be rid of the notebook. He felt relieved. As if he'd had a lump in his throat and was now free of it.

There are no streetlights along the access road to the town. Two rows of tall cypress trees block out the light of the moon, casting the road in further darkness. The two beams from the jeep's headlights slice through the black.

Avner will know what to do with the notebook. He always knows what to do, Amiram thought.

He reached out and turned up the volume on the sound system. He was listening to an argument on Army Radio between the program's host and a listener who'd called in and was on the air. One was saying that celebrating New Year's is a Christian practice and has no place in the Jewish state, and what's with all the parties that take place, and that it isn't right; and the other was arguing that there's nothing wrong with it, and why is a fuss made about every bit of nonsense in this country, and that we have no self-confidence if we're scared to celebrate a holiday that the whole world celebrates, and that we're a country of paranoid people.

He must start dealing with moving, Amiram mused. Avner's right, he can't afford to take any risks at all. He'll speak to his wife tonight. She probably won't like the idea, but it has to be done.

The host of the program ended the argument by abruptly hanging up. "And now let's listen to 'If You Go' by Idan Raichel, followed by a news update."

Amiram pressed on the lighter button in the car and, while waiting for it to heat up, reached for the box of Marlboro Lights in his shirt pocket, took out a cigarette, and slipped the box back into his pocket. He withdrew the lighter from its socket and directed its glowing red end toward the tip of the cigarette in his mouth. His lips could feel the heat of the metal coil. Even if he hadn't taken his eyes off the road in that second, he still wouldn't have been able to see the thick steel cable, painted black, that had been tied to two thick-trunked cypress trees and stretched across the road.

The front end of the jeep struck the cable and the back end was catapulted into the air, causing the vehicle to somersault and land on its roof in a ditch by the side of the road. The cigarette flew out of Amiram's mouth and the lighter was thrown from his hand. The seat belt saved his life; but because the old Land Rover was not fitted with an airbag, his head slammed hard into the steering wheel and Amiram lost consciousness. He remained strapped in the seat of the overturned vehicle, its engine running and its wheels pointing skyward, still spinning.

* * *

A figure dressed in black emerged from the ditch by the side of the road and quietly walked over to the steel cable. The person released one end of the cable and crossed the road to untie the other, cheerfully humming. After rolling up the cable and inserting it into a backpack, the dark-clothed figure then walked casually over to the overturned Jeep, looking up and down the road to make sure no other vehicles were approaching.

At closer range, the figure looked like a young man. He peered into the jeep and waited for a moment, stroking his beard. He then reached out and removed the Jeep's key from the ignition. The engine went silent. The Jeep's wheels stopped spinning. The man switched off the vehicle's lights, removed the pistol from the unconscious driver's belt, and emptied his pockets. Wallet. Cell phone. He removed his ID card from the wallet and looked at it.

"It's really very good," he said to himself.

The bearded man then sat on the ground in front of the open door of the overturned Jeep, crossed his legs, and stared with interest at the unconscious passenger.

* * *

Amiram didn't know how long he'd been lying there like that, upside down in the Jeep. But what he did know when he came to was that something was wrong. His head was throbbing, both from the blow it took on the steering wheel and also due to the fact that he was strapped upside down in his seat. How had the Jeep flipped like that without him crashing into anything? He had indeed been fiddling with the lighter, but there was no car coming in the opposite direction at the time and there had been nothing on the road. He was sure of that. His reflexes kicked in.

Hand to the right hip.

The gun wasn't there. It must have been thrown aside by the force of the crash, he thought.

His cell phone wasn't in his pocket either.

Amiram groped around in the dark for the release mechanism of the seat belt. He pressed down on the button, taking another blow to his head as he fell from the driver's seat onto the roof of the overturned vehicle.

He noticed after freeing himself that the Jeep's door was open. He crawled out of the vehicle, freezing in place at the sight of the bearded man sitting in front of him, legs crossed and a gun in his hand.

"What's going on here?"

"Hi. I've come to get you. Take these handcuffs. Use one pair to shackle your legs and then tie your wrists with the other pair. Drink this when you're done."

NIGHT. APRIL 1992

It's raining and we're stuck in an endless traffic jam on our way home from up north. The windshield wipers squeak monotonously.

Squeak

Squeak

Squeak

Squeak

The lights of the cars around us are reflected in shades of red and white on the wet pavement. The traffic ends when we come upon an accident—2 smashed cars and a few police vehicles. Their lights reflect blue-red-white on the wet road. There's an ambulance alongside them. Its lights are revolving red. A paramedic in a light blue uniform is leaning against the side of the ambulance and smoking a cigarette. 4 bodies covered in white sheets wet from the rain lie neatly on the road next to the cars—3 large adult bodies and 1 small body of a boy.

Or maybe a girl.

I wake at 1:30 and go to the fridge.

I measure the level of the water in the bottles and notice that someone has added water or something to one of them. I empty it into the kitchen sink, wash it well with dish soap and refill it to the level the water was at before I went to bed.

The next day at school I'm sitting at recess and reading a chemistry book. Yoav, David, and Amir from my class come in and shut the door. "The nerd's got his nose in a book again," Yoav says, and he grabs the book and throws it out the classroom window.

18

"Go outside and bring me back my book," I say.

"Screw you," Yoav replies.

These 3 boys have been bullying me ever since the start of middle school. I didn't care much about this until now but the book I'm reading is very interesting and I want to finish reading it without interference, so I decide to put an end to it. I remove a pencil from my pencil case and begin to sharpen it. Yoav laughs, "Now the nerd's going to do his homework."

I put the sharpener back in the pencil box, close it, put the pencil case in my schoolbag, and attack Yoav. He manages to turn his head slightly so the pencil misses his eye, but pierces through his cheek and comes to a stop against his tongue. He pulls the pencil out of his cheek and screams.

I quietly say that if any of them reports me to the principal, I'll probably be suspended from school for a week or 2 or maybe even for good, but if that happens I'll come back and find them one by one and ram the pencil through their eyes and into their brains. And it'll come as a surprise and they won't be able to turn their heads in time. Maybe I'll sneak into their rooms at night while they're asleep.

"Go get my book," I say to them before they leave the classroom.

Amir runs out and returns with the book.

I continue reading. I'm already on page 106 and there's an explanation there about reactions in theoretical chemistry. Halogenation, for example, is a reaction in which a halogen atom is added to an organic compound.

The bullies and the rest of the kids at my middle school keep their distance and don't bother me anymore.

MORNING. JULY 1993

I don't feel well today and I'm staying home. I have fever: 38.6 Celsius.

Mom asks if I can manage on my own and I say I can. Before she heads off to work she leaves me a plate of schnitzel and mashed potatoes in the fridge. I don't eat it.

I read a book for 2 hours and then take a piece of shoulder of beef out the freezer.

I thaw the meat in the microwave and eat it raw. I dip my finger in the pool of blood that collected on the plate and smell it. The smell seems familiar but I can't tell why. It is like a mix of earth, mildew, and decay.

I imagine the piece of meat when it was a living muscle along the back of the cow and still performing the operations a muscle should.

Flexing and relaxing.

Flexing and relaxing.

Flexing and relaxing.

I go over to the medicine cabinet and find a sterile syringe. I thrust it into my thigh muscle and it slides in all the way up to the green tip without any resistance. I leave the needle in my leg and walk across the living room. Flexing the muscle and then relaxing again. Getting used to the stab wound.

And again.

One last time.

I then pull the needle out of my thigh. A small drop of blood remains on the spot where it went in.

Later I'll check what happens when you jab the needle into your stomach. If I jab it into my belly button it won't leave a mark.

"Avner, are you coming to bed?"

The voice came from over his shoulder and startled Avner. He was completely engrossed in the notebook.

"Soon, hon."

Avner looked back and caressed Efrat's hand.

"You gave me a fright," he smiled.

"Were you just speaking to someone or am I imagining things?"

"Someone from work stopped by to bring me something to read."

"At eleven at night?"

"Yes, something urgent. You know how it is. Go upstairs, I'll join you soon."

"It'll be worth your while," she smiled.

"I'll be up in a minute."

Efrat went up to their bedroom on the second floor and smiled to herself. She knew her husband well—he'd spend the entire night reading through the material he received from work. She gazed out the window at the orange and lemon trees in the backyard dimly lit by the moon peeking between the clouds and went into the bathroom. Looking at the mirror she paused for a moment. Her face suddenly looked unfamiliar, like she was looking at someone else. Short black hair, black eyes, wrinkles at the edges of the eyes, this person looking back at her from the mirror looked like an older version of her. She brushed her teeth and re-turned to the bedroom, undressed, put on a big T-shirt and got into bed, then reached for the cable TV remote and turned on Channel 10 to watch the late night news. She missed the times when the kids were still living with them. Such a big house is a waste of space for just two people. And too quiet. Way too quiet.

Avner placed the notebook on the table and went to look for something to eat in the fridge. He took out a tub of cottage cheese and spread some on a slice of brown bread. When he returned to the table he set the notebook aside for a moment and quietly ate the small late-night snack he'd prepared for himself. Although he would have liked a break, his well-trained mind was already racing.

There's something here.

Avner flipped quickly through the pages of the notebook he'd already read. He didn't recall seeing anything in the autopsy report about a girl's tooth being found with the remains of the body. He needed to check that out.

The solutions to many puzzles are found within the pages of this notebook, he thought to himself, but why the notebook was sent at all was the real mystery. And why specifically now, years after the death of 10483?

A wry smile appeared on Avner's lips. Now there's a number he'll never forget.

NIGHT. NOVEMBER 1995

The walls in my room are painted white.

I'm lying in bed and looking at them.

Brown stains are starting to appear on the ceiling and walls, and brown water has started to drip down the walls and collect in brown puddles on the floor.

Brown drops are falling onto my bed from the ceiling, dirtying the white linen and wetting me.

The water is hot and steam is rising.

Vapors begin to fill the room.

They have an acrid smell.

The air in the room is hot and damp.

It's hard for me to inhale the brown fumes.

I try to get up, but remain in bed paralyzed, unable to move.

The water is dripping down my cheeks and leaving brown streaks.

It's dripping into my eyes and I can't blink to clean them.

My eyes are burning.

I wake up at 1:30.

On the way to the kitchen I hear my mother crying. She's speaking to Dad. I stop outside their room and listen.

"Dandush, it'll be okay," he tells her.

Mom answers him. "No. I don't want any more children."

"We need another boy or girl in the family," he says to her. "We can't remain just as we are. We've been waiting a long time."

"And what if they turn out like him?" she says.

I quietly return to my room and wait for them to fall asleep. Then I go to check the door and the fridge.

Last year's calendar is still hanging on the fridge. Mom and Dad haven't replaced it. But I know that it's 1995. I'm in 11th grade now.

Lying on the kitchen table is a newspaper with a big headline, "Rabin assassinated; Israel mourns," and there's a bottle of orange juice in the fridge. I didn't measure it yesterday and I don't know if anything's been added to it. I take the bottle and empty the orange juice down the sink. I open the tap and watch the remains of the juice disappear in a circular motion down the drain.

I wash the empty bottle and throw it into the trash can under the sink.

I light a candle and stare at it and think hard about the candle going out. Sometimes, if I'm very focused, I see the flame dancing a little. Once I looked at a streetlight and thought really hard and it went out.

I hold my foot over the flame to see how long I can withstand the pain. I could manage just 6 seconds when I was younger. Now I can leave my foot over the flame of the candle until there's the smell of burning flesh. I focus my thoughts on something else and ignore the pain. I no longer do the exercise with my hand because Mom and Dad see the mark and ask me to explain the burn.

"I accidentally leaned against the stove after making myself an omelet," I reply.

Maybe it's good that I don't have a brother or sister.

I look back through the pages of the notebook and read about the trip we took to Spain over the Passover holiday. We visited the Salvador Dalí Museum in the town of Figueres. The collection at the museum included a life-size sculpture of a naked woman in a glass case. 4 blue fluorescent lightbulbs run the length of the glass case and cast a bluish-white light on the sculpture from 4 different angles.

I copy down the text alongside the artwork:

Female Nude

Dimensions: 166×53×45 cm

Technique: Painted polyester sculpture

When I grow up I'll have a collection of works like these in my house.

It begins with small movements. Things that are barely detectable. The blink of an eye.

It takes me a while to realize that everything I do is being mirrored by the people in front of me.

I sneeze, and the person opposite me, on the other side of the table, sneezes at the very same second.

I can't control it at first. It comes and goes.

When I open my mouth to say something to someone at school he says the exact same word and we both stop, unable to understand how we can read one another's thoughts.

But I realize with time that it's just me and my mirror images in the people I encounter.

With time I learn to control it. I run my fingers through my hair and everyone near me does the same.

I take my telephone out of my pocket to check the time, and all the people at the mall make the exact same motion.

I'm expanding my spheres of control. My influence is getting stronger.

When I enlist in the army, the commander doesn't believe me until I show him how all the trainees on the base scratch their heads at exactly the same time. That's how I make it all the way to meet the Chief of Staff.

It happens during a long war. The situation on the front is bad. I sit in the office of the Chief of Staff, listen to my mission and say, "Yes, Sir. I'm willing to carry it out." I understand there's no alternative.

Armed with a large commando knife I'm dropped by parachute deep behind enemy lines. And there, after I hit the ground and fold my parachute, I take the commando knife and drive it straight into my heart.

And all the enemy soldiers do the exact same thing.

I wake up at 1:30.

My chest still hurts from the knife wound.

I go to the kitchen, measure and replace the water in the bottles.

I pour myself a glass of water and sit on a chair in the kitchen.

Facing me, fixed to the fridge door with a pineapple-shaped magnet, is the draft notice that arrived yesterday in the mail.

"In one dream I see her on the backdrop of the sign at the Geneva Airport. A small girl in a long blue coat with her parents holding each of her hands. They're smiling for the camera, but she isn't. She gives me a piercing look from her slanted black eyes. I can't really see her eyes behind the sunglasses she wears, but I know exactly what they look like. Then the image fades and I wake up."

Carmit fiddled with the teaspoon in the cup of coffee she'd ordered. She was sitting across from Elliot in a comfortable chair at the Starbucks in Hammersmith, not far from the Underground station. People in coats rushed past outside on their way home from work.

"I think the work is starting to have an effect on me despite all my defense mechanisms."

Elliot remained silent. He watched as Carmit stirred her coffee and then retrieved a folded piece of paper from her backpack. Then she placed a drawing of a Japanese girl on the table between them. He leaned forward to look at the picture, which was almost as precise as a photograph.

"Did you draw it? I didn't know you could draw."

"Yes, I drew it. I didn't know I could draw either until I picked up the pen. I've been dreaming about her more and more. She didn't appear in the initial dreams. Only after a few. I dreamed at first about three angels in a large control room who were looking at some sort of giant control screen. I saw it frozen. Like a realistic three-dimensional image in front of me. It's hard to explain, because it wasn't an ordinary dream. It was as if I was there. For a few seconds after I woke up, too. Until the image faded. The girl's name is Keiko."

Carmit wrote Keiko in English characters alongside the drawing.

"That's how it's written in English. When a child is born in Japan his parents choose the kanji characters that will make up his name. Ko is written with the kanji for girl, and mi means beauty, so they are common endings for girls' names. Japanese has 50,000 kanji characters. You don't have to know them all these days. If you know around 2,000, you can get by in Japan. The kids at elementary school learn about 1,000 characters. It's easier than it looks. Keiko can mean 'a lucky and blessed girl' or 'an appreciative and respectful girl' or 'a sunshine girl' or 'a katsura tree girl' or 'girl of the square diamond' or 'girl with the open eyes that herald the springtime' or simply 'happy girl.' But I don't have the kanji, so I don't know the meaning of her name. I haven't seen it. I've only heard her speak it to me. But she doesn't look like a happy child, so I think we can rule out that option."

Carmit took a pen out her bag and jotted down seven symbols alongside the drawing of the girl.

恵子

敬子

景子

桂子

圭子

慶子

啓子

"One of these is her name," she said. "A person's name means a lot. Much more than you yourself usually know. Your name influences the course of your life."

Carmit looked at the sheet of paper on the table. She ran her finger over the hair of the sketched figure, caressing it.

"I was fluent in Japanese after dreaming about her for the first time. I understood it in the dream and it remained with me after I woke up. I don't understand how it happened."

"Don't you use protective glasses?"

"What do you think? Of course I use them. I have no idea how it happened. It affected me somehow. I don't know why."

Elliot finished his croissant. "I think you need to stop the work you're doing. It's all well and good as long as the effect remains just a dream; you can live with that. But the Japanese stayed with you. It's affecting you, changing you. Go get another degree or open a flower shop. What do you need this for? You've already got more money than you could ever spend."

She'd thought about it often. She doesn't do it for the money, she does it for the adrenaline rush. And because it's hers. It's her technique and no one's going to take it from her.

"You are messing with people who don't like leaving evidence behind and you are one hell of an evidence. I don't want to see you hurt. I promised myself I won't let you make the same mistakes I did when I left The Organization."

"You're sweet."

"How are things with him?"

"With whom?"

"With Guy."

"Okay, I guess. I mean, fine. Actually good. Why?" she was caught off guard. Elliot has the tendency to catch her like this.

"Just wondering."

"Elliot, one day you'll have to accept I'm a family girl now."

"It's hard for me to think of you this way."

"Believe me, I've changed."

"Sure." Elliot almost started laughing. "All you need is a little push. Like that film with the perfect wife, you know, when she cuts carrots in the kitchen and then realizes that she was a government assassin in her past life and throws the knife into the kitchen cabinet and says to her husband and daughter 'chefs do that.' "

"She had amnesia. I don't. I know exactly who I am."

"I should have waited for you. I ditched first and left you there with all these sharks." All these years after he left The Organization and he still feels the largest mistake was not taking her with him at that time. He had to disappear fast and he didn't want them to think she had anything to do with this so he didn't tell her a thing. He just vanished and left her alone. What a mistake. He loved her then. He still does. He placed his hand on hers. Her hand was warm. She did not pull back.

"You had to. I did the same two years later. If you asked me then to come with you I would have said no. It took me some time to understand I needed to run away, too."

"I'll never let anything bad happen to you. Carmit, you have to stop. It's not worth it. you are hurting yourself. Don't make the same mistakes I did. This transformation process links you to your targets in a way you'll be able to understand only years from now. Get out of that business."

"Eventually I will, but not just yet. Elliot, what happened today? You're gloomier than ever and too nostalgic."

"I'm worried. You know Japanese now, you can draw, the dreams are intensifying, it is happening to you much faster than what I have experienced."

"You got over it."

"Took me years after I quit."

They sat drinking their coffees in silence and then got up, put on their coats, and went outside.

Elliot kissed Carmit on the cheek. "Take care of yourself," he said.

Carmit slung her backpack over her shoulder. She smiled at Elliot, pressed her hand to her lips, and blew him a kiss. Then she headed off in the direction of the Underground.

Elliot looked around him trying to identify anything unusual and smiled to himself. He'd left The Organization years ago and was still acting paranoid. They entrenched it into him.

NIGHT. AUGUST 1997

The whole world stops one day and only I keep moving.

I walk through the quiet streets and look at all the people who are frozen in place. Some are hurrying to work with bags in their hands and some are sitting in their cars or at cafés.

I take a seat at a café next to a woman who's looking out through the large glass window at the frozen street.

I sip her coffee.

It's sweet.

Not good.

I move among the tables and sip from all the cups of coffee until I find one without sugar. I take the cup of coffee and sit down in front of the woman again. She's looking outside with a worried expression. Maybe she's waiting for someone who hasn't shown up.

It's morning, and the sun, too, remains fixed in place, an ongoing morning that could stretch over several days or even a lifetime.

I place my hand on the forehead of the woman sitting in front of me. It's cold.

It's 1:30. I get up quietly, taking care not to wake Ronen, my roommate, who's sleeping in the adjacent room.

I make sure the apartment door is locked and that no one has touched the drinks and food in the fridge.

Ronen serves at the Kirya army base and I'm serving in the Decoding Unit of the Military Intelligence's Computer Division.

"Who has a background and experience in computer programming?" they asked at the Induction Center on the day I enlisted.

I raised my hand.

They sent me off to do a series of professional tests and I completed them quickly. It was material I was familiar with. I had all the tests printed out at home from a server I hacked into on the Internet.

I also completed all the personality tests and provided all the answers that were expected of me. I really wanted to get into the Decoding Unit. It involves a lot of mathematical work.

The unit has bases throughout the country and some have ammunition depots. That's important. I need ammunition to defend myself.

NIGHT. JANUARY 1998

I'm on my way home from the base. The sky is pitch-black. I can't see the moon or the stars. The road is dark, no street lamps. My car lights are the only ones on the road.

The air is cold.

My car is traveling fast.

I see something flash past me and immediately hear a boom. The car makes a clunking sound and the steering wheel pulls to the right. I pull over to the side of the road.

I get out and see that the front right tire is flat and the bumper has buckled. The right side of the car is smeared with blood.

I notice a pile of rags on the road some 30 meters away. It's moving.

Slowly I approach the writhing clump on the road. I may have hit someone.

I lean over the pile of fabric.

It's wrapped around a large rat, the size of a man. It's injured. It looks up at me with bloodshot eyes and bares its teeth.

I wake at 1:30 and walk around the apartment. Ronen's gone down south to visit his parents. The apartment's empty.

No one has touched anything in the fridge.

I've been in Decoding Unit for a year now. It's my job to go to all the unit's bases and install relay systems that send input back to headquarters for deciphering.

I use some of my visits to bases in the north to accumulate supplies. I already have 8 full magazines, 10 blocks of plastic explosives, 2 fragmentation grenades, 20 detonators, and 50 meters of ignition fuse wire in my room.

Every Sunday night I log into the Adjutant Corps' database computer using a system admin account I cracked and check my personal file. If they've written anything wrong, I jot down a reminder to myself to amend it before my discharge—like, for example, to change "introverted and asocial" to "professional and diligent."

December 4th 2016

Avner glanced at the round clock hanging on the kitchen wall and saw that another half hour had gone by. It was a little after midnight. He placed the notebook on the kitchen table, stood up, and stretched.

He went up to the bedroom. Efrat was fast asleep already. The midnight news was on the television, an anchor was reviewing the stock market's performance for the day.

Avner turned off the TV and covered Efrat with a blanket. A light breeze was coming in through the open window. Avner closed it completely. Tomorrow would be a rainy day.

With a worn black bag in his hand he returned to the kitchen. He withdrew his laptop, placed it on the kitchen table, plugged it in, and turned it on.

- Fingerprint reader
- User Name
- Password
- Key Phrase

He opened a new Word document and wrote:

10483–Additional Conclusions in Light of New Information

1. We obviously made some serious errors. 10483 was recruited despite the fact that he was clearly suffering from paranoia and obsessive-compulsive disorder. He successfully kept this hidden from us during the recruitment stage but the notebook that has now come to light clearly indicates his condition.

2. We've been relying on the army's findings and
information systems. We need to rethink this.

3. The army needs to be made aware of some of this
material so that it can fix its procedures.

Avner opened one of the kitchen drawers and found a
packet of Turkish coffee. He filled the electric kettle and
turned it on. While waiting for the water to boil, he added
two heaping teaspoons of coffee to a glass cup. He had a
long night ahead of him.

The water in the kettle boiled and Avner filled his glass
and stirred it well. He returned to the kitchen table,
moved his computer to the side and proceeded to examine the several sheets of paper that had been inserted between the pages of the notebook. They were A4 sheets of
paper, without lines, and bore the same tight handwriting
that appeared in the rest of the notebook.

There were sketches of some building with bars, something
that looked like the façade of a building with several floors, a
bridge, something that appeared to be a network of pipes, a
drawing of a round container with rods inside it, a number of
hand-drawn maps, and various math and physics formulas
that Avner didn't understand. He placed all the drawings in a
single pile and put them aside. He'd go through them later. He
returned to the rest of the sheets of paper. Some looked
like revision notes in preparation for various kinds of psycho-
metric exams. There were examples from Rorschach tests
with various interpretations, tests that involved images with
stories written alongside them, geometric shapes from Bender-
Gestalt tests, explanations about the MMPI-2 test, analyses

of the Myers-Briggs tests, and summaries of sentence-completion and shape-completion tests. Some of the pages showed drawings of various trees with a psychological profile for each tree image.

There was also an army release document with references that brought a smile to Avner's face. The password to access the Adjutant Corps computer had certainly proved its worth.

Attached to the flattering Army release document was a summons from The Organization to admission tests along with a photocopy of a complete classification booklet in the same neat handwriting—and with them, one of The Organization's standard employment contracts. The Civilian Profession section read: "10483 has agreed to biology, chemistry, and mathematics studies at the expense of The Organization and employment in a pharmaceuticals firm (or a company that provides customer service in the field) that includes travel to Europe and North America."

A few more stapled pages contained summaries from one of The Organization's basic courses. There were a number of polygraph test printouts with some of the graphs colored with a yellow marker. Avner assumed they were from the polygraph training section of the basic agents' course.

There were undergraduate diplomas in biology, chemistry, physics, mathematics and computer science, and an approval for a full scholarship toward a master's degree.

A small envelope was taped to one of the pages. Avner opened it. Inside was a flash drive bearing a small sticker with the word, SLOWPOKE, written on it in black ink. He had no idea what the writing meant and he refrained for the time being from checking its contents on the laptop. He first wanted to finish reading through the notebook. He'd get to it afterward.

Avner typed some more:

> **4.** Today, in the age of the Internet, one can very easily study all the psychological and personality tests and provide the optimal answers that the examiners expect. We need to significantly reduce their weight in the recruitment process and rely more on personal interviews, group behavior, (unmediated) observation, and stress-simulation exercises.

That psycho fooled us all, Avner thought to himself. He mouthed the word, SLOWPOKE. He seemed to recall encountering the term at some point in the past, and then it struck him—the Bernoulli Project. A chill went down his spine.

MORNING. MAY 2000

I'm sitting in Ullman hall and listening to another lecture in discrete algorithmic geometry. The material is easy to grasp and I use the time to connect to the building's wireless network from my computer and hack into the other students' laptops.

If I find any interesting pictures, I download them to my laptop.

On one of the laptops I find a rental contract for an apartment and a username and password to access an account at Bank Leumi. I copy them, too. I may need them one day.

I thought the studies at the Technion would move at a quicker pace, but I was wrong. Everyone is still slower than me. Most of the lectures bore me.

I no longer live with Ronen in Tel Aviv. I live in Haifa in a ground-floor rental with a roommate, Sigal. Every night I check to make sure no one is poisoning our food and drink in the fridge, and sometimes I go into her room while she's sleeping to check that she's still breathing.

Our kitchen and living room window face a garden, where Sigal is growing herbs and marijuana.

In the analytical introduction to theoretical geometry you're also taught to calculate the areas and volumes of circular forms. Most of the formulas include a multiple of pi, which is rounded off to 3.14. The moment I begin calculating pi in my head I break away from the lesson and go back to the apartment and mentally run through the sequence of numbers. Pi is the circumference of a circle divided by its diameter. I lie on my bed and calculate pi.

Meanwhile, a large black ant crawls out from under the bed. It's the size of a pack of cigarettes.

3-point-1-4-1-5-9-2-6-5-3-5. I've been on the bed calculating pi for a few hours by now. Starting afresh every time I reach a few hundred digits. The ants continue to emerge from under the bed and are walking slowly around the room. A week ago I dropped a box of Moxypen Forte tablets under the bed and left it there. The ants gnawed through the packaging and ate the antibiotics. It caused them to grow.

8-9-7-9-3-2-3-8-4-6. Sigal comes into my room. She asks if I've seen her sneakers. I motion with my hand to indicate I haven't. 2-6-4-3-3. She returns to her room.

A thin man with razor-cut spiky hair and black eyes is standing next to my bed. "Do you know what a mouse and an elephant have in common?" he asks.

I signal with my hand that I don't. I can't speak. I continue my calculations. 8-3-2-7-9. The giant ants are emerging from under the bed. A convoy is heading for the kitchen. If Sigal sees them she'll scream.

"The thing they have in common," says the man next to the bed, "is that their teeth never stop growing. That's why an elephant has to chew all the time and a mouse has to gnaw all the time. That's how they grind down their teeth. If they stopped, their teeth would grow too large, their mouths wouldn't close properly, and they'd eventually starve to death."

5-0-2-8-8. One of the ants is gnawing at one of the wooden legs of my desk chair. A noise is coming from the kitchen. I shouldn't have left the antibiotics under the bed. 4-1-9-7-1. "You're the same," the man says. "You gnaw away at things, too. You have to gnaw. You gnaw on numbers."

6-9-3-9-9. I continue to gnaw away at the ratio between a circle's circumference and its diameter. The man beside the bed leaves the room and shuts the door on one of the ants, slicing it in two. Music is coming from Sigal's room. 3-7-5-1-0. One of the ants has crawled up onto my bed. I can see it moving toward me under the blanket.

I wake at 1:30.

There's a jar of sodium that I took from the chemistry lab on the small bedside table. The gray lump of sodium with its plasticine-like texture is immersed in oil. If you take a small piece and drop it into water, the lump ignites in white flame and bounces off the surface of the water leaving white puffs of smoke in its wake.

I take the jar of sodium and go to the bathroom. I fill the bath with cold water, take my clothes off, enter the bath, and sit in the water. I take a few lumps out of the jar and place them in the water around me and they ignite and dance around me in the water. Whenever one of them reaches too close to me I push it away with my hand feeling the sting of fire when I do that.

The bathroom is filled with white smoke.

I wonder what will happen if I swallow one of these lumps. Would I spit it out as soon as it ignited or would I swallow it and then would it burn in my stomach? And if it were to burn in my stomach would I explode?

It's interesting.

I record it later in my notebook so I don't forget.

September 13th 2016

"It must be a mistake."

The three angels on duty looked at the large gray wall, which was divided into hundreds of thousands of flat rectangles adjacent to one another, stretching as far as the eye could see in both directions. A red LED light was flashing furiously in the middle of one of the rectangles and the flashing quickly spread to the surrounding rectangles to create an increasingly large patch of thousands of red flashes in the center of the gray wall.

"When was the last system test conducted?"

"Just a week ago. Everything's in order."

By now a large part of the wall was covered with tens of thousands of blinking red lights.

"Okay, we've got no choice. We need to file a report. Which sector is it?"

"Take this down: 6-August-1945/Japan/Chūgoku region, San'in-San'yō / Hiroshima."

"Got it. I still think it's a mistake. How could eighty thousand units stop all at once within a few seconds?"

* * *

Carmit woke up and rubbed her eyes. The clock on the nightstand next to her bed displayed 1:30 a.m. in glowing green numbers. Even central London was quiet at this hour.

She remembered that dream. She couldn't quite recall the faces of the angels, aside from their eyes, which were completely white, without pupils. Their wings were folded behind their backs. They spoke Japanese.

And she understood every word.

She got out of bed, went to the refrigerator and poured herself half a glass of cold water. She returned to bed after drinking it and tried to fall sleep, without success. She spent a few minutes tossing and turning from side to side before jumping out of bed and putting on a pair of gray sweatpants and a black tanktop. After opening the living room window and peering out for a moment she returned to her bedroom and put on a gray sweatshirt.

She took a key, left the apartment and quietly locked the door behind her. She didn't take the elevator, she took the stairs instead, skipping down from the third floor two steps at a time until she reached the bottom and stepped out onto the empty street.

She looked right and left.

There was no one suspicious around.

Carmit started to jog.

NIGHT. JULY 2002

I sit up in bed and place my feet on the floor.

I feel a sharp pain on my right side.

I remove my shirt and see a large cut down the right side of my body, above my pelvis. The cut has been crudely stitched with black thread and there are knots at each end.

I turn on the light in the room and see a large blood stain on the sheet. A Stanley knife. Its exposed blade marked with dried blood lies on the floor next to me. Next to it is a pair of small scissors. They're stained with blood, too.

I walk slowly to the kitchen to drink some water.

When I open the fridge there's a closed jar with a kidney floating inside of it in oil. I must have performed surgery on myself in my sleep and removed one of my kidneys. I was extremely tired when I went to bed.

I lift the jar to my face and take a closer look at my kidney. The lid of the jar is stained with blood, smeared in the form of the fingers that were holding it when the container was placed in the fridge.

From the kitchen window I can hear the voices of 2 people.

One of them says, "The anesthetic will hold until tomorrow afternoon," and the other responds, "He'll find the kidney in the refrigerator, but not the one we transplanted in its place."

They both laugh. Their laughter sounds inhuman.

They leave.

I wake at 1:30 and drink a glass of water in the kitchen.

Sigal wakes up, too, comes in and sits down in the chair across from me.

She rolls a cigarette and lights it. She gives it to me and rolls another for herself.

She runs her nails along the back of my hand and asks if I'd like to spend the night in her bed.

"Yes," I say to her.

MORNING. AUGUST 2003

I receive a letter from The Organization to my flat in Tel Aviv. I moved back from Haifa 4 months ago.

They've called me in to take entrance exams.

I've been expecting the letter. Everyone who serves in my unit in the army gets one at some point while studying at university.

I complete a stack of forms and send them back. I receive a test date.

I prepare for the test. I read all the psychological studies conducted by the test creators and know what is expected of me.

On the day of the test I place 2 tacks in my shoes and walk with my feet arched. When I'm summoned to do the polygraph test I sit down, flatten my feet and allow the tacks to pierce my flesh.

They ask me if I'm studying at the Technion. I say, "Yes."

They ask me where I served in the army and I reply.

They ask me if I have nightmares. I say, "No."

They ask me if I've ever physically harmed anyone. I say, "No."

They ask me if I've ever stolen anything. I say, "No,"

They ask me if I've ever used drugs. I say, "No."

I get a call from them 2 weeks later. "Hi, this is Amiram from The Organization."

We meet. He tells me that I've been accepted into The Organization, and that they see I'm studying computer science. He asks me to study additional subjects so that afterward I can find work that involves overseas travel.

He tells me he'll be my operator and that we'll be in touch after I finish my university studies and The Organization training after that.

MORNING. MAY 2004

Toward the end of the second stage of core training they send a group of 15 of us to perform our first surveillance mission outside of Israel. We are supplied with Australian, Canadian, and French passports and new names. I look at my passport. My name is James Wilson and my picture appears on it. I also have a new MasterCard that I got from The Organization with the same name. James Wilson.

At the briefing before the exercise they explain to us what needs to be done. Each one of us receives a target to follow in Greece. They are scattered over a few cities. We need to arrange everything alone. Each one of us will need to independently purchase the airline tickets, book a hotel, build a cover story, and trace a target for one week. We get the target's details and are told that our grade will be based on the accuracy and detail of the surveillance report we submit at the end of the training mission when we get back in exactly 7 days. We'll need to reach the training base by ourselves. We are not allowed to work together or contact each other during this week.

I am following Nikos Demetriou, a Greek Palestinian citizen living in Rafina, a 40-minute drive from Athens. I leave my suitcase in the hotel room and I pass the next 3 days sitting in coffee shops, walking the streets, and bathing in the sea. I found Nikos's house easily using the Internet on the first day of my mission and since then I am following him around from the minute he leaves his house in the morning until the time he goes to sleep. I prepare a well-documented surveillance log, for example:

- 12:56—meets 2 people and has lunch with them. One of them looks Greek and the other European (blond hair and a lobster tan)
- 14:13—comes back to his accounting firm office and sits by his desk (seen from the second-floor window)
- 15:20—descends to the street and hands a package to a woman with curly hair. He returns to the office and I follow her until she enters a car parked 2 streets away from the office. The car's license plate is ICL-5835.

The training mission is not that interesting but we were told to notice every detail. It is important.

On the 5th day my target goes beyond his habit of eating lunch. He walks on foot for a few blocks, with me at a safe distance behind him, wearing shorts and a white T-shirt. He enters a large warehouse-like building with 2 open doors. I take a look around before following him inside. On the ground, not far from the warehouse entrance I spot a crumpled empty pack of cigarettes that I identify as the Israeli Noblesse brand. I understand that the situation I am in right now is the actual exercise I need to pass, and I walk into the warehouse.

Before my eyes can get used to the darkness something hits the back of my head and the world around me siwils and disappears.

I wake up later unaware of how much time has passed. My neck hurts, I try to touch it but I can't. I remember that I'm in the warehouse, the doors are closed now and I do not know if it is day or night. Maybe they have moved me to an internal room inside the warehouse. It is dark. I am lying on my back strapped with my arms and legs to a metal base of a bed with no mattress. I can't move. Tucked in my mouth is a small towel that tastes and smells like garlic.

I hear a switch click and a small lightbulb above fills the room with yellowish light. 3 men are standing above me. One of them is Nikos. He pulls the towel out of my mouth and says something in Greek. I answer him in English, telling him I don't understand what he says.

He switches to English "you are following me."

I say "would you happen to know if there is a Hertz car rental place somewhere around here? I have been looking for it for hours and could not find it."

One of the men throws his cigarette at me and punches my stomach.

Nikos asks again why I was following him. I explain him that I am a tourist who got lost. I am searching for a car rental agency in order to rent a car for the day and drive to a nudist beach that another tourist told me about yesterday. I do not know who he is and what he and his 2 friends want from me. I tell them that I have heard that the Greeks are a very hospitable nation and that they should adhere to this norm.

They slowly insert a needle below the nail of my right index finger. I lie in the metal bed focusing on the pain making its way in fast pulses from my finger to my hand, then to my brain, then it explodes all over my body.

A couple of hours later my kidnappers are tired of abusing me. 2 of them speak Arabic. I understand them. I learned Arabic in the first stage of core training.

"Are you bringing the syringe?"

"Yes, get rid of his body at sea, put it on the yacht and tie him to a diving belt with weights, dump him at least five kilometers from the beach, we don't want him surfacing at the shore before the fish finish eating him."

In the corner of the room there is a small trash can made of some kind of gray metal netting. I saw it when one of them opened a door to a different room and a bright light briefly exposed its contents of a few cramped papers and a crushed green pack of cigarettes, same as the one I saw outside.

One of the men goes out of the room and returns a moment later with a syringe full of pale white liquid. He bends down and injects it into my arm above the place where I'm tied to the bed frame. I feel dizzy. The 3 men look at me and laugh. Nikos says "James Wilson, you are going to live with the fish." I black out.

I wake up again. I am not on a yacht with diving weights on my waist on the way to the bottom of the sea. I'm lying on the roadside. I check my pockets. My wallet is not there. It's a good thing that I left my passport with most of my money in the hotel room safe. I enter a nearby restaurant, go to the restroom and wash my face. My finger hurts and the nail color has turned purple. It will probably fall off in a couple of days. Besides that, the damage is relatively minor. I drink some water from the bathroom tap and take a cab to the hotel.

I pass another day at the hotel and decide to go back to the building where Nikos works, wait for him on the roof and drop a brick on his head when he enters the building. But I change my mind thinking The Organization will not be happy with me killing one of their trainers and instead I relax in the swimming pool and drink straight tequila. To those who wonder what the bruises all over my body are and why my finger is bandaged I explain that I fell down the escalator at the airport minutes after I got out of the airplane but I would not let this ruin my vacation and I intend to have fun.

On the 7th day I leave the hotel, take a cab to the airport and fly back home. I drive to the training base at the rendezvous hour. In our training class there are only 3 students. Myself, a man named Zohar and a woman named Keren. 12 did not arrive. All 3 of us have our fingers bandaged.

Our instructor comes into the class. He tells us "usually two or three out of fifteen pass this stage, you stand nicely within the statistics but don't get too excited, you have more to go. We have had courses that ended up with zero certifications."

Keren asks him what happened to the others.

"Some broke the minute they got captured, some broke at the finger phase and the rest lost it when the needle approached their arm. You have a week off now, use it to rest and recover. The next stage is the hardest. You'll need to use your brain." The instructor laughs. He has bright white teeth and a face with the marks of chicken pox that he got when he was a kid.

I ask him where to place the well-written and organized surveillance notes I made.

He points at the trash bin.

MORNING. SEPTEMBER 2004

I get a job with a company that develops software for pharmaceutical firms. It's software that centralizes quality-assurance and manufacturing-control data.

Most of the company's customers are in Europe and North America.

Just like The Organization wanted.

I write a small program and remotely install it as a rootkit on both my manager's computer and on her boss's computer.

The software saves a screenshot in a hidden directory on their computers every 30 seconds. When they're connected to the company network, the hidden directories are emptied onto my laptop once an hour.

My manager's name is Nurit.

I discover that she spends a few hours a day browsing through chat forums on the Internet.

She's also in love with Assaf from the accounting department.

She writes him an email: "My husband is out of town tomorrow. Come over at 11 p.m. after the kids are asleep. I can't wait any longer."

Yaron is my manager's boss.

He's a department head.

He likes to give us speeches about the dire state of the market and why we won't be getting bonuses again this year.

He also enjoys a certain kind of pornography and submitting inflated travel-expense accounts to the company.

I save their screenshots onto an external hard drive every month as back-up.

September 19th 2016

The doors of the Underground train opened at Hammersmith station and the rushed human contents of the cars spilled out onto the platform. Carmit hurried to the Way Out escalator and walked quickly up its left side, passing by the commuters who were standing on the right. The escalator took her straight into the shopping center that formed part of the station and she headed for a small bookstore adjacent to a noodle bar.

"Good morning, Mr. Chong," she called out to the owner of the eatery who was busy preparing to open for the day.

"Good morning, Jennifer. Is the new J. K. Rowling in yet? My son told me to ask you."

"I don't know . . . maybe. I have a stack of packages that arrived yesterday evening just before I went home and now I have to open everything and do some sorting. I didn't have the strength to deal with it yesterday. If I see it's arrived I'll let you know."

"Thanks, sweetie. Have a good day. Come in at noon, we'll have lunch together."

Carmit opened the door to the small store and deactivated the alarm system. She removed her backpack from her shoulders and placed it on the counter, and then turned on the light and the heat. "Brrrr, it's freezing in here," she said to herself.

She walked to the small alcove at the back of the store, filled the white electric kettle with fresh water, turned it on, and then went over to the stack of cardboard boxes at the entrance to the shop. She opened the packages and sorted the books. Every book got scanned with a barcode reader to up-date the computer's inventory. Some books went directly onto shelves and others went to the storeroom. After finishing with the box marked *Before I Go to Sleep,* she opened another brown cardboard package. It contained rows of small glass bottles with white labels bearing tiny writing:

Halorhodopsin (NpHR)
Enhanced halorhodopsin (eNpHR2.0)
Enhanced halorhodopsin (eNpHR3.0)
Archaerhodopsin (Arch)
Leptosphaeria maculans fungal opsins (Mac)
Enhanced bacteriorhodopsin (eBR)

Carmit removed the bottles from the package and re-corded their contents in a notebook she kept in one of the drawers under the register. She took a red pen out of the same drawer and wrote the date on each bottle. She then locked the front door from the inside, hung up a sign that read RUNNING ERRANDS, BACK IN 10, on the glass, and went to the alcove at the back of the store. This time she removed a set of keys from her pocket and opened two locks on a heavy metal door that squeaked slightly on its hinges. It opened inward into a darkroom.

She left the door open, collected the bottles, and arranged them all on a shelf labeled Optogenetics—Silencers. Under that shelf was another labeled Optogenetics—Neural Excit-ers, also laden with rows of small glass bottles.

She retrieved her backpack from the counter, went into the darkroom and closed the door behind her, leaving herself in total darkness for a moment before flipping a switch. The interior of the room was illuminated with the weak glow of blue LED lights. In addition to the shelves of bottles, the room was packed with other shelves bearing various types of materials, medical equipment, and small cages.

Carmit slipped on a pair of white disposable gloves, went over to one of the shelves, removed several syringes, and attached a sterile needle to each one. She then took a number of bottles off the Neural Exciters shelf and drew out a measured quantity from each bottle, using a separate syringe for each liquid. After mixing the contents of the syringes in a test tube and drawing up a portion of the solution into another syringe, she went over to one of the cages, took it off the shelf and placed it on the table in front of her.

The cage contained four white mice. She removed them from the cage one at a time, injected each one with a small amount of the solution, and then put them back in their cage. The mice appeared indifferent to the treatment and started to nibble away at the food Carmit scattered on the floor of the cage for them.

Then she reached for a switch on the wall. The instant the color of the LED lights changed from blue to red, the mice flew at one another in a mad rage, creating a white mass of fur and gnashing jaws. Carmit quickly switched the lights to green and the mice relented and scurried away in fear, each one pressing itself into a corner of the cage, trembling uncontrollably. When she changed the color to yellow, the four mice immediately fell asleep.

Carmit restored the blue light and the mice returned to the center of the cage, sniffing at one another for a moment and then going back to nibbling their food as if nothing had happened. Carmit stroked them with her fingers. "Sorry, sweeties. Bon appétit," she said softly, before putting on a pair of orange goggles, picking up her iPhone and opening an app that started to display a countdown. She aimed the phone's screen at the cage and turned her head to the side. The iPhone flashed a rapid series of colors in the direction of the mice and then turned black after a few seconds. Carmit turned her head back to the cage. The four mice remained fixed to the spot for a few seconds and then walked together in a single line toward one of the walls of the cage, tapped on the wall at the same time with their right front foot, froze again for a second or two, and resumed eating.

"Excellent," Carmit said to herself and emptied the contents of the test tube into a sterile vial. She placed the vial in one of the pockets of her backpack along with two sealed sterile syringes. She then removed the goggles, put them back, and scattered food in the remaining cages in the room.

The room's extractor fan is on a timer that operates automatically, in sync with the business hours of Mr. Chong's noodle bar. The smell of the noodles overshadows all the odors that come from her laboratory. That's why Carmit opened the bookstore in this location.

She picked up her backpack and left the room, locking it behind her. She placed her bag on the floor behind the counter, went over to the door to the store, and took down the sign. Two girls were waiting outside. They came in and asked her if she had a copy of *Looking for Alaska*. She found the book. One of the girls bought and paid for it and they both left the store, each with her eyes fixed on the screen of her phone. Carmit remembered the kettle, boiled it again, and made herself a cup of Earl Grey tea.

Hardly anyone came into the store in the early morning hours. Carmit worked through the remaining parcels of books and arranged another box of vials labeled Fear Conditioning on the shelf. She went through her emails and sent off some orders for books.

Waiting in her in-box was a message from a Chinese client with a name and address in Japan and an encrypted conversion file. She'd have to make her way to Osaka in two weeks to look for Takashi Hoshimaru. She smiled to herself.

Carmit left the store for a few moments and approached Mr. Chong, who was stir-frying vegetables in a wok.

"The book your son wanted is in. I'll put a copy aside for you."

MORNING. MAY 2005

Today is Thursday. The phone rings. It's Amiram from The Organization. "I see your work is sending you to the Netherlands," he says.

I realize The Organization must be tapped into El Al's network.

"Yes, I have an installation job at a German pharmaceutical company with branches in the Netherlands," I tell him.

"I have an installation job for you, too," Amiram says. "I need you to rotate a lightbulb for me."

"No problem," I reply.

Amiram says he'll call me when I'm in Amsterdam.

For work trips I fly with a small carry-on bag. That way no one can plant anything in my suitcase.

I always go to baggage collection and randomly select a suitcase from the conveyor belt. I only open it and check what's inside once I'm in my hotel room. Sometimes I find an interesting book or a perfume with a pleasant aroma. Sometimes it's just clothes.

The suitcase this time contains a few dresses, shirts, pants, panties, bras, and a white stuffed rabbit. I place the rabbit on the television set in the hotel room. I don't watch TV. I've already downloaded all the seasons of CSI from the Internet. I use them to learn and memorize all the techniques I need to conceal evidence at a crime scene. I know they'll be of use to me further down the line in my work for The Organization.

I spend the week installing the system for the client and on

Thursday I receive an encrypted email from Amiram with the instructions for my first mission.

There's a conference room on the second floor of the Iranian Embassy in the Netherlands. The Hague—Duinweg 20.

Hanging from the ceiling of the conference room is a decorative light fixture.

The light fixture is actually a listening device.

It's audio-surveillance equipment that can't be detected by conventional means because it has no electronic components.

It's made up of a few small ordinary mirrors.

One of them faces the building across the street.

There's a rental apartment on the second floor of that building.

The sign on the door there reads THE DE JONG FAMILY, but 2 technicians from The Organization are the real residents.

Positioned in the De Jong apartment, in the room facing the conference room, is a small laser device that's aimed at the light fixture in the embassy.

You can't see the laser as it emits an infrared beam that lies outside the color spectrum visible to the naked human eye.

The beam strikes the light fixture in the conference room and is reflected back to the apartment, where it strikes a painting hanging on the wall.

The painting is of several colored circles, with a larger black circle at its center, all on a white background.

When anyone in the conference room speaks, the sound waves cause the mirror to vibrate and this causes the laser beam to dance lightly over the black circle in the middle of the picture.

The circle is made up of sensitive light sensors and codec software that converts the beam's movement back into sound.

A laptop connected to the Internet encrypts the audio files and transfers them to The Organization's computers in real time.

Soon I'm in the apartment with Britt de Jong.

Britt has long golden hair tied in a tight ponytail. Her eyes are cold.

Sleeping in a cradle under the picture on the wall is her baby.

She's 5 months old.

She's wearing a white jumpsuit with pink stripes.

Britt points out the conference room in the building across the street.

"Three weeks ago, someone replaced a lightbulb and touched the mirror," she says. "The angle of the beam is off now and it's striking the building outside the window. We tried to adjust the angle of our flashlight, but the deviation is too large and the mirror in the room itself needs to be repositioned."

She hands me a small laser flashlight fitted with a clip so that I can attach it to the mirror on the light fixture in the conference room and use it to make sure I get it into the correct position.

I call Nurit. "There's a problem with the database server," I tell her. "I'll deal with it over the weekend and return on Sunday."

"It's best you stay on for another week to make sure that everything is functioning properly and no other problems arise," she says.

"I already do too much traveling; there's no need for another full week," I say.

"I'd really like you to, it's very important," she says. "We need this customer to be satisfied."

"Okay," I reply.

The trip from The Hague to Amsterdam takes 45 minutes by

train. Sufficient time to do some planning. I go to the train's bathroom with my bag, close the door and make sure it's locked.

And again.

And again.

I make sure there are no security cameras in the train's bathroom.

I remove my laptop from my bag.

Turn it on.

Place a curly red wig on my head and use make-up to cover my face in freckles.

Take a photograph of myself with the laptop's camera.

Clean the freckles off my face.

Remove the wig from my head and return it to the bag.

Pick up the bag and laptop and return to my seat.

Clean up the image using Photoshop and give it a white background.

I then use a cellular modem to connect to the Internet and do a search on Google for "300 tips for selling on eBay."

It takes me to The Organization's European website. There I click on "Click here for more info" and enter an encrypted order:

Order 10483-1:

Expenses

1. Commercial vehicle
2. Paint and logo for the vehicle
3. Domain name for Internet website
4. Inflatable double mattress
5. 12V car battery + jumper cables
6. Basic toolbox (cutter, screwdriver set, insulation tape, etc.)
7. 12V blower

8. Pack of matchboxes
9. 1 meter-long piece of garden hose
10. Plumbing tools for opening blockages and sewer pits
11. Prepaid cellular telephone
12. 2 overalls
13. 2 sets of clothes
14. 2 pairs of shoes
15. 1 roll of large garbage bags
16. 20 packs of baby wipes.
17. Black spray paint
18. GPS
19. Flashlight
20. Business cards
21. Receipt books
22. My Salary
23. €40,000

Required
1. A Dutch identity card in the name of Gerald O'Connor (photo attached), country of birth—Ireland
2. Visa credit card in the name of Gerald O'Connor with a withdrawal facility of at least $400
3. A Dutch driver's license in the name of Gerald O'Connor

I go into the Municipality of The Hague website and look over the floor plans of Duinweg 20.

I buy myself a pizza on the way back to the hotel. I don't order deliveries to my room to prevent anyone from poisoning my food.

I go into a Vodafone store and buy a prepaid cell phone with credit of €100.

It's Friday and I have a lot to get done.

I open The Organization's 300-tips site and waiting for me is an encrypted message. It tells me that an envelope has been left for me in the hotel lobby.

I collect the envelope. It contains a ticket for a storage locker at Amsterdam Centraal Station.

I go into the bathroom adjacent to the hotel lobby where I re-apply Gerald O'Connor's freckles and put on his wig, then I flush the toilet and wash my hands.

I ride the Metro to the Centraal Station.

Someone in a black coat and blue woolen hat is on my tail. I saw him talking to the bellboy in the hotel. This is one of the things they taught us in core training. If you see the same person 2 times at different places—assume he is following you.

The luggage storage locker at the Centraal Station contains an envelope. I remove it and shut the locker door.

I go into a public toilet, lock the door, and open the envelope. Inside I find a driver's license and ID card in the name of Gerald O'Connor, a Dutch citizen of Irish descent. The envelope also contains €40,000 in hundreds. I put the ID card and driver's license in my wallet.

I then rip the envelope to shreds and flush the pieces down the toilet. I put the money in my bag with the laptop.

I wash my hands, leave the restroom, and go to a café. I order a large cup of coffee and a croissant at the bar and then sit at a corner table with my back to the wall. That way no one can see what I'm doing on the laptop and I have a better view of the black-coat-blue-hat who's been following me. He's sitting at a table on the other side of the café and pretending to read the newspaper.

Using Gerald O'Connor's credit card, I buy an Internet domain name, gerrytheplumber.co.nl, and set up a simple website for Gerry the plumber. I advertise the number of the mobile phone I purchased yesterday and post the picture with the red wig.

I fill the site with words of praise and warm recommendations about Gerry the plumber's excellent service and post pictures of equipment used to unblock drains and sewers in both English and Dutch.

I then go to a second-hand site and find a plumber selling his car and equipment. His name is Ben. I call him and we agree on a price of €14,000 in cash. We arrange to meet in 2 hours.

Black-coat-blue-hat blinks impatiently and orders another coffee.

I use the laptop to design a business card for Gerry the plumber with the number of the cell phone I purchased and the address of the website I created. I also prepare receipts in the name of Gerald O'Connor—Plumber.

I search on Google for a printing shop nearby. I find one. They print everything, their site says. Signs, too.

The printing shop is just 2 Metro stops away. I go to the Metro platform and stand as close as possible to the opening of the tunnel from which the underground train will soon emerge.

A gust of charred moist air hits my face. The train is about to come out of the tunnel and pull up alongside the platform.

Black-coat-blue-hat is standing next to me. He doesn't want

to miss the train and lose me. I turn to him and smile. "Pleased to meet you," I say and offer my hand.

A look of surprise in his eyes.

He shakes my hand.

I tug forcefully on his hand and quickly turn my body to the left.

He loses his balance and falls backward onto the Metro track.

Freeze frame.

I'm looking at black-coat-blue-hat. He's at an angle of 45 degrees, his hands outstretched toward me, trying to clutch the air. His eyes are wide. His mouth is closed.

I can see the first Metro car from the opening of the tunnel to his left.

I remember the taste of the blood of the girl who crashed into the fence. Her tooth is still around my neck.

Release frame.

A dull thud.

The discordant shriek of metal on metal.

The screaming.

I use the ensuing commotion to leave the Metro station and hail a cab instead. Black-coat-blue-hat is not following me anymore.

The police will see Gerald O'Connor on the footage from the Metro's security cameras, but he'll be gone by then.

December 4th 2016

"Son of a fucking bitch!"

Avner wasn't in the habit of swearing, but he jumped to his feet from the kitchen chair, placed the notebook on the table, and paced back and forth like a caged lion.

"Son of a fucking bitch," he hissed again. "He killed him."

Avner closed his laptop and returned it to the computer bag. He slipped the notebook into the bag, too, and put his coffee cup in the sink. "Good morning, honey, I'm at the office and can't be reached on my mobile," he scribbled quickly on the magnetic board on the refrigerator and then left the house. Tossing the bag onto the passenger seat beside him, he sped off.

Had he been driving more slowly and been more focused on the road, he would certainly have seen the dark and empty upside-down Land Rover lying in the ditch a short way from the entrance to the town.

The Organization's computer network is inaccessible from outside its offices. Some of the data it contains is restricted to the main branch or to one of the authorized satellite branches. To access the information he wanted, Avner had to go to one of the branches.

The satellite branch closest to Avner's home was in Ganei Yehuda. It was one of forty-two branches scattered throughout the country. This particular branch is designated a "Hotel" and serves The Organization's employees as a secure location from which to access information or conduct secure video calls without having to go to the main office. Avner rarely visited this place. His office was at the main base, which was a more robust facility. This place was bare-bones.

Avner parked his car near the villa. Decorative lighting in shades of green illuminated the trees and flowers around the fenced-off house. The night air was cool and damp, and drops of dew rested on the shrubs and extensive lawn that surrounded the building.

He got out his car and walked to the gate. He would have turned around and gone elsewhere had the lighting around the house been red—a sign that there were people there who couldn't be seen, or if there was a security problem. But that night, all was well at the villa, and hence, green.

The sign on the doorbell reads THE GREENBAUM FAMILY, and next to it is a fingerprint reader. Avner passed his finger over the scanner, heard a soft buzz, and with a light push, he opened the gate and made his way up the stone path toward the front door.

The interior of the residence appeared quite ordinary. A living room and kitchen on the ground floor and stairs going up to bedrooms on the top floor and down to the basement. The lights in the house were on and rhythmic background music was coming from the living room, but there was no one there. The residence was empty.

Avner followed the stairs down to the basement to find another locked door and above it a camera. He looked up and the door buzzed open, taking him into a small passageway that ended in a glass wall. Behind the glass sat a guard.

"You know the drill."

Avner placed his bag in the drawer that extended through the glass partition, adding the contents of his pockets and his firearm. He removed the battery from his cell phone and placed both items separately in the drawer. He then took a step back, raised his arms in the air and slowly turned a full circle.

The guard looked over the scanned images of Avner's body and the contents of his bag and pockets and opened a door for him in the glass wall.

"Welcome. If you need help with any of the equipment, just let me know."

"All I need is access to a computer."

"Something to drink?"

"Thanks, maybe later."

The basement looked like a regular office. Wall-to-wall carpeting covered the floors and a cold white neon light glowed from the ceiling. The space was divided into several small offices, a kitchenette, and a conference room with video-conferencing equipment.

Avner went into one of the offices and locked the door behind him. He sat at the desk and passed his finger over the fingerprint reader to gain access to The Organization's information system. He loved the outdated user interface.

```
-   USERNAME

-   PASSWORD

-   KEYPHRASE

                    WELCOME TO THE ORION SYSTEM,

                    WAITING FOR INSTRUCTIONS

"SEARCH"

→ SEARCH FOR WHAT?

"SURVEILLANCE REQUEST AMSTERDAM 2005"

                    WAIT . . .
```

→ SEARCH RESULTS "SURVEILLANCE REQUEST AMSTERDAM 2005"

DISPLAYING FIRST 5 RESULTS:

1. 2005 – SURVEILLANCE REQUEST
    MINISTER OF COOPERATION AND DEVELOPMENT
    AGNES SCHMITZ
2. 2005 – SURVEILLANCE REQUEST
    STATE SECRETARY OF JUSTICE
    ALEXANDER VAN DER STAAIJ
3. 2005 – SURVEILLANCE REQUEST – SEGEV G.
4. 2005 – SURVEILLANCE REQUEST – 10483
5. 2005 – SURVEILLANCE REQUEST
    STATE SECRETARY OF ECONOMY FOR EXPORT
    WILLEM VAN BUITENEN

"OPEN DOCUMENT 4"

→ ACCESS TO THIS DOCUMENT REQUIRES REIDENTIFICATION

Avner swiped his finger over the reader again, entered his password, and the document opened in a new window:

DATE 4/21/2005

CLASSIFICATION: BLACK

TO: NETHERLANDS DIVISION – HEAD

FROM: RECRUITMENT   TRAINING WING

DISTRIBUTION: DEPARTMENT HEAD   RECRUITMENT EUROPE

DEPARTMENT HEAD   OPERATORS EUROPE

DIVISION   NETHERLANDS – OPERATIONS WING

SYSTEM: ORION / BASE: MTR / EXPIRY: __ / __ / ___

RE: SURVEILLANCE REQUEST, AGENT 10483

/

IN KEEPING WITH YOUR REQUEST DATED MAY 11, 2005, AN AGENT WILL BE
DISPATCHED TO REPAIR LISTENING SYSTEM #17

THE ABOVEMENTIONED AGENT WILL BE OPERATING FOR THE FIRST TIME
AND WE REQUEST THEREFORE THAT YOU MONITOR HIS STAY IN AMSTERDAM
IN ORDER TO:

    1. IDENTIFY WORK PATTERNS

    2. CONDUCT A RELIABILITY / CREDIBILITY CHECK

SURVEILLANCE STARTS – 5/9/2005 (MONDAY), 06:30, FROM RENAISSANCE
HOTEL

SURVEILLANCE ENDS – 5/30/2005 (THIS IS AN ESTIMATION, ACTUAL DATE PER
AGENT 10483 RETURN FLIGHT), AIRCRAFT BOARDING TIME, SCHIPHOL

ON COMPLETION OF SURVEILLANCE, PLEASE SEND REPORT TO THE
RECRUITMENT TRAINING WING

SINCERELY

/

Avner returned to the findings document and typed:

> **5.** Agent 6844 was assassinated in Amsterdam by 10483
> and not by the Iranian secret service, as was believed
> until now. The file can be closed.

NOON. MAY 2005

The cab drops me off at the printing shop.

I pay the driver and give him a tip.

I hand over the files I designed and order 10 receipt books, a package of business cards, and two 2-meter long and 1-meter wide transparent stickers bearing the words Gerry the Plumber—Service from the Heart in dark blue, with the number of the cell phone I purchased printed in sewage-green below that. The shop assistant smiles at me and tells me everything will be ready in 4 hours.

"Thanks," I say, in an Irish accent.

I walk to the closest Metro station and take the train to Ben's house. There's no way my picture is out there already. This is the Netherlands.

Ben's a plumber. He's selling his van and old equipment because he's sick and tired of working in the sewers. He'll be focusing solely on home installations from now on. He calls it "clean work."

I pay him in cash and we transfer the van into my name at the nearby post office. My ID card works perfectly.

The van is a Volkswagen Transporter. It's covered in scratches and dents. I tell Ben it's fine.

"You don't look like a plumber," Ben says to me.

I tell him I'm just getting started, and he offers to teach me a little about the pieces of equipment. He has a water pressure pump and rods that fit into one another, with the end of one fitted with a coil to release blockages when the assembled pole spins.

I go for a drive in my sewage car.

A slight stench wafts up from the back.

I quickly get used to the smell and head off to do some shopping.

I use the Internet to locate the stores that stock what I need.

At a department store I purchase an inflatable double mattress, 2 blue overalls that are a little big for me, high black boots, a role of large garbage bags, twenty packs of baby wipes, black spray paint, a basic toolbox, a short length of garden hose, a package of matchboxes, a flashlight and batteries.

From a car accessories dealer I pick up a small battery, jumper cables, an air pump, and a GPS device. I enter the address of the printing shop and drive off. The device gives me directions in Dutch, which I don't understand, but the map it offers is clear enough.

My order is ready by the time I get to the printing shop. I collect it and add all the items to the pile of equipment in the van and head out of the city.

The houses become fewer and farther between. I turn onto less crowded roads.

I get onto a dirt road and pull over to rest. I eat a sandwich I bought on the way and drink a bottle of water. The sun is about to set. There's no one else around.

I put on the overalls and boots and get to work.

I spray-paint the rear windows of the van black from the inside.

I cut off one end of each jumper cable and connect them to the air pump. I then connect the jumper cables to the battery I bought.

The blower works.

The battery is charged.

I disconnect the cables from the battery and put them aside. Remove the inflatable double mattress from its packaging.

Insert the batteries into the flashlight and check that it works.

I stick my logo to both sides of the van.

I rub some gravel over the stickers so they don't appear new.

I take the 8th receipt book and tear out the first 11 receipts and burn them along with all the remaining books. I now have only one used book. I add all the tool packaging and the mattress box to the small bonfire.

I put my ID card and driver's license on the ground and tread on them a little so they won't appear too new. The boots and overalls no longer look very new either. I remove them and put my clothes back on. The wig goes back into the bag, and I use a wet wipe to remove the freckles.

I enter the address of the hotel into the GPS device and it guides me back. I park the van 2 streets away from the hotel and walk the rest of the way.

I shower and go to bed.

NIGHT. MAY 2005

I'm back at the Metro station.

The platform is completely deserted.

I stand close to the edge and wait for the train to arrive.

I hear a noise from beneath me.

I bend over and look down.

A dirty hand lunges out at me from below and tries to pull me onto the tracks.

The lights of a train are approaching from the Metro tunnel.

I look at the hand that's pulling me down.

It's attached to a headless body.

I wake at 1:30 and check that the door to the hotel room is locked.

Click

Click

Click

It doesn't open.

I check the door of the safe in the room. I enter the 4-digit code and it opens. I close it.

Open and close it again.

And again.

One last time.

I relock it and go back to sleep.

Today is Saturday.

I get into the van and drive to The Hague.

It's 6 in the morning, the roads are empty and the drive doesn't take long.

The GPS device directs me to Duinweg street. I park at the top of the street and move to the back of the van. I put on the wig and apply Gerry's freckles, change into the blue overalls, and pull on the high boots I bought. I get out.

I walk down the street carrying a crowbar designed to open manhole covers and a black backpack. The nearest manhole cover is outside Duinweg 16—about 40 meters from the embassy.

I open the manhole cover and climb down a few metal rungs. I then close the cover above me.

I'm in total darkness.

There's a powerful stench of feces.

I turn on my flashlight and descend further until my feet touch down in wastewater.

I crawl through the sewer on all fours for about 40 meters. I pass by the sewer opening of Duinweg 18 and continue on to Duinweg 20.

A sewer shaft measuring about half a meter in diameter leads to the building. I remove the inflatable double mattress from my bag and lay it out lengthwise in the shaft. I connect its valve to the air pump and the air pump to the battery.

The pump comes to life and fills the air mattress.

It takes 3 minutes for the sewer shaft to be completely blocked.

I disconnect the air pump from the mattress and make sure the valve is tightly closed. Then I crawl back to the manhole opening, lift the cover and climb out.

I return to the van, get in through the back door and remove the filthy overalls. I place them in a trash bag and put on the clean ones. I move the van and park outside the embassy on the other side of the street. Then I get out of the van and go for a walk.

I return some 30 minutes later, open the back doors of the van, ready the equipment, and whistle out loud.

An embassy guard from the building across the street comes over.

"Are you a plumber?" he asks.

I respond in an Irish accent: "No, I'm a pilot. This is just a hobby."

The guard laughs. "Our entire first floor is flooded with sewage and the plumber we work with is sick," he says. "Lucky you're here."

I know their regular plumber is sick. Britt de Jong took care of that. She told me that she will make sure to put enough laxative in everything he has in his kitchen to make him stay at home the whole day, attached to his toilet seat.

"I don't have time right now," I say to him. "I've just finished opening a blockage across the road and I have a big piping-installation job to get to an hour and a half's drive away from here. Who's going to pay me for being late?"

The guard asks me how much I want, and I tell him it will cost them €200 and that he should know I am doing them a favor because I like Italians and that I saw they have an Italian flag on the roof.

The guard asks for identification.

I give him my ID card and a business card.

The guard disappears into the building, probably to check my website and credentials, and returns 2 minutes later.

"I'll escort you," he says.

I take 2 poles and the coil out the van and go inside with the guard. He doesn't let me out of his sight. While I am walking with him I get a phone call from an unidentified number.

"Gerry the plumber. How can I help?"

A girl's voice is on the line "Hi, I need help here, the whole apartment is a mess!" Her voice sounds stressful. "Can you come quickly to Katerstraat 14?"

"Sorry hon." I reply with an Irish accent. "I am doing a very urgent job at the Italian embassy and it will take some time. At least an hour. I can call you when I finish if you give me your number."

"I can't wait that long. I'll find someone else. Thanks." She hangs up the phone.

I put the phone back in my pocket. They probably made this call from their lobby in order to verify that the phone on the business card is indeed mine, the guard next to me is here to verify that.

The first floor stinks. My mattress is doing a good job and sewage from the entire building is rising up from the toilets.

I ask the guard to take me to the bathroom.

I attach the coil to one of the poles and insert it into the toilet, make an attempt to swivel it and stop.

I inform the guard that I don't have a good angle from there and that I need to go up to the bathroom on the second floor and try to get to the blockage from above.

On the second floor I point toward the conference room and ask if there's a bathroom in there. I already know there is one. I saw it on the building's floor plan.

The guard opens the door to the conference room and I go inside. Hanging over a large and dark wooden table is a decorative light fixture adorned with mirrors.

I join the 2 flexible metal rods to one other and attach the coil to the one end of the pole.

I turn to face the bathroom door. The coil knocks against the light fitting and gets entangled. I climb onto the table to release the coil. The guard looks at me.

"No damage done," I say.

The coil comes away easily. I move the small mirror facing the window so that it points directly at the window in the building across the street. The guard's in the room with me, so I can't use the laser flashlight Britt de Jong gave me.

I jump off the table, open the bathroom door and insert the coil into the toilet as far as it will go and turn it. Nothing happens.

I curse in an Irish accent and tell the guard that the blockage appears to be in the building's main sewage pipes and that I'll have to get into the central sewer to release it. "It'll cost you another two hundred euros," I say.

I'm back in the sewage pipe from the street. I crawl on all fours toward building number 20. I cut the mattress that was serving as a plug and a torrent of sewage washes over me. I put the deflated air mattress into a trash bag and take it with me.

I emerge drenched in putrid wastewater and walk over to

the guard. He looks like he's about to throw up. He gives me a check for €400 and quickly escapes back into the embassy building.

I disassemble the rods and coil, put them into the back of the van, and climb inside. The overalls and boots also go into the trash bag. I go through several packages of baby wipes to scrub the stench of sewage off my body.

Again.

And again.

I drive toward the exit from The Hague and park the van about 500 meters from the train station.

I remove the wig and toss it into the trunk and wipe away the freckles with the baby wipes.

I put on a pair of rubber gloves.

Using the piece of garden hose I bought I syphon some gas from the tank into an empty jerrycan and pour the fuel over the seats of the van, the roof, and inside the trunk.

I move back a little, set fire to one of the matchboxes, throw it into the van through the open driver's window and then head on foot to the train station.

There's a small post office at the train station. I purchase a small box, pack the laser flashlight inside and send the parcel to the De Jong family at Duinweg 33.

The train to Amsterdam arrives 3 minutes late. When I'm seated I turn on my laptop. I delete Gerry the plumber's website from the Internet.

Back in my hotel room I put the bag with the laptop and the remaining money in the safe and go down to the bar. I order a beer. The beer comes with a small bowl of salted peanuts. I eat them. The news is on. The TV hangs from the ceiling behind the bartender. The police are seeking the public's help in locating the subway murder suspect.

The TV displays a blurred video of a man pushing someone onto the tracks just as the train is pulling into the station.

Someone sitting on the chair next to me turns toward me and says in English with a British accent, "People are crazy."

"True, people are crazy," I respond.

Amiram calls me that evening on my cell phone. He calls from a telephone with caller ID and my phone displays an odd six-digit number. This number is divisible by 3. "Well done," he says, "I received a message that everything's in order."

"It wasn't very difficult," I say to him.

"Did you notice anyone following you?" Amiram asks.

I tell him I did, but that I managed to shake him at some point.

"Great," he says.

He asks me if I think I can carry out more serious tasks in the future.

"Yes," I reply.

Amiram hangs up.

I continue to work with the Dutch client for a further 5 days. Then I return to Israel.

November 27th 2005

Carmit wasn't bothered by the cold weather and the icy rain. Wearing a long gray tracksuit and running shoes, she was completely focused on her run. As she circled Hyde Park's large lake, she overtook the other joggers, not bothering to skip over the small puddles of rain on the ground. Her iPod rested in an inside pocket she'd purposefully sewn into the top of her gray tracksuit. She wore a pair of white waterproof headphones that poked out from her hood via a small hole she'd made. The Prodigy's music set the pace of her run and rhythm of her breathing.

Her body ran on autopilot, but her eyes weren't focused solely on the path. She constantly scanned the trees along the route, a squirrel moving on the grass, every individual in the vicinity. She knew every corner of the park, it was her favorite place to run.

The cell phone buzzing at her hip caused her to slow down. Carmit reached into the pocket of her sweatshirt and paused the rhythmic music. She eased off into a walk, retrieved the cell phone, and looked at the display. An unlisted number.

"Angela speaking, who's calling please?"

"Hello."

She recognized the voice.

"It will cost you fifty thousand pounds."

"You don't know what we want yet."

"True, and it'll cost you fifty thousand."

"Are you available in early 2006? The first week of January?"

"Just a sec, let me see."

Carmit muted the call and returned the phone to its pouch. She walked for another 30 seconds or so, retrieved the phone again and continued the conversation.

"Three days. From December 31st in the morning to January 2nd at night. Excluding flights. Fifty thousand pounds into account number 016497725 at Credit Suisse. Transfer within three business days. Today is Monday, so I'll check on Thursday afternoon to make sure the money's come through."

"Don't you trust me?" asked the voice on the other end of the line.

"Don't take it personally, but I don't trust any of you. And I say that as someone who cleans up your shit off the grid."

"We'll need you in Geneva for one night of headphones and glasses. You'll get started on January 15th at the Crowne Plaza. It's near the airport."

"Send me an encrypted image and encrypted conversion file to the following email address: angela.fields.116@gmail.com."

"You'll get them today."

"I won't look at them before Thursday afternoon."

"Greedy bitch."

"Evil manipulator."

Carmit hung up and returned again to The Prodigy. She broke into a jog, upped her pace again and looked over at a group of ducks that were trying to evade the charge of a small child. After the money arrived she'd withdraw it in cash and redeposit it into two different accounts. She'd open the two accounts when she got home, after showering and having breakfast. She quickened her pace and took pleasure in the heat generated by her body. It contrasted starkly with the cold London air. She was in excellent shape.

NIGHT. JUNE 2005

I'm in the shower.

The water flows over my body and washes off the still faint stench of sewage.

The light outside the bathroom is on and my eyes are fixed on the illuminated gap between the floor and the bathroom door.

2 shadows move across the floor outside the bathroom.

Someone is out there.

I leave the bathroom faucet on and go over to open the door.

Standing behind the door is an old man dressed in a black suit. He's carrying a black leather bag.

"I've come to get you." he says.

He removes a rope from his case.

"Here, hang yourself."

He offers me the rope with the palms of his hands turned upward.

Steam is rising from the hot water behind me.

Drops of water are running down the fogged mirror.

I wake at 1:30 and get up to continue digging my basement.

I live in a ground-floor apartment in a residential building with 4 floors. I've been digging under the apartment's living room for the past 11 months. It was hard to get through the layer of concrete under the floor, but it was plain sailing thereafter.

I set aside 2 hours for digging every night. I place the earth I extract into construction sacks, and I put those into regular trash bags that I throw into various garbage bins around the neighborhood every morning before I head off to work.

I'm using timber to support the sides of the basement, and when the work is done I'll cast concrete to construct the basement walls. No one comes into my apartment, so the large hole that begins just before the front door and stretches into the living room remains unnoticed by anyone.

I remove 8 bags of earth from the apartment early every morning, and at this rate the basement will be ready in 5 months. If all goes according to plan it should reach a depth of 6 meters.

I'm fitting the basement with a bathroom, storeroom, battery and generator room, ventilation system, electricity, plumbing, and CCTV cameras.

Close to the middle of the room, under the front door to the apartment, I'm building a 4-meter-high steel cage with thick bars. The cage has a steel door with a lock. The cage also has a small 10-centimeter-high opening adjacent to the floor.

There are 2 ways to enter the basement—either through the metal bottom of my bedroom closet and down a ladder fitted below it, or by falling into the steel cage, once I finish rebuilding the floor. Anyone entering the apartment and heading straight to my room will open 2 doors in the floor and fall straight into the cage.

The open roof of the cage can be shut and locked with 2 steel plates that slide on rails on either side of the cage. Landing on the floor of the cage after the fall will trigger this locking mechanism automatically.

I plant blocks of explosive material I collected over my years in the army in 10 different places in the basement. I connect them all together with fuse wire, thus turning the basement into one giant bomb, with an electronic detonator fitted to an ordinary light switch located near the ladder. Someone who isn't familiar with the basement and who wants to turn on a light will blow it all up.

I fill the storeroom with canned produce, dehydrated food-stuffs, and gallons of bottled water.

When they come to kill me I'll be ready.

December 4th 2016

Avner placed the notebook on the table and rubbed his eyes. He stood up, raised his arms above his head and stretched. He took his laptop out of his bag, plugged it in and continued working on the document he'd started at home.

- **For action tomorrow morning**—The building in which 10483 was living before his death needs to be evacuated and a sweep must be made of the basement he writes about, if it does indeed exist; and if so, the explosive charges need to be neutralized. Take into account the fact that not everything that appears in this notebook is the truth (it may be his imagination or deliberate deception). Take care not to flip any light switches on the way down into the basement. Send agents in fire engines and dressed as firefighters to evacuate the building due to a reported gas leak. Coordinate with the police, the ambulance service, and the fire and rescue services.

Avner left the office, closed the door, and walked over to the guard station.

"Is that coffee offer still valid?"

"Sure, come with me. I've got an espresso machine. Much better than the regular shit The Organization provides."

The guard filled the small espresso machine's water tank and turned it on. He placed a capsule of coffee in the designated slot and two small glass cups under the spouts.

"Long night?" the guard asked.

"Through to the morning and afterward, too, probably."

"My shift ends at seven. Whenever you feel the need to wake up a little, come see me. I'd give you a Vodka and Red Bull if I had it—that would wake you up a little more," the guard laughed.

"That's all I need. . . ."

They both sat down to drink their coffee in the kitchenette before hearing a short buzz from the area of the offices.

"I need to get going," the guard said, rising quickly out of his chair, his cup of espresso in his hand. "Someone's approaching the building."

"I thought I was the only one who comes here at this time of night."

"Yes, these are usually dead hours. We're a small branch. I'm outta here."

"See you later."

Avner returned to the office with his cup of coffee. He placed it on the table, sat down in the chair, and continued to read from the notebook.

MORNING. DECEMBER 2005

I go out this morning with a regular trash bag. I'm no longer clearing earth.

The basement is ready.

Someone said to be a member of a crime family lives on our street.

He approaches me.

He shoves his face up close to mine.

I can sense the pulsing of his blood flowing through his body.

"You parked in my space," he says.

"I parked on the street," I respond. "And there aren't any private parking spaces here."

"The space outside the entrance to the building is mine. Park there again and I'll beat the crap outta you."

"I'm going to park there again," I say.

He punches me hard in the nose. I close my eyes and focus on the feeling. The blood flows down from my nose into my mouth and I collect it with my tongue.

"I know where you live," he says to me.

"In the building across the street, on the ground floor, the door on the right," I tell him.

He turns around and walks off.

Before leaving for work I go back inside, change my blood-stained shirt and put a Band-Aid on my nose. It may be broken.

Nurit meets me in the corridor at work. She asks me to report to Yaron's office in 15 minutes and quickly disappears.

I know my name appears on the list for the next round of layoffs. I have the system admin's password to get into the company's human resources management program and I conduct daily checks on the wages of all the company managers and any other interesting information I can find.

I stop by my office, retrieve a flash drive from the top drawer of my desk, put it in my pocket and report to Yaron's office.

Yaron and Nurit are there, fixing me with frozen stares.

"I'm sure you're aware of the state of the global pharmaceuticals market and the effect the recession has had on the entire sector in general and our company in particular," Yaron says.

I notice he's reading the text from a sheet of paper resting on his desk.

"I broke my nose today," I say to them.

"We've been forced to let you go," Nurit says. "This booklet contains a presentation that outlines your compensation package," she adds.

"I need to remain in this job," I say. "It's important."

Nurit looks at Yaron.

"The decision is final," he says.

"I have a presentation, too," I say to them. "You should see it." They look at each other and then at me.

I plug the flash drive into Yaron's computer and open the presentation I've prepared. It's made up of selected screenshots of their respective hobbies.

Nurit's face turns bright red and Yaron's goes white.

"This material gets uploaded to YouTube within an hour after I'm fired," I say to them. "Ten minutes later, an email with a link to the material will be sent to all company employees, and five minutes later it gets sent to your extended families."

"I believe we can change the list of layoffs," Yaron says. "You can go back to work."

"Yes, I believe you can change the list," I respond.

Yaron asks me for the flash drive.

I tell him he can keep it as a souvenir, but that I still have several more copies of the presentation so it doesn't really matter.

I return to my office and continue working.

My phone rings at 4 in the afternoon. Amiram is on the line. He informs me he has sent an encrypted email to my account at The Organization and that I should open it and read it.

I tell him to wait a moment and place the receiver on my desk.

I access my web-based email account at The Organization and open the message.

It reads: "There is someone we want you to kill for us. You need to organize a trip to a customer in Switzerland."

I close the message and it's deleted and disappears from my account. I delete my browsing history and shut down the computer.

I pick up the phone. "Got it," I say.

NIGHT. DECEMBER 2005

The sensation of pleasure begins at my fingertips and courses through my back and neck all the way to the top of my head. Shivers run through me and I can feel every hair on my body. It's more powerful than sex, better than a good meal.

It's hard to press down on the pedal. Every time the wave of pleasure begins to dissipate I have to press down on it with my foot with all I've got. Otherwise the next wave won't come. It gets harder and harder every time.

I don't know if it's the mechanism of the pedal itself or because my body, which is usually young and strong, is showing signs of weakness and confusion. Perhaps it's because I haven't eaten in a long time. For several days now. Okay, I'll go get myself something to eat.

But first just one more small press on the pedal.

Ooooooooha, another wave passes through me. I close my eyes and again surrender to the sensation. The need to eat or sleep fades once more. I try to think when I last slept and where, and that, too, evades me.

No.

I can't.

I have to break away from this cycle. But my body won't listen to me. It remains standing in front of the large glass wall from which this pedal emerges. I came across it by chance. I mean it's always been there just like all the rest of the furniture in my house, and my life was just fine before I began messing around with it.

My foot presses down on the pedal again and another wave of pleasure washes over me. Everything around me is spinning in colorful sparkling light and I lie down on the floor alongside the pedal, too tired and spent to press down on it again, and finally fall into a deep sleep.

"Look—the rat is dead."

2 white coats are looking down at the floor of my cell. My body is sprawled there. I am watching the scene from above.

"Yes, it chose to press the handle until it died of exhaustion and hunger, even though there was a pile of food right next to it, just four steps away. It didn't even touch the food."

One of the white coats is wearing yellow rubber gloves. He picks up my body and disconnects the electrode from my head. The other white coat is holding an open plastic bag. Yellow gloves tosses me in. He ties the top of the bag and throws it in the trash.

"This proves without doubt that the brain's pleasure center is more powerful than the centers of sleep or hunger."

"Yes, but I'm concerned about taking things to the next level."

"Why? Just think of the huge potential in terms of alleviating the suffering of terminally ill patients or patients with chronic pain. It's a drug-free treatment with no side effects."

"Right, no side effects . . . except for the fact that the rat's dead."

"It's a rat."

"In this context—we're exactly the same. What do you think a person would do if he had direct and unadulterated access to the pleasure center of his brain? The same thing. All the rat did for exactly five days was press and press the pedal until it died of exhaustion, thirst, and hunger. It didn't care about anything else."

The 2 white coats remain silent for a moment. I continue to observe them from above.

"You may be right."

"I'm not saying that we aren't going to publish, but there's no way we're going to take it to the practical level. Never."

"Okay, let's get out of here. It's one in the morning already. We'll start working on the final report tomorrow." The rows of neon lights in the laboratory go out one after the other. The cleaner will show up early tomorrow morning to empty the trash bin.

I'm lying in my bed again.

The lights in my apartment are off.

There's someone in the apartment.

I can sense it.

I hear light rustling and breathing from the direction of the front door.

I know who it is.

I hear a loud noise, a scream, a thud, the grating sound of metal against metal and then silence again, disturbed occasionally by weak screams that seem to come from far away.

I turn over and go back to sleep.

I wake at 1:30 and get up to go see the man in the basement.

I climb down the ladder under my bedroom closet and turn the basement light on using a hidden switch.

Sitting in the cage in the middle of the basement is the guy who punched me last week.

The sudden light causes him to cover his eyes. "I'm going to slaughter you like a pig!" he screams.

I get myself a chair and sit down in front of the cage.

I stare at him while waiting for him to stop yelling.

He goes silent after a few minutes.

"This basement is sealed," I say to him. "If you scream with all your might, you'll be faintly heard in the apartment above, but it, too, is sealed with thick acoustic insulation and no one outside will hear a thing. So don't waste your energy. You're going to need it."

He tries to move the bars. He can't. The steel bars are 2 centimeters thick, welded together, and they've been cast into the concrete floor of the basement. He kicks out angrily at the floor and the bars and looks up at the steel plates that shut the cage 4 meters above him.

I take a ladder and place it about a meter and a half from the cage.

I press a switch that opens one of the cage's steel ceiling panels and say, "You'd do good to move aside."

I climb up the ladder several times and throw some things into the cage. 3 cartons of mineral water. A box of mixed dried fruits, rice cakes and pita bread, and a bucket filled with trash bags.

I shut the ceiling of the cage again, turn out the basement's main light and leave just a small lamp glowing.

I turn on the basement's ventilation system.

"I'm going away now for two weeks," I tell him. "That's your food and drink. The trash bags are for you to shit in and then tie shut. You can piss into the bottles after you drink from them. Work out how much to drink and eat each day so that you don't run out too quickly. Use the time to kick your smoking habit."

Before climbing back up into the apartment, I turn to him and say: "I may need your fingers. That's why I'm keeping you alive."

MORNING. JANUARY 2006

I'm flying to Switzerland today at 5 in the evening to carry out a routine system-performance check for a client. Nurit approved the trip.

Amiram asks me to stop by The Organization's home base before leaving for Geneva.

I meet him there and he instructs me to go to the Crowne Plaza Hotel near the airport, identify myself as Peter Connor and ask if anyone has left a parcel at reception for me. There I'll receive an envelope with the details of the target.

I ask Amiram why he doesn't simply inform me of the target now and save me the trouble. He says that he does not know the identity of the target.

He gives me an Irish passport in the name of Peter Connor, €50,000 in cash, one of The Organization's encrypted cell phones, and several make-up accessories.

"Thanks, they'll be put to good use," I say. "I'll submit a detailed list of expenses when I'm in Geneva."

"It's vital you complete this mission," Amiram says. "Success will see you move up in The Organization."

"Good."

I purchase a pair of pants, a shirt, underwear, socks, a belt, shoes, a new bag for the laptop, and a can of Coke at the airport before the flight.

I drink the Coke from the can and then go to the bathroom to change into my new clothes. I transfer the laptop and the money and some of the make-up accessories to the new bag and shove the clothes and shoes I was wearing before into the old one, along with all the other things that Amiram gave me.

I go over to the DHL branch at the airport and pack the old bag into a cardboard box. I pay in cash and send the parcel to Dusit Zoo, Bangkok, Thailand.

That's how I rid myself of all the tracking and listening devices that they planted on me without my knowledge when I was at the home base.

I fly to Dublin and from there to Switzerland.

In Geneva I go over to the reception desk at the Plaza and wait in line. I look around. A decorated Christmas tree stands near the entrance to the elevators, small lights flashing. A boy and a girl are standing there looking at the lights while their parents wait in the line to check in. The boy touches one of the glass decorations on the tree.

When it's my turn I ask the clerk if there's a message there for Peter Connor.

He asks me if I'm a guest at the hotel and I tell him I'm not.

He goes off to check and returns with 3 white envelopes.

He asks to see an ID card or passport and I show him my passport. Then I take the envelopes and go to a hotel in the city center.

I unpack the random suitcase I picked up from baggage claim at the airport when I get to my room. In it are the clothes of an ultra-Orthodox man and several Jewish books about the Bible.

I open the first envelope.

It contains 2 photographs of a young woman. 1 photograph is a close-up of her face, and the 2nd shows her playing with a small girl who looks about 4 years old. The woman is chubby and has long blonde-brown hair and brown eyes.

The same text appears on the back of both photographs:

CERN—European Organization for Nuclear Research

VErtex LOcator (VELO)

The second envelope contains another 2 photographs. An elderly man—a close-up of his face and a photograph taken from farther back that shows his build. He is tall and thin and has short blond hair.

The back of his 2 photographs reads:

Universidad Nacional de Cuyo, UNCuyo

Instituto Balseiro

There are no names in the envelopes. Only the photographs and locations.

I open the 3rd envelope, in it there are 2 photographs of an elderly man. He looks about 60 years old, bald with a black goatee. 1 photograph shows him standing and smiling on the backdrop of a garden with trees and flowers. The other is a close-up of his face.

Again, the same text appears on the back of both photographs:

École Polytechnique de Montréal

SLOWPOKE (Safe Low-Power Kritical Experiment)

As I'm in Geneva, my first target is the young woman. I'll kill the 2 men on my next trips.

I go to a restaurant near the hotel for lunch.

I'll go to the client tomorrow and to CERN the day after.

December 4th 2016

Avner put the notebook down. Why three envelopes? And on three different continents, too! It doesn't make sense. According to the findings in the official report, agent 10483 was believed to have embarked on an assassination campaign of his own volition and somehow managed to get his hands on a portion of the Bernoulli Project target list; but according to the notebook, he was given three envelopes. Unbelievable. Did someone make a mistake and gave him three targets from the Bernoulli list? Who would want to do that?

WELCOME TO THE ORION SYSTEM,

WAITING FOR INSTRUCTIONS

"SEARCH"

→ SEARCH FOR WHAT?

"BERNOULLI, TARGET LIST"

WAIT . . .

→ NO SEARCH RESULTS FOR "BERNOULLI, TARGET LIST"

"SEARCH"

→ SEARCH FOR WHAT?

"BERNOULLI"

WAIT . . .

→ NO SEARCH RESULTS FOR "BERNOULLI"

Avner squinted at the computer screen. Someone's erased the project from the system. Or perhaps they've upped the security clearance level required to view documents related to the project? But it doesn't make sense. Why would anyone want to erase the material, some ten years after the project?

A decision was made after the lessons learned in Berlin to drop the big-team format and revert back to the lone-assassin system. Large groups are more likely to be spotted these days as there's hardly a public location anywhere in the world that isn't covered by cameras operating 24/7, and computer systems can easily cross-reference both identities and the movements of large groups. But when it comes to a lone individual who switches identities, tracking becomes a lot more difficult. And if he's caught, then it's just one individual and not an entire group.

Following his creatively executed work in the Netherlands, 10483 underwent training to operate as an assassin under the new system. Alone, not as part of a team, without any backup. If he received three envelopes and acted in keeping with the system, he would have gone dark from the moment he received the missions and through to their completion.

10483 had done exactly what was expected of him.

He had acted in accordance with the new system.

The problem was that he had done so far too enthusiastically and with the mind-set of a psychopath.

Avner glanced again at the open notebook on the table and the computer screen in front of him. The clock in the bottom corner of the screen read 02:42. Time for another cup of coffee. He left the office and closed the door.

"Is your coffee machine still functioning?"

"Full steam ahead."

"Another round of espresso?"

"Gladly."

"I'm Avner. I haven't even asked you your name yet, very rude of me."

"Benny. It's a pleasure."

Benny filled the machine with water and removed two clean cups from the drying rack.

"What was that buzzing earlier?"

"An alert about an outside camera that stopped functioning. The one that covers the area of the parking lot. I had a walk around and didn't see anything suspicious. The very same camera malfunctioned last week, and a technician came over to repair it. Apparently, he didn't do a very good job. The guard who replaces me in the morning will call in another technician. I left a note for him on the on the desk."

"How long have you been with us?" Avner handles the recruitment of agents, and "the human resources bug," as he calls it, frequently takes hold of him.

"A year and a half. I've been told I can sit the tests for the basic course in six months."

"Are you thinking of going for it?"

"I don't know. I have two more years at university and I don't want to leave in the middle, so I'll complete my degree first and then decide."

"What are you studying?"

"Information Systems and East Asian Studies. Here, take a look at what I was reading before you interrupted me with your coffee request." Benny smiled and offered Avner a book written in Chinese.

"It's all Greek to me."

Benny laughed. "Our lecturer has some interesting ideas. She decided that we're going to study Chinese philosophy in the original language this year. That way we'll make more progress with the language and understand original intent without the need for a translation, which is never as exact as it should be. Especially when it comes to Chinese. She's killing us though. I don't even have time to shave in the mornings. I decided to grow a beard."

"Chinese is good for The Organization. But not in my department. You don't look like a typical Chinese." Avner allowed himself a smile. The thought of taking someone with a European look and trying to pass him off as Chinese for the purpose of carrying out fieldwork as an agent in China amused him.

"You should think about a position at the home base after your studies. There's a big demand for Chinese speakers."

They sat in the kitchenette for a few more minutes and drank their coffee. Avner was happy to give his mind a rest from the notebook. Something about the way in which it was written bothered him, and Avner suddenly realized what it was. Almost the entire notebook is written in the present tense. There's no past and no future. As if it was all one long-running, ongoing, and exhausting continuum. And the text was completely devoid of any emotive language. It's all completely objective, seemingly related by someone on the sidelines, an observer, even though everything was written very close to the time it actually happened and by 10483 himself. Or so it seems.

Or perhaps it's all one big scam?

Perhaps he has a partner or partners who are still alive?

Avner left Benny and returned to the office.

He sat down and picked up the notebook again.

January 1st 2006

The Crowne Plaza lobby is as dull as any European hotel. Armchairs, low tables, a bar, a drowsy bellboy standing alongside a baggage trolley with a couple of suitcases on its padded bottom, and two reception desk clerks sitting behind a large wooden desk, cost-effective lighting above their heads.

When Carmit landed in Geneva, she rented a car at the airport and drove to the hotel. She took a seat on one of the armchairs facing the reception desk and ordered a Diet Coke and a plate of fruit. She retrieved her laptop from her black leather bag and started a game of Solitaire, one eye keeping constant watch on the people entering the hotel. Every now and then she sipped her drink and ate a grape or segment of orange from the fruit platter.

An hour and a half later or so, her target appeared. She recognized him from the photograph she received a month ago. He cast a wary glance around the lobby and went over to the reception desk. Carmit continued with her game of Solitaire until he turned around again and left the hotel. At the same moment, she quickly slipped her laptop into the bag and exited the hotel.

While the target waited outside for a cab, Carmit got into her rental car, which was parked a few dozen meters away. She started it, but left the headlights off. A cab pulled up alongside the target at the entrance to the hotel. The target got in. The cab pulled away and Carmit followed, switching lanes and always leaving a gap of a few vehicles between her car and the cab.

The cab stopped at the entrance to the Tiffany Hotel. The target paid the driver and went into the hotel. Carmit handed her car over to the hotel's valet service, along with a 10-franc tip, and walked inside. Instead of approaching the reception desk, she sat on one of the armchairs in the lobby and was reminded again just how much she despised hotels.

With his hotel room keycard in hand and two suitcases in tow, her target entered one of the elevators. Carmit watched it stop on the fifth floor. She got up from the armchair and went over to the front desk.

"Good evening. I'm from the group; I have a reservation under the name of Angela Fields." Before handing her car over to the valet service, she'd seen them parking a car bearing a Cymedix logo.

The desk clerk checked his computer. "Sorry, I don't see your name here."

"I have a reservation number," Carmit said, quickly whipping out a blank piece of paper from her pocket and reading out an imaginary number. "Five six three four two five."

"That's a strange number," the clerk responded. "Someone seems to have given you the wrong one."

"I can't believe it! The travel department does this to me every single time. I just came in on a twelve-hour flight from Santa Clara, I'm dying to crash on a bed, and they fucked up my booking again? It's always me who gets screwed. Look, that guy you just gave a key to is also here with Cymedix for the same conference. But surprise, surprise! His reservation's fine. And I'm the one screwed, again!"

"Who? Room 513? He arrived without a reservation, actually. He took a regular vacant room."

"You have vacancies? Well, why didn't you say so? Screw the company, they'll just pay double. Here's my business card. Just don't give me a room adjacent to 513. He snores like a buzz saw. He was right behind me on the flight; I thought I was going to lose it." Carmit's burst of rolling laughter prompted a chuckle from the desk clerk, who swiped the credit card and gave her a key to room 544, a nonsmoking room.

Carmit went up to the fifth floor and made a quick inspection of both its layout and the location of the emergency exit doors to the stairs. She then went back down to the lobby and found an empty armchair. She ordered a soda and grilled cheese sandwich this time. Half an hour later, her target left the hotel on foot, with Carmit trailing right behind him.

The target walked a short way down the street before entering a restaurant and taking a seat at a corner table with his back to the wall. Carmit walked in and took a seat at the bar. She glanced over at her target, who was talking to a waitress. The waitress smiled and nodded. From that moment, Carmit's eyes never left the waitress.

"*Ein Glas Weizentrumpf, bitte.*" Carmit smiled at the bartender and placed a ten-franc note on the countertop. The bartender nodded and poured her drink. He offered her change but she waved it away. "*Halten die Änderung.*" He nodded again and put the coins in the tip jar on the bar.

The waitress who had taken her target's order went over to the kitchen and then spoke a few words to the bartender, who was pouring beer into a row of glasses on the bar in front of him. As she spoke to him, the bartender turned momentarily toward the kitchen, and Carmit seized the opportunity to quickly pass her hand over the glasses and release a single drop of liquid into each one from the ring on her finger. She had her back to the target. Her hand and the glasses were not in his field of vision. No one saw what she did.

Carmit took a sip from her beer. Then she asked the bartender to point out the bathroom. He gestured toward a wooden door to her left. On her way over she watched the waitress collect the glasses of beer from the bar and serve them to the diners. Her target received one of the glasses. Carmit went into the bathroom, waited three minutes, washed her hands and then exited the bathroom and the restaurant. She crossed the street after looking left and right at the crosswalk to make sure no car was approaching and also to make sure that the target was drinking his beer. There were no cars. The target was drinking.

Carmit walked back to the hotel. She had four hours before the material would take effect. Her target would sleep particularly soundly tonight.

She used the time to take a shower in her room. The hot water flowed over her body, relaxing her and washing away the "airport smell" as she uses to call it. She then organized all the equipment she'd need during the course of the night and packed everything into a medium-size backpack. After completing her preparations, she got into bed and set her alarm for two in the morning.

Getting into room 513 posed no problem at all. Carmit inserted an electronic keycard that was attached to her iPod into the slot in the door. Some 15 seconds later the light on the door handle turned green and Carmit entered the room, quietly closing the door behind her. Her target was in the bed, fast asleep.

Carmit placed the backpack on the carpet at her feet. She opened it, removed her laptop and started taking pictures. First she took stills of the entire room, the bathroom and the bed in which her target was sleeping. She then switched the camera to video mode and repeated the same exercise. From the backpack afterward she retrieved an inhalation mask, which was connected by means of a transparent flexible tube to a small device, and positioned it over the target's face, fixing it in place with a rubber band stretched around the back of his neck. Carmit placed the device on the bed next to the target and turned it on. The device emitted a low buzzing sound and a fine mist-like vapor began flowing through the tube into the target's lungs.

Carmit removed a white towel from her bag and laid it out on the carpet. She arranged all her equipment on the towel and checked that everything was in working order. She then proceeded to assemble the system on the sleeping target. She placed her laptop on the nightstand next to the bed and plugged a micro card into its USB port. Leading out from the card were two fine wires that each ended in an electrode, which she adhered to the target's temples. She then opened an app that divided her screen into three sections, two of which remained black while the third flickered to life and displayed a green graph of the target's brain activity across a time axis. Carmit went into the bathroom and retrieved two small towels. She rolled them up and placed them on either side of the target's head. She then connected a set of headphones to the laptop and placed them over her target's ears. Then she plugged a pair of black glasses into a socket at the base of the laptop. She applied two small bandaids to the target's eyelids to keep them open, then she gently placed the glasses over his eyes.

Carmit reached for a small syringe. She removed a sterile needle from its wrapping and fixed it to the syringe. From a small glass vial she drew up a pink liquid into the syringe, and tapped it, making sure it was free of any air bubbles. She folded and positioned one of the target's legs, knee pointing toward the ceiling, foot flat on the bed, and injected the solution into a vein at the back of his thigh, in a spot where the target would not be able to see the puncture mark.

"Here's a little sauce for you," she said to the sleeping target.

After withdrawing the needle, Carmit wiped the puncture area with a small ball of cotton and checked to make sure no mark remained. There was none.

She entered a five-digit code into her laptop and pressed Enter. The other two sections of the screen came to life. One displayed an equalizer and a pattern of sound waves, and the other showed a digital timer that began a 120-minute countdown and a blue bar that flickered frantically at a fluctuating rate.

The dark glasses began emitting a series of blue flashes at the same rate as the blue bar on the laptop screen. Carmit put on a pair of sunglasses with orange lenses and turned to face the screen again for a few minutes. Everything was in order. She removed a checkered tablecloth from her knapsack and spread it out on the carpet next to the towel. On the tablecloth she placed a wine glass, a package of salted almonds and a small bottle of wine from the minibar in her room. She sat down on the tablecloth at the foot of the bed, opened the package of almonds, poured some wine into the glass and raised it in the air, "Cheers," she said to the figure on the bed.

Carmit then rested her hand on the target's head and ran her fingers through his hair. She whispered:

Sleep, sleep my little child
And dream of oceans blue and wide

The blue light continued to flicker, and a soft, monotonous voice cycled through the headphones. Using a long pipette, Carmit made sure to carefully place a drop of distilled water into each of the target's eyes every few minutes without removing the glasses.

She still remembered the lecture she attended at the Department of Molecular Neurobiology of Behavior at Georg-August University in Germany, when she was still working for The Organization. They sent her there to complete a postgraduate degree. She hadn't planned on going to that particular lecture. The subject of the lecture wasn't even related to her field of specialization. But when she saw the title of the lecture on the sheet of paper fixed to the door of the hall, she decided she had to go in. It said: "The Smell of Blue Light."

Olfaction is one of the most important senses throughout the animal kingdom. It enables animals to discriminate between a wide variety of attractive and repulsive odorants and often plays a decisive role in species-specific communication. In recent years the analysis of olfactory systems in both vertebrates and invertebrates has attracted much scientific interest. In this context a pivotal question is how the properties and connectivities of individual neurons contribute to a functioning neuronal network that mediates odor-guided behavior. As a novel approach to analyze the role of individual neurons within a circuitry, techniques have been established that make use of light-sensitive proteins. In this review we introduce a non-invasive, optogenetic technique which was used to manipulate the activity of individual neurons in the olfactory system of Drosophila melanogaster larvae. Both channelrhodopsin-2 and the photosensitive adenylyl cyclase PAC α in individual olfactory receptor neurons (ORNs) of the olfactory system of Drosophila larvae allows stimulating individual receptor neurons by light. Depending on which particular ORN is optogenetically activated, repulsion or attraction behavior can be induced, indicating which sensory neurons underlie which type of behavior.[1]

She'd listened wide-eyed to the explanation about how scientists caused flies to be able to smell blue light by adding a light-sensitive protein to their olfactory neuronal receptors. Contrary to their natural aversion to light, fly larvae were attracted to blue light simply because their olfactory system neurons interpreted the blue light as the smell of food.

It was a window to the brain!

If we have precise mappings of the human brain, why shouldn't we be able to do the same thing? The lecture posited. *Blind people would be able to see by means of their sense of smell, or be able to listen to their environment instead of seeing it. And deaf people could see sounds.* The power of the notion left Carmit astounded.

---

1. "The Smell of Blue Light: A New Approach toward Understanding an Olfactory Neuronal Network" by Klemens F. Störtkuhl and André Fiala

All one would need is an exact topographic image of the individual brain and a suitable cocktail of light-sensitive proteins that would fix themselves to the relevant areas of the particular brain, with the eyes serving as windows through which light would enter the cranial cavity. Eyes that can't see.

That lecture changed her course of studies.

She corresponded with experts at The Organization's home base about the incredible potential. But at some point, they broke off all contact with her. She assumed they'd decided to leave the matter to the civilian sector.

Upon completing her studies and returning to home base she learned that they had in fact gone with the notion, but in a completely different direction.

Carmit drank the wine and ate the almonds as she monitored the process through the course of its 120 minutes. She then disconnected and gathered up all the instruments, folded the tablecloth and towel, and packed everything into her backpack again; she returned the rolled-up towels to their place in the bathroom, removed the two small adhesive bandages from the target's eyes, and wiped clean the areas of his face where the plasters and electrodes had been.

Before leaving the room she compared the pictures and video she'd taken with her laptop on first entering to the room to its present state. She moved the blanket and pillow a little to ensure an exact match and returned the laptop to her backpack.

Carmit opened the door to leave. She turned to give one last look at the room. On the bed, still sound asleep, lay 10483.

The pressure on me at a depth of 30 meters is about 4 atmospheres.

For every 10 meters of depth in water, the pressure increases by 1 atmosphere; so at a depth of 30 meters, the ambient pressure is 4 atmospheres—1 for the earth's atmosphere, plus 3 for every 10 meters of depth.

That's why the air from the scuba tank makes a soft whistling sound when you're breathing. The regulator in your mouth makes sure that the pressure in your lungs is equal to the surrounding pressure so that you can breathe. Otherwise your lungs would collapse together with your sinuses. And that's also why if for example you have a cavity in a tooth that's partially hollow and hasn't been filled properly, the tooth could collapse and disintegrate at such depths.

Because my life is dependent on this small regulator, there's another one connected to the tank, dangling in the water during the dive and waiting for its twin to malfunction. But it never malfunctions.

When I'm at a depth of 30 meters and inhaling air at a pressure of 4 atmospheres, I can't rise quickly to the surface because my lungs could explode like 2 small pink balloons.

If I ascend rapidly, even if I ensure to expel air from my lungs all the way to the surface, my lungs will remain intact but my blood, which grew accustomed to 4 atmospheres of pressure, will release nitrogen bubbles like a Coke bottle fizzes when you open it, and these bubbles will accumulate in my veins and arteries and block the flow of blood to my legs or

117

arms or brain. If I'm lucky, I'll end up paralyzed; if I'm not, I'll have a stroke.

That's why I have 2 regulators.

And that's why you should always dive with a partner who can give you air from his second regulator if both your regulators malfunction.

Dive partners protect one another against decompression sickness.

I dive without a partner.

I'm surrounded by silence.

All I hear is the sound of my breathing.

I check the tank's depth and air-pressure gauges.

And then again—depth and air-pressure gauges.

One last time.

The sun's rays at the depth I'm at no longer break directly on the corals but instead they move over them in waves of light that cast an aura of deep blue over everything. The Lighthouse diving site in the Sinai is teeming with corals.

Eilat's coral reef looks like a desert compared to the abundance here. Sea fans and giant corals cover the steeply sloped underwater rock face, and swimming among them are endless species of fish in every color imaginable. The fish are indifferent to my movements and the bubbles rising from the regulator, they allow me to approach. They think I'm one of them.

Every now and then, a cloud-like school of tiny fish swimming in perfect harmony flashes through the corals. I see streaks of dark and light blue running over the body of an octopus and watch as it attaches itself to one of the corals, blends in with it, and disappears. The octopus's body perfectly mimics the coral beneath it and the color and movements of color produced by the darkish-blue ray of the sun from above.

And then I see her.

She's swimming naked below me. Her long white hair reaches down to her waist and flows around her in the water, weightless. She has no scuba gear and there are no bubbles coming from her mouth. She's unaware of my presence and swims on, passing by a few meters below me and descending farther along the wall of corals. I descend in her wake.

40 meters.

50 meters.

I can feel the pressure of the water around me increasing. The air that the regulator is forcing into my mouth turns cooler. More compressed. I move my jaw slightly to release the pressure in my sinuses.

80 meters.

110 meters.

270 meters.

Total darkness. It's harder for the sunlight to penetrate the thick blanket of water here. I'm cold. I almost touch her.

288 meters.

She turns to me.

Her eyes shine bright blue. Her long silver hair flows around her.

She puts a finger to her lips, "Shhhh," and I know that everything will be fine.

She clasps my head in her hands and brings her face to mine. The deep blue light of her eyes shines brightly into mine.

I wake at 5 in the morning and not at 1:30.

My head is heavy. My eyes hurt. I go over to the sink in the bathroom and splash water on them. I put my head under the faucet and allow the water to flow over my hair and wash down my face for several minutes.

I pull my head away from under the faucet and stand up straight. Water from my wet hair drips onto my shirt.

I go over to my desk, turn on the laptop and open the website for CERN, the international organization that runs the world's largest particle accelerator. It's located near Geneva. Scientists there from all around the world are testing physical theories and that's where my target appears to be working.

I browse through the site for information on how to join one of the guided tours at the facility and sign up for one. I also learn the location of the entrances to the facility, the parking lots, and the employees' entrance.

I sit in my car close to the entrance from early in the morning and watch the people going in. It takes me 3 days to find my target. She's not alone. Someone clearly wants to keep her alive. She's never without security detail. Bodyguards ride with her in her car and in 2 additional vehicles. One in front of her and one behind.

I follow her car from a distance.

The bodyguards take off when her car enters CERN. But security at the facility is high and it's impossible to get in. She's inaccessible when she's in the car, too.

I perform some calculations to see if I could remotely bring down a metal girder from a bridge she passes under in the mornings.

I need t seconds for the girder to drop to a height of 1 meter above the ground.

The height of the bridge is 7 meters. So if $d=6$ and $g=9.8$, that gives us approximately 1.106 seconds.

$$\frac{110000}{3600} * 1.106 = 33.8$$

The target's vehicle travels at about 110 kilometers per hour. In the time it takes for the girder to drop 6 meters and be at a height of 1 meter above the ground (precisely in line with windshield), the vehicle will travel approximately 33 meters and 80 centimeters.

I'd have to place a marker on the side of the road at a distance of 33 meters and 80 centimeters from the bridge and cause the girder to fall at the exact moment the target's vehicle passes it.

To remotely release the bolts holding the girder in place and cause it to drop would require timing-precision of less than 1/10th of a second, and the chances of success are small. The speed of the vehicle and wind direction are also unpredictable factors. It won't work. I need to get to her in her home.

MORNING. JANUARY 2006

My target lives in an old apartment building in the city center. The building has 7 floors and there are 2 apartments on every level. I take a seat in the morning at the café across the street from the building and watch the entrance from the table adjacent to the window, going through emails from work and eating breakfast.

The target and her family live on the second floor. They took apartments 3 and 4 and combined them into a single unit so they wouldn't have any neighbors. Bodyguards live in apartments 1 and 2 on the first floor. They're posing as students.

Bodyguards also live in apartments 5 and 6 on the 3rd floor, thus, access to the target's apartment is blocked from both below and above.

The building is old, but all the windows on the second floor are brand new. They must have replaced the old windows with armored bulletproof glass.

The target has 2 children. An older daughter who looks about 6, and a younger one who is about 4 years old. I try hacking into CERN and looking in the target's folders on their file servers but their servers farm is well protected from outside penetration. I Google CERN employees and scientists, find her picture and her name and then search for more information she may have on the web like a Myspace page but find nothing. I keep following her for a few more days and learn by the lights in the apartment going on when she returns home that her bedroom is located at the southeastern end of the building. I learn where she shops for groceries and where her kids go to kindergarten and school. One day she also buys a large Gustav Klimt framed poster. I see her take it from her car and the guard downstairs helping her to carry it in.

I open my website and enter the password. A matrix of 9 simultaneous videos opens on my laptop screen, these are live feeds from all areas of my apartment back in Israel. In the feeds from the living room and kitchen, everything looks fine. Then I check the feed from the infrared camera in the basement. The man in the cage is naked and on all fours. He must be hot. He's trying to dig into the floor with a piece of plastic from a broken bottle of mineral water. I observe his efforts while I finish eating my breakfast.

I leave a 5-franc tip for the café's shift manager, who is also a part of the target's security team. I know as much because I see him communicating on occasion with the security chief, whose silhouette appears in the window of the building across the street. When the shift manager places a call, the security chief removes his cell phone from his pocket and the 2 men converse.

I go to my client's office to work on the existing computer system's performance report prior to the upgrade.

That afternoon I get a shirt made with the logo and telephone number of a florist in Geneva that I copy from a local website.

MORNING. JANUARY 2006

I wear the florist shirt under my coat. I buy a bouquet of flowers and an accompanying greeting card. I scribble "Happy Birthday, Olga" on the card and head for the target's home.

I park my rental car a block away from the target's building, leave the coat inside and put on a colorful woolen hat. We were taught at The Organization that if you're wearing 1 conspicuous item of clothing, people will focus their attention on it and remember it rather than your facial features.

It's 9 in the morning and the target and her family have already left the house. The bodyguards are less vigilant.

I approach the building.

I walk into the building and press the elevator button to the 7th floor. It's an old elevator. It has large buttons for the different floors. The button to the 2nd floor has been replaced by a cylinder lock, and the floor can be accessed with a key only. Fitted into the elevator door is an elongated pane of tinted glass. I see the silhouette of a bodyguard as I pass the 2nd floor. He's standing in the hallway. The apartments above and below the 2nd floor are also permanently manned with bodyguards, even when the target and her family aren't home. I exit the elevator on the 7th floor and check the door to the apartment on the south side of the building. An oval-shaped sign on the door reads ADRIANA KARSON. I place the bouquet of flowers at the door to the apartment across the hall and turn toward the stairwell. I open the door to the stairwell and peer down. There are no bodyguards in the stairwell.

I take the elevator and leave the building and head to work.

I stop at the Geneva Holiday travel agency on Route de Saint-Georges.

I tell the travel agent that a good friend of mine was diagnosed recently with terminal cancer and that I want to treat her to a holiday package for 2 to Rio. It's pancreatic cancer. "She doesn't have much time left," I say, and explain to the travel agent that she must make it appear as if my friend has won some sort of prize because she wouldn't agree to accept such an expensive gift from me.

I pay in cash and tell the travel agent that I'm going to write my friend a letter, which will appear to have come from Swissair, to tell her to pick up the tickets that she won.

"No problem," the travel agent says, "anything to make her happy."

"Yes, it's the last holiday she has left," I respond. "And one more thing, can you please give her a call later today and tell her that you are the agency dealing with these tickets and that she has won and will receive them soon by mail? I am afraid that if I just leave the tickets in her mailbox she will think it is junk mail and throw them away."

"No problem."

"And don't mention anything about her cancer."

"Of course."

I meet with the client to discuss my suggestions on how to improve his system's performance. I get the go-ahead to perform an upgrade to the operating system and the database on Tuesday night.

I use the time at the client's offices to write a letter.

Dear Mrs. Adriana Karson,

As part of a customer maintenance and reward program, we conduct a weekly prize drawing in which we give away free tickets for vacant seats on flights to a wide variety of destinations.

We are pleased to inform you that you have won a vacation package that includes two air tickets to Rio de Janeiro and five nights at a five-star hotel.

Your prize can be claimed at the Holiday Geneva travel agency on Route de Saint-Georges.
Please hurry, as the tickets are last-minute vacancies.
The flight (LX2815) departs Thursday evening!

I use Google to translate the letter into German and French and print out 1 copy in each language on sheets of paper bearing the Swissair logo.

I print the Swissair logo onto an envelope, insert the 2 folded pages and seal it, and mail the envelope to Adriana Karson.

I place a new order on The Organization's website:

Order 10483-2:
Expenses
1. Commercial vehicle
2. Paint and logo for the vehicle
3. Domain name for Internet website
4. Painting equipment (brushes, paint, buckets, masking tape)
5. Ladder
6. Large hydraulic jack
7. Thick metal bar

8. Iso-Flex sealant
9. 200 tubes of silicone + dispenser
10. Rubber sheeting
11. Prepaid cellular telephone
12. Overalls + overalls logo printing
13. 5-night holiday package for 2 to Rio de Janeiro
14. 1 pair of shoes
15. Shirt + printing
16. Woolen hat
17. Coat
18. Miscellaneous printing costs
19. Boxes of matches
20. Short length of garden hose
21. Jerrycan
22. My salary

Required
1. 52,000 Swiss francs
2. 200,000 Canadian dollars
3. 400,000 Argentine pesos
4. Swiss identity card in the name of Alberto Lombardi (photo attached), country of birth—Italy
5. Visa credit card in the name of Alberto Lombardi with a withdrawal facility of at least $5,000   6.
   Swiss driver's license in the name of Alberto Lombardi
7. Swiss passport in the name of Alberto Lombardi

I attach a photograph of myself with a full beard and brown contact lenses to the order. I'm not using the passport I received in the name of Peter Connor for now.

I design a website, "Alberto Lombardi, Painting and Carpentry," and include various pictures of apartments that are undergoing renovations and paintwork.

I place an online order for business cards, receipt books, and 2 large stickers for a commercial vehicle that read LOMBARDI PAINTING AND CARPENTRY—UNCOMPROMISING QUALITY. They'll be ready this evening.

I print out a work order for an apartment painting job and sign it "Adriana Karson."

I browse the Internet to find a commercial vehicle for sale and check where I can buy all the items I need to kill the target.

I leave the office in the evening and return to the hotel in the rental car.

There's an envelope waiting for me at reception. It contains a credit card in the name of Alberto Lombardi and a note. The note informs me that a locker has been reserved for me at the Gare de Cornavin in Geneva and that the credit card will open it.

I slip the card into my wallet go to the bathroom, where I tear the note into small pieces, drop them into the toilet, and flush.

I apply Alberto Lombardi's beard and drive to the Gare de Cornavin, collect a large brown envelope from the locker, and go into the station's public bathroom.

I'm not being followed.

I remove all the items I ordered from the envelope. Everything's there—the passport, ID card, driving license and several bundles of cash. Swiss Francs, Canadian dollars, Argentine pesos. The Organization doesn't ask questions. If a field agent requests something, he gets it. I'll need the money to complete the mission in Canada and Argentina.

I take a cab to Rue du Stand near the river. There, Lisa sells me a Fiat pickup van.

Lisa has a flower shop and uses the van for deliveries and to pick up flowers and equipment from nurseries. She's upgrading to a new Toyota. She asks me to be kind to the Fiat. "No problem," I say. I pay her in cash. We manage to complete the ownership transfer before the Licensing Office closes.

I drive the pick-up to a large Carrefour shopping center and purchase equipment. Tins of white paint, a ladder, masking tape, and all the other items on the list I drew up in the notebook.

The shop assistant cocks his head and fixes me with a stare when I ask him for 10 large boxes of Iso-Flex sealant and 200 tubes of silicone. "It's for a big sealing job, a swimming pool," I explain. He also offers me a special kind of water-resistant paint. I buy that, too.

I buy a vehicle jack and a 60-centimeter-long metal rod in a different section of the mall.

I put all the equipment in the back of the van, cover everything with a length of tarpaulin I bought, and tie it down well.

I stop off at the print shop on my way back to pick up my order, and in a parking lot behind a gas station, after I make sure there's no one around, I apply the stickers to the van. I park the van 2 blocks from my hotel and walk the rest of the way.

I'll complete the first part of my mission this weekend, the first envelope. Then I'll go back to Israel to kill the man in my basement.

MORNING. JANUARY 2006. FRIDAY

I park on the street outside the target's building and begin offloading the contents of the van onto the sidewalk. It takes less than a minute for one of the security guards to come over. "What are you doing here?" he asks me.

"Is this 21 Rue de Délices?" I ask.

"Yes," he says. "What business do you have here?"

"I have a work order here from someone named Adriana Karson," I reply. "Seventh floor. Do you know her?" I show him the page I printed with Adriana's name and the signature I scribbled.

He tells me Adriana has gone away and isn't home. He saw her leaving last night with a suitcase.

"That's right," I say, "I'm painting her apartment, and she won't be able to sleep there for the next two nights. She went to a hotel and left me a key to the apartment."

I load the tins of paint in the meantime onto a carry cart. "Do you want to keep an eye on my gear while I take the paint up?" I ask the guard. "I'll give you five francs."

The guard looks at me. His eyes narrow. He lets out a snort, turns back toward the building and walks inside. Before reentering the apartment on the first floor he turns and says, "Don't wander around the building and don't make a mess in the lobby or elevator."

"I work clean," I say.

I take the equipment up to the 7th floor. I remove the jack and a metal rod from a large tool box. I have to open Adriana Karson's door without making any noise, so as not to arouse the suspicion of the guards in the apartments below.

The door and frame are made of metal. The deadbolt lock looks new. I position the jack parallel to the floor at the height of the lock, surface pressed against the doorframe. I then position the metal rod between the other end of the jack and the opposite side of the doorframe, holding the rod parallel to the floor. I turn the handle of the jack and it takes no more than 30 seconds to widen the doorframe by 3 centimeters without making a sound. I push the door and it opens inward into the apartment. I return the jack and metal rod to the toolbox.

I offload the paint and go down to the van twice more to get the rest of the equipment. I then park the van in a nearby lot and return to the apartment.

I take a 10-liter tin of paint and empty it down the sink. I place the empty container under the faucet in the bath and turn the knob. It takes 72 seconds to fill up. I turn off the faucet and proceed to paint one of the walls.

I then spread a layer of Iso-Flex over the floor and cover it with plastic sheeting. I seal the windows with silicone and then cover them with rubber sheeting that I adhere to the walls with adhesive tape.

I accurately measure the dimensions of the apartment with measuring tape. I go through all the rooms.

And measure again.

One last time.

I wrap impermeable rubber sheeting around the toilet bowls and use plastic sheeting and silicone to block the drain openings in all the sinks. I collect all the empty tubes of silicone, paint containers, and Iso-Flex packaging in large garbage bags.

On the inside of the front door I stick a length of rubber

sheeting that extends 5 centimeters beyond the doorframe on all sides.

At 11:30 a.m.:

I open the bathroom faucet and the tap in the kitchen,

Take the garbage bags and tools with me,

Widen the doorframe again,

Close the front door,

Return the jack and metal rod to the tool box,

Load all the equipment into the van,

Wave goodbye to the guard, who ignores me,

Drive to an empty campsite outside of town that's close to the train station,

Torch the van,

Catch a train back to the city center,

Walk for 15 minutes back to the hotel,

Shower,

Drive my rental car to another day of work at the office of the client.

Everything has to be ready ahead of the system upgrade on Tuesday, and I'm planning on working late into the night.

Yasmin woke with a strange sense of apprehension. Something wasn't right. She was aware of a dull rumbling noise all around her, the sound of metal snapping and bending, and loud booms one after the other that shook the apartment. She thought for a moment that she was dreaming. She glanced over at the clock on the bedside table. It was 3:40 in the morning. Albert isn't next to her in bed. He went to speak at a conference in Stockholm. It must be an earthquake. She should go get the girls who are asleep in the adjacent room.

She sat up and the world came to an end.

The ceiling of her apartment gave way and came crashing down onto her bed, together with the five additional apartments above it and a huge torrent of water. Chunks of concrete and steel, furniture and household objects, bodies, drywall, clothes, and water. So much water.

The adrenaline in her body completely blocked out all sense of pain. Even when she felt the bones of her legs bend and break under the immense pressure of the concrete beam that fell on them. All she could do was try to cry out the names of her 2 daughters.

She couldn't.

The pressure on her chest was enormous. She couldn't cry out. Or breathe. The screams around her faded.

The last image etched in her consciousness before everything came crashing down, in a flash of light that sparked an electrical short, was the picture of a tree in shades of brown, orange, and yellow. The tree's swirling branches that twisted and turned into spirals adorned with spotted geometric shapes. There was a signature at the bottom of the picture: Gustav Klimt.

January 15th 2006

The encrypted phone in Amiram's home rang at seven in the morning. The department head for Western Europe was on the line. He didn't sound happy.

"So this is the way you do things now? You turn an entire building into a pile of rubble just to take out one target? Do you have any idea how this is going to affect our relations with Switzerland? What do you think—that Switzerland's DDPS isn't going to guess who's behind it? Who is the idiot you sent there? Do you have any idea what you've got us into?"

"I don't understand what you're talking about."

"Target six on the Bernoulli list—that's what I'm talking about. She's on your list and now she's gone and so is an entire building. You blew up an entire building in Geneva—residents and all, that's what I'm talking about. And I hear about it from the Public News Monitoring Unit who just caught it on a BBC newsflash."

"Let me look into what happened there and I'll get back to you."

"You do that. Be in my office at eight. Come with preliminary details."

Amiram left his half-eaten breakfast on the kitchen table and got up. He's responsible; he's the one who gave the mission to 10483. But who could have imagined that he'd take down an entire building? And where did he get the explosive material? He would have needed at least 100 kilograms to cause such extensive damage.

We'll have to throw him out of The Organization. But he knows too much. Who can guarantee his silence?

And why did the micro tracking device that was fixed to him and the cell phone he gave him indicate that he was in Thailand? What was he doing in Thailand before the mission in Switzerland?

I'll send two agents over to his home when he returns from Geneva to intimidate him a little. They'll tell him to look for another job and that he best keep his mouth shut.

So that's how he brought down the building! Avner marveled at the simplicity. They never figured out how a single agent without access to explosives had managed to flatten a seven-story building on top of a target. Or more precisely, on top of the target and her family and an additional thirty-eight residents, who were all killed in the collapse of the building at 21 Rue de Délices.

Avner recalled seeing a page of figures and calculations in the bundle that he hadn't been able to figure out. He looked for it again among the pile of papers and reviewed it carefully. The page showed a sketch of a small apartment. It read:

First measurement—83 square meters

Second measurement—83 square meters

Third measurement—83 square meters

Area of apartment: 83 square meters

500 kilograms per square meter = $83 \times 500 =$

 41,500 liters = 41.5 tons

Filling rate per liter = 7.2 seconds

Total $7.2 \times 41,500 = 298,800$ sec = 4,980 minutes = 83 hours

2 taps simultaneously:

83/2 = 41.5 hours

To achieve a load of half a ton per square meter at 5 in the morning on Sunday, the taps need to be opened 41.5 hours prior to then = 11:30 on Friday morning.

It's an old building. It won't hold up under the pressure of half a ton per square meter.

Avner needed to get some fresh air. He left the small office he was in, locked the door behind him, and went out through the door to the basement.

"That's it? Done for the day?"

"No. Just going upstairs for a while to get some fresh air. I'm leaving all my stuff here with you, okay?"

"No problem."

It was a little after three in the morning and it felt cool and pleasant outside. It smelled like winter, narcissus in bloom. He could hear the dull hum of a jet taking off from Ben Gurion International Airport in the distance, but all else was quiet. A sudden movement behind a row of bushes caught Avner's attention, and he reached instinctively for his gun, remembering as he did so that he'd left it downstairs with the guard. He crouched down and waited.

A cat emerged from the bushes. Avner stood up and stretched. He went back down to the office. Had he thought to look back, he would have seen a black shadow moving silently toward his car.

The black shadow sped through the section of yard normally covered by the malfunctioned camera, taking care not to stray into view of the rest of the cameras that covered the villa. First he dealt with the camera, now he'd take care of the car. The shadow crawled under the white Mazda, retrieved a screwdriver and cordless power drill from the small bag he carried, and went to work.

Back in the basement of the villa Avner went through the screening process in front of the glass wall one more time, returned to the small office, sat down, and picked up the notebook again.

January 4th 2006

The wheels of the plane touched down on the runway at Heathrow and the large Boeing shuddered a little and slowed on the tarmac. Carmit woke up and stretched. She peeked out from under the thin blanket she'd covered herself with during the flight, and scanned the interior of the plane. Everything appeared to be in order, except for the passenger who sat a few rows behind her and was making an unnatural effort to avoid eye-contact with her. Now he was pretending to be asleep. So transparent, she thought to herself. The assholes dispatched someone to keep track of her. Really?!

The doors opened and passengers began streaming out of the plane. Carmit decided she wanted to have some fun with the man sent to follow her. She tucked her head under the blanket again and waited.

When the plane was completely empty a flight attendant gently touched her shoulder. "We've landed," she said, smiling. Carmit smiled back and stretched again. The only other passenger still on the plane was the man she'd suspected earlier. Carmit moved the blanket aside and slowly put on her sneakers. She took her time retrieving her backpack from the storage compartment above her. The man made his way out the plane. Carmit smiled at him as he passed by. He realized she had him. They both knew he was out of the game.

Carmit exited the aircraft and walked through the terminal toward the baggage claim area, taking careful note of all the people she could see on the way. She went into the bathroom and closed the door behind her. In addition to what one normally does in the bathroom after a flight, she removed her iPod and laptop from her bag and shut them down completely so they couldn't be used as tracking devices.

Although she was traveling with only the backpack she carried, Carmit stopped at the baggage carousel and waited. Slowly but surely the passengers from her plane all headed off with their luggage and were eventually replaced by passengers from the next flight. Carmit spotted one passenger who'd stayed behind, seemingly waiting for a suitcase that never showed up. She looked at him and smiled until he cracked and headed off. Follower number two burned.

She spent the next few hours traveling through the various London Underground stations, buying lingerie at Victoria's Secret, visiting the London Zoo (she didn't skip over a single exhibit, and acquired two stuffed animals—a giraffe and a lion—in the process), eating fish and chips at a street stall, and constantly messing with the people who were following her. New faces kept replacing old ones. The last one was a curly-haired man who looked Middle Eastern, wearing a yellow shirt.

Carmit stopped on the street next to the most intimidating skinhead in sight.

"Excuse me, but I'm terrified. Perhaps you could help me?" She blinked her eyes at him in total panic.

"What's the problem?"

"That man back there, with the yellow shirt, he's been following me now for the past hour. I don't know what to do. Can you hold him up for a while so I can get away from him? Here's a fifty."

"I won't just hold him up. I'll bury the motherfucker. Go."

Carmit continued down Oxford Street toward the Marble Arch as all hell broke loose behind her. She crossed to Hyde Park Corner, tightened the straps of her backpack, and broke into a sprint through the park as she gave the entire surveillance team the slip.

MORNING. JANUARY 2006

I land back in Israel and go through passport control. Someone's on my tail from the moment I leave the airport. I take a cab to the health clinic.

I walk into the clinic and request an urgent appointment. I tell the receptionist I'm suffering from dizziness and blurred vision and that the right side of my body isn't functioning as well as my left side. The receptionist immediately slots me in to see a family doctor. I'm next in line.

Truth is I don't have any of those symptoms; I'm making them up. What I am suffering from is a constant buzzing in my head. I believe it's a listening device that they planted in my head while I was sleeping and is now transmitting my thoughts. That's why I'm making an effort to think only of petty things that don't have any value as intelligence. The people following me must be enemies of The Organization. One of them is sitting just a few meters to my right down the hall outside the dermatologist's door.

The family doctor gives me an urgent referral to the emergency room. I can barely lift my right arm for her and my right leg appears lame. I speak strangely, too, as if my tongue is numb.

On the way out I buy 2 packages of sleeping pills from an elderly man. I saw him buy them earlier from the clinic's pharmacy; they're mine now for 400 shekels.

I leave the clinic. Someone new is following me, and I see the man who was following me previously approach the elderly man I bought the pills from. He must be questioning him now.

I take a cab to the ER at Tel Hashomer Hospital and I'm

rushed off for an MRI. I receive the results burned onto a CD within 40 minutes. I'm told to take the disc to the Neurology Department, but I leave the hospital. My limp is gone.

I take a cab home. On the way I take my laptop out of my bag, turn it on and insert the CD. I take a close look at my brain through all the MRI scans, including the 3-D imaging. There's no listening device in my head. The buzzing has stopped.

I get home and go inside. I make sure not to walk straight in but turn immediately to the right toward the kitchen, and then left and left again toward the bedroom. Thus I avoid falling into the cage in the basement. I peer out the window and see the car that was following my cab parked a little farther down the street. Its windows are tinted and it's impossible to see how many people are inside apart from the driver and the woman in the passenger seat.

I go down to the basement through the bedroom closet.

I turn on the light in the basement.

The man in the basement is sitting down in the cage, with his back resting against the bars. His legs are stretched out in front of him. "Water," he says. His eyes are closed. He's become accustomed to the dark over the past weeks. The light blinds him.

I see he's out of water bottles.

"You have to die now," I say to him. "I have no need for you."

I take a bottle of mineral water and sit down in front of the cage. I take out one package of sleeping pills and crush them one by one into the bottle. The package contains 40 tablets. I shake the bottle well and throw it into the cage.

The man in the cage is thirsty. He hesitates for a moment but his thirst overpowers him. He gulps down the entire bottle. Drinking and crying.

"With your permission, I'll perform a brief religious ceremony," I say to him.

I reach for a sheet of paper I prepared in the basement ahead of time and recite the Kaddish prayer out loud to him while he drinks the contents of the bottle:

> *Yit'gadal ve-'yit'kadash sh'mei raba . . .*
> *Throughout the world which He has created according to His Will.*
> *May He establish His kingship, bring forth His redemption and hasten the coming of His Messiah*
> *In your lifetime and in your days and in the lifetime of the entire House of Israel,*
> *Speedily and soon, and say, Amen.*
> *May His great Name be blessed forever and to all eternity.*
> *Blessed and praised and glorified,*
> *Exalted and extolled and honored,*
> *Adored and lauded be the Name of the Holy One, blessed be He.*
> *Beyond all the blessings, hymns, praises*
> *And consolations that are uttered in the world, and say, Amen.*

He continues to cry. "Don't worry, you won't feel a thing," I say to him.

I go back upstairs to shower. On my way to the bathroom I look outside. The car with the tinted windows is still parked down the street.

I thaw a frozen chicken breast in the microwave and cook it for dinner. It'll be dark soon. I return to the basement. The man in the basement is in the same position, his back against the bars, the empty bottle of water lying on the floor next to him, his eyes open, his mouth open. He isn't breathing.

Fitted into a niche in the wall of the basement is a large aquarium I constructed before my trip to Geneva. It's 2 meters high, 1.8 meters wide and half a meter deep. 4 LED lights add a blue glow to the tank.

I unlock the side door to the cage and drag the man out. I wash him down with a hose and move him into the aquarium. He isn't heavy. I fill the aquarium to the brim with cooking oil that I've stockpiled in the basement. It'll stop the body from decomposing. Formaldehyde would have been better, but buying such a large quantity of formaldehyde would raise questions.

I turn on the LED lights.

To complete the picture I get a blank sheet of paper and stick it to the bottom right corner of the aquarium with 2 strips of adhesive tape. I write on the page in block letters with a black marker:

TIME
HAS FOLDED ITS GRAY WINGS
AND WILL NO LONGER SPREAD THEM
OVER YOU

I take 3 steps back and look at the piece. Perfect. No need to add a thing.

I clear away all the trash that accumulated in the cage while I was in Geneva, dump it all into large garbage bags, and wash down the cage with a hose and an entire container of bleach. I carry the bags up from the basement. I'll throw them away in the morning.

NIGHT. JANUARY 2006

Tel Aviv.

I'm standing at the entrance to a floor of offices.

I press the button for the elevator.

There are 3 elevators. The middle one comes down from the 8th floor and stops at mine. The 2nd floor.

The doors open and a wave of water spills out and washes through the hallway.

The flow doesn't stop. It intensifies.

The hallway begins to fill up with water. The level keeps rising. I swim in the water until it almost reaches the ceiling. I try to press my mouth to the ceiling to keep breathing. The water is almost touching the fluorescent lighting in the hallway. Sparks fly from the electricity. The hallway fills with a charred smell. I start to breathe water.

I hear the sound of muffled bangs and wake up.

The sounds are coming from below.

From the basement.

Someone is firing a gun.

I go back to sleep.

I'll wake at 1:30 to check what's going on down there.

Erez and Limor stood in the cage.

They aren't rookies; they're burned field agents.

A burned field agent is an agent who was caught on camera while carrying out a mission abroad and whose face is now a target for facial recognition software in public locations around the world. The moment such an agent were to step foot in an airport somewhere, he'd be arrested on the spot. A beard or wig would be of no use. The software measures dozens of parameters, like the distance between the eyes, the shape of the nose, the chin line, and the circumference of the skull. It can't be fooled. Even plastic surgery doesn't help.

The Organization looks after such agents and arranges work for them within Israel, at one of the intelligence analysis departments or in the form of easygoing and risk-free fieldwork inside the country.

This was supposed to have been one of those jobs.

Breaking in posed no problem at all.

They planned to make their way to 10483's bed and jolt him out of sleep with their guns to his face. They would explain that he no longer worked for The Organization, that he would be under surveillance, and that if he breathed even a single word, they wouldn't bother waking him next time. They'd just put a bullet in his head.

Three steps into the apartment, and the floor gave way beneath them. The six-meter fall left them stunned for several minutes. After getting back on their feet, Limor switched on a small flashlight to see where they were.

The beam of the flashlight shone directly on the aquarium in which a naked body, arms outstretched and eyes and mouth wide open, appeared to hover before them in a yellowish solution. An involuntary scream escaped Limor's lips and she aimed her pistol at the tank, but Erez stopped her.

"There's no point, it's a corpse."

"What is this place?"

"I have no idea. Shine the light here for a moment."

"They're bars; we're in a prison cell! How could there be a prison inside a residential building in the heart of Tel Aviv?"

"Let's have a go at shooting this bar out. Maybe we can break it. Move back a moment; I'm going to fire my weapon."

I leave the dentist's office and get into my car. I run my hand over my left cheek and realize that he pulled my left molar instead of my right one.

I start the car and drive off.

There's a pair of sunglasses on the seat next to me. They aren't mine. I realize that the car isn't mine either. The color of the upholstery is different. Strange that my key opened it.

I have a slight sense of déjà vu. I remember that I left the kettle on the stove, and then remember that I have an electric kettle.

It's like déjà vu backward. As if I remember having been in this place yet I know I never was. Or I was, but I didn't do what I'm doing now.

I reach up to my shirt pocket for a cigarette and realize that my shirt has no pocket. Then I remember that I don't smoke.

Had I taken the pill in the small box on the bookshelf in my safe room, I might have been able to remember everything.

Then I remember that I don't have a safe room.

I wake at 1:30 and go down to the basement.

I peer into the darkness from the bottom of the ladder. A shot fired from a pistol flies by—mere centimeters from my face. It's hard to aim in the dark.

I get a glimpse of 2 figures in the cage. I pull back.

I assume the shots I heard earlier were their attempts to break out the cage. They don't have a hope in hell. Not even with an M-16 assault rifle would they be able to pierce or cut through

2-centimeter-thick steel bars without killing themselves first with the ricochets. They must have realized this and stopped shooting pretty quickly.

"You missed," I call out to them.

"It was an accident," a woman's voice replies. "We just want to talk. We've been sent by The Organization to update you about the mission."

"Then throw your weapons out of the cage," I reply. I don't believe a word they say.

Nothing but silence from the basement. I don't hear the sound of weapons falling.

"You're both going to die anyway," I say to them. "I can't afford to let you live. If you throw out your weapons, I promise it'll be quick and painless."

The man responds with a torrent of curses. He spits out, "So you can put us in your exhibit, too? You're sick in the head! We've contacted the home base; the entire organization is on its way over."

These enemies are trying to deceive me. They're lying. First of all, the basement is fitted with a cellular signal jamming device. No cell phone is going to work down there. And surely they can't be from The Organization. The Organization wouldn't send armed individuals in the dead of night to its best agent, and certainly not right after an operation as successful as the one I carried out in Geneva.

But they're familiar with the home base. Someone in The Organization must be collaborating with them. I'll leave a message about it on The Organization's website before I fly out to complete my next mission.

"See you in twenty-four hours," I say, and return to my bedroom via the floor of the closet. I have a few errands to run. I use the control panel next to the ladder to turn off the dim light and ventilation system in the basement.

I open the Lufthansa website and book a flight to Frankfurt in the name of Peter Connor.

I browse the net for information on Instituto Balseiro and find out that it's an academic institution, located in Bariloche, Argentina, chartered by the National University of Cuyo and the country's National Atomic Energy Commission. The institution offers studies in physics, nuclear and mechanical engineering.

I read through background material on the nuclear engineering projects in Bariloche that started after World War II. German scientists who'd worked on nuclear projects in Nazi Germany fled Europe after the war. Some found a partner in the continuation of their nuclear endeavors in the form of Juan Domingo Perón, who was in power in Argentina at the time. Huge sums of money went toward setting up a secret project on Huemul Island, off the coast of Bariloche, where they constructed nuclear laboratories with the purpose of producing controlled nuclear fusion using cheap materials. The project failed, but the structures that were once the reactor and laboratories remain scattered and crumbling on the island as a reminder.

Instituto Balseiro, on the other hand, remains active to this day. I'll fly from Frankfurt to Buenos Aires and get a connection from there to Bariloche.

I reserve a room for 2 weeks at Bariloche's Hotel Premier. It's a small hotel located 200 meters from the lake.

I save a map to the institution on my laptop, along with its operating hours and pictures of the buildings and academic staff members. I see based on the photograph in my possession that my target is Professor Federico Lopez.

It's 3 in the morning. I go back to bed to sleep for a few more hours.

MORNING. FEBRUARY 2006

I get up at 10 in the morning and call the municipality to report a car with tinted windows that's parked illegally in a place reserved for vehicles belonging to Tel Aviv residents. The car doesn't have a Tel Aviv resident tag.

I clean the house well and scrub the plate, fork, and knife I used yesterday.

I go out to the mailbox and retrieve a stack of letters that have accumulated there. Outside I see the car being loaded onto a tow truck. There's already a citation on its windshield.

I browse through the mail at the entrance to my building. The junk mail goes into the trash bin and the letters and bills remain in my hand.

I return to the apartment and open all the envelopes. I pay my water, municipal tax, electricity, and gas bills online with a credit card. I then throw out the trash, which includes all the bags I filled from the cage after I washed it.

I head off to the gym, then go for a long run.

At night I sit in the living room and watch the video feed on my laptop from the camera in the basement. The camera's infrared beam allows me to see in the total darkness down there.

I see them sitting in the cage. After leaving them for 24 hours without water, in complete darkness and without fresh air, I check to see if they're willing to cooperate.

My laptop's microphone is connected to a powerful speaker in the basement, and a microphone in the basement is connected to the speakers of my laptop.

"Hello again to you down there," I say. They jump up in fright and point their weapons in the direction of the ladder to the bedroom.

"I advise you to throw your weapons out of the cage so that we can move forward," I say to them.

"Okay. We'll cooperate." He says and takes a Zippo lighter from his pocket and throws it through the bars of the cage. The lighter makes a metallic sound as it falls to the floor.

"What about the second gun?"

"Come on, throw yours out, too," the man says to the woman; and she wraps a belt with a large metal buckle around her wallet and throws it out through the bars. It too makes a metallic sound when it hits the floor.

"There you go," says the man, "we've thrown out our weapons. Now let's talk."

"You're very thirsty. You also must have noticed, that the oxygen level in the air down there is dropping and it's getting harder for you to breathe. That's because I turned off the basement's ventilation system. I don't need your lighter or your wallet. See you in twenty-four hours. If you're still alive by then."

They both throw their weapons out the cage and scream for water.

I go to my bedroom, open the closet, lift up the floor panel and climb down the ladder. I collect the guns off the floor and throw 2 bottles of mineral water to the couple in the basement. They drink them. I turn on the ventilation system and sit down on a chair in front of the cage.

The woman remains silent. The man looks panicked. "Don't you understand?" he says. "Amiram sent us. You mistakenly received three envelopes instead of one. You have to suspend the missions. We've been sent by The Organization to explain it all to you. Geneva was your only mission, and there, you killed too many people."

I don't believe him. Amiram has to be notified. The mission has been exposed. I can't allow myself to be confused by the enemy. There must be a mole in The Organization. Someone from the very heart of The Organization is relaying information about the most confidential missions. I can't let them stop me.

"I put sleeping tablets in your water," I say to them. "Ten tablets for each of you. You'll soon fall asleep."

They both start to scream again. I tell them they each received just 10 tablets. "I promised you'd die slowly," I say to them. "The tablets won't kill you."

I wait for them to fall asleep. They try as hard they can to fight it. They beat themselves and bang their heads against the bars in an effort to neutralize the effect of the tablets.

I watch them for about half an hour, then open the cage door after they both fall asleep.

I drag them out and position them in keeping with the picture I have in mind. Before going back upstairs I turn around to look at them one last time. Perfect.

I photograph them and the man in the aquarium.

Back upstairs in the apartment I print the 2 images on small sheets of glossy photo paper.

February 2nd 2006

"Janet speaking, how can I be of assistance?"

"Hello."

"It'll cost you seventy-five thousand pounds."

"You're out of your mind."

"That's what you get for the bullshit with the surveillance team last time." Carmit was digging into a bowl of spaghetti pomodoro. She sucked noisily on a string of pasta, and drops of tomato sauce spattered and landed on the tip of her nose.

"You almost killed one member of the team," the voice on the other end of the line sighed.

"Admit it was a brilliant idea," Carmit grinned. "You don't give up, do you? You're wasting your time." She took a sip from the glass of red wine on the table in front of her and signaled the waiter with a thumbs-up and a smile that she was ready for a refill. "When do you need me?"

"Next week. Friday. Bariloche, Argentina."

"Ah, a little pressed for time, are we? Perhaps I should have asked for more. Three days. Thursday morning to Saturday night. Excluding flights. Seventy-five thousand British pounds into Credit Suisse account 016502381. By tomorrow evening at the latest. Headphones and glasses?"

"Yes."

"Encrypted image and encrypted conversion file to janet.wong.73@gmail.com."

"You'll get them today. The payment, too."

"It's a pleasure doing business with you."
"Fuck you!"
"Die already"

NIGHT. FEBRUARY 2006

My headache stops abruptly.

I place the bottle beside me. It takes immediate effect.

When the pain subsides I'm extremely focused. Sharp as butcher's knife. No, sharp as a surgeon's scalpel. I'm able to analyze everything clearly, as if a black veil was shrouding my brain before and is now gone.

My brain, usually inhibited, begins to realize its potential with full force. That's why I always have a small pencil in my pocket. So I can make a note of things before the veil comes down again and dulls everything.

But I don't take my pencil out this time. This time I look inward.

I scan my insides from the bone of my little toe all the way through to the fine capillaries in my brain. My awareness splits into several paths, each scanning a different system or organ— kidneys, digestive system, sex organs, respiratory system, heart, metabolism. All the data is gathered and processed quickly.

I understand now that in order to prolong the effect of the juice I need to adjust the pH levels in my stomach and slow my blood flow. I do so. I can now consciously control these functions.

I can't understand why I never thought to do this before. I buy myself a few more minutes before the black veil takes over again.

I know that every sneeze takes 14 minutes off an individual's life. I know this because I can read the capillaries in my brain and understand the erosive effect the pressure of a single sneeze has on the walls of the blood vessels.

I think for a moment that perhaps I should write it all down in the notebook, but there's no time now. I have to delve deeper.

I slightly adjust the rate of flow of oxygen into the red blood cells in my lungs, and my eyes fix momentarily on the back of my left hand. I play with the skin pigmentation on the back of my hand such that my beauty spots and freckles appear and disappear with every passing second and display the current time.

I notice I have less than a minute. I'm dwelling on trivialities again. I breathe in, totally suspend the functioning of my stomach, and move directly into my brain. The effort to comprehend all these connections is huge, and my body temperature rises despite the fact that I channel more blood into my brain to rid it of excess heat, and produce as much perspiration as possible to cool my body.

Then, mere seconds before all the alarm lights begin flashing red and the black veil again sets in, I understand it all. My brain is laid bare to me, completely decoded, I am aware of the function of every single cell in that gray sponge, every interneuron, every tiny electrical current.

I temporarily shut down a problematic neural circuit, apply a number of bypasses and restore normal functioning to all my body's systems. The black veil won't return again.

I get up and throw the bottle in the trash. I won't be needing it anymore. The bottle lands in the bin and knocks out a piece of crumpled paper. Instinctively, I bend down to pick it up, but then I stop.

I concentrate for a moment and the piece of paper rises up off the floor on its own, its folds straighten out completely, and it floats smoothly through the air and comes to rest gently on the table next to me. I take the small pencil out my pocket and write on the page: "Remember not to sneeze anymore."

I wake up at 1:30.

I check the bottles in the fridge and the displays in the basement and go out for a run. It's quiet outside and the street is empty. I go around my block and then all the way to Yarkon Park, then I continue along the running track toward the sea.

When I run I don't have to think or dream.

It's almost 2 in the morning yet it's hot outside. I'm sweating.

I hear someone running behind me.

I run faster until the breathing fades into the distance and disappears.

I turn around.

There's no one behind me.

I have to remember not to sneeze anymore.

MORNING. FEBRUARY 2006

I'm at Ben Gurion Airport, waiting to check in.

Earlier, I'd emptied the contents of the fridge into the trash and threw out the garbage. I'll be away from home for a long time.

I call the office and speak to Nurit. I tell her I need to take 2 months unpaid vacation due to a family emergency. "Okay," she says.

I use my laptop to connect to The Organization's 300-tips website.

I leave a message.

"Amiram, you're being watched. Two people came to my home and told me you sent them. Someone outside The Organization is aware of the mission you gave me. They tried to stop me, unsuccessfully. I invited them to dinner in Milan. I think you need to leave The Organization. It'll be safer for everyone. I'm sure they're monitoring you as well. Careful they don't poison you. Check the bottles in your fridge before you drink from them."

I board the plane to Frankfurt.

I've stashed the money in several inside pockets.

The material about Instituto Balseiro is on my laptop.

The girl's tooth is around my neck.

The 2 photographs from the basement are in my wallet.

The flight attendant asks me what I'd like to drink. "Orange juice and water with ice," I say to him.

I'm on my way to my second target.

February 2nd 2006

Limor came to first. Her head hurt and she wanted to place her hand on her forehead but wasn't able to. Then she noticed that the basement wasn't in complete darkness—there was a bluish glow coming from the aquarium in front of her, and two spotlights were casting yellow circles of light around Erez and herself.

She was seated next to the empty cage in the basement on a heavy iron chair at one end of a table made of thick wooden beams and covered with a white tablecloth. Wooden bowls containing pieces of cooked meat and potatoes, and several loaves of bread were set out on the table. She looked at Erez, who sat on the other side of the table and had yet to wake up, and noticed he was wearing a light blue robe. She looked down and realized she was dressed in a robe, too. He had removed their clothes and dressed them in robes while they were unconscious. Her mouth was gagged with strips of duct tape wrapped several times around her head. She could only breathe through her nose.

Limor tried to work out why she wasn't able to move her hands. She looked down at her arms and legs and saw they were tied firmly to the chair with hundreds of small zip ties. She tried to fall backward together with the chair but wasn't able to. The chair was bolted to the floor. A long metal cord was wrapped around her stomach and then dozens of times around the back of the chair. She wasn't going anywhere. The only part of her body that wasn't tied to something was her head.

Erez was tied to his chair in the same manner.

She noticed an intravenous drip hooked up to his arm.

Limor looked at her right arm and saw an IV tube coming from it, too. The two tubes inserted into their bodies were connected to a single tube that emerged from a container the size of a water cooler bottle. The container sat on a high shelf outside the cage and the tube connecting them to it was long. Drop after drop left the container and flowed through the tube, split into two and made its way into their veins.

The drip would keep them alive for weeks. The basement's ventilation system was on.

He promised they would die slowly.

Fixed to the tablecloth with two strips of adhesive tape was an A4 sheet of paper. The page read: "L'Ultima Cena."

December 4th 2016

Avner closed the notebook and sighed. His throat was dry and he went to the kitchenette to get a glass of cold water.

The notebook said "I drag them out and position them in keeping with the picture I have in mind." Avner wondered what that picture was.

The trail of bodies 10483 left behind was getting longer. Another unsolved case was now resolved. Two more agents died at his hands. Two agents with families that don't have graves to visit to this day. "Missing in action in defense of the country"—that's the version the families get; but Avner knows no rest until all the loose ends are tied up. As the man who heads the recruitment department, he holds himself personally responsible for their fate. And now, finally, he knows he can give three families graves over which to mourn.

He wrote:

> **6.** Agents 6452 and 7274 were killed by 10483 in Tel Aviv. File can be closed.
>
> **7.** Make sure that the team going into the basement this morning comprises long-serving agents who've seen a thing or two in their lives. The basement isn't going to be pretty.
>
> **8.** Arrange for a female American agent to travel to Amsterdam to look for her "brother" who disappeared in May 2005 so that we can get the remains of the body. Equip her with 6844's DNA sample.

Dinner in Milan . . . They'd racked their brains for ages after the two agents disappeared. The strange message Amiram received from 10483 had thrown them completely off track. Every available agent in Italy at the time was sent out to look for the three agents in Milan. They thought that perhaps 10483 had managed to persuade the two agents to help him with the rest of his mission and that's where they'd met their deaths. He thought they'd agreed to it because they hoped that the airport cameras in Italy would pick them up so that they could all be arrested by Interpol. But they were down in the basement the whole time.

And how had they forgotten to issue a stay of exit order against him? What an endless succession of screw-ups! But perhaps he left the country under a different passport. Avner paged back through the notebook and read again:

I open the Lufthansa website and book a flight to Frankfurt in the name of Peter Connor. I still have his passport.

Avner sighed again. Such amateurism. How had they not thought to cancel the passport? He entered "6452, 7274" into the system's search engine and browsed through the collection of resulting documents. Surveillance requests, hospital checks in Europe, lists of unidentified corpses in Italy, compensation payments to the families of the agents, wiretaps on foreign agents, hacking of Interpol computers. So much energy spent looking for something that was right under their nose the whole time. How had they missed the basement when they'd searched the apartment after the fire?

An individual who kills for his country will eventually do so for himself, for personal motives. If someone cuts him off on the road, for example. Violence breeds more violence.

How do we channel this violence is the question. It can be done—with the right kind of training and guidance and ongoing psychological treatment and assessment. Of course that's assuming the agent is sane to begin with.

Avner's jaw dropped the first time he laid eyes on the Bernoulli Project hit list. It included the names of twelve of the world's leading physicists and chemists. All twelve were to be assassinated within four years. 10483 took out three of the targets; the remaining nine were killed one after the other by lone agents. For each target—a different agent, who was unaware of the other targets. Accidents, suicides, heart attacks, a stroke. The fact that no one around the world linked the series of deaths to a single entity was quite surprising. The notion was so insane that apparently no one even thought to do so. Who would want to kill a Nobel Laureate in physics? A scientist working on a medical breakthrough in the field of antiviral vaccines?

Avner was still missing one key piece of the Bernoulli Project puzzle: He knew the "what" but not the "why." Ten years down the line, it was time to find out.

Avner lifted the receiver of the office's encrypted telephone. It was already past three in the morning, not exactly the best time to trouble The Organization's top-ranking directors. But Avner wasn't able to contain himself. He needed answers now. Before the teams were sent in the morning to the apartment in Tel Aviv.

The person on the other end of the line picked up after two rings.

"Hi, Grandpa," Avner said. "I need your help."

December 4th 2016

Grandpa put the handset back on the dresser next to his bed. He pulled off his blanket, sat down, and put his feet into his slippers. Then he got up, stretched, and went to his home office. He sat down in front of his desk and passed his finger over the fingerprint reader. Three computer screens arranged in an arc on the desk in front of him came to life.

> It was clear that this would happen.
> That charred body was too easy.
> We should have kept looking.

Grandpa opened his Outlook contacts folder, found the phone number he needed, picked up his office phone, and dialed.

December 4th 2016

Rotem Rolnik was sound asleep.

On the living room carpet.

She was lying on her stomach, arms stretched out to her sides. The short tank top she wore left her upper back exposed, and the wing tips of a colorful fairy tattoo peeked out from under the fabric. The fairy's feet appeared in the space between the lower end of her tank top and the black sweatpants she was wearing.

Her hand rested on a stack of printed pages and next to her was a pile of books with small yellow notes stuffed between their pages. Two open laptops were perched on the coffee table by her side. Both displayed aquarium screensavers.

The house looked like a tornado had swept through it. The carpet, floor, and living room couch were littered with jumbled heaps of clothing. An empty pizza box lay on the carpet, and two empty Carlsberg bottles, one upright, the other on its side, were on the table next to the laptops, along with a half-eaten slice of pizza.

The shrill ring of a telephone startled Rotem out of her slumber, and as she opened her green eyes she banged her head on the coffee table.

"Ahhhhh . . . Dammit. Shit! Shit! Shit! Double shit! My head's gonna explode."

She stumbled through the living room, rubbing her head while rummaging through the piles of clothing for the encrypted cell phone, before retrieving it from under a black skirt.

"It's three thirty in the morning!" she roared into the mobile.

Her expression changed the moment she recognized the voice on the other end of the line.

"Grandpa?"

Rotem listened for a few seconds and then rattled off in quick-fire bursts. "You're fucking kidding me!—I don't believe it!—Tell him not to move and not to touch the notebook—To just leave it on the desk—He's probably poisoned the pages with arsenic or cyanide—He needs to go and wash his hands right now—With lots of soap—I knew he was alive!—I can't believe it!—That wasn't his body—How did his DNA disappear from the database?—Clearly he deleted it intentionally—He must have acquired an admin password—Just like I said all along—You know he was a hacker, right?—I have to see it!—Where did you say it is?—Ganei Tikva?—No, Ganei Yehuda?—I'm on my way—You coming too?—I don't want him touching it anymore!—I'll bring gloves!—Tell him—Tell him to just leave it alone—I'm on my way!!!"

Rotem tossed the cell phone onto the living room couch and headed quickly for the shower, throwing off her clothing as she scampered to the bathroom. Her tank top landed on another pile of laundry and she kicked her sweatpants and panties off and left them on the carpet. She had to wake up. A jet of cold would will do the trick.

Rotem wrote a research paper on 10483 when she was seventeen. It was part of her thesis for The Organization's course in micropsychoanalysis.

She was recruited at fifteen. Her name came up together with those of two other students from the Education Ministry's program for gifted teenagers. "Exceptional EQ capabilities in addition to a particularly high IQ," read the report, to which the director of the program had added in her own hand: **"Don't let her slip. She's something special."**

The Organization allowed her to study whatever she wanted, and she grabbed at the chance to focus on her passion—psychology. After breezing through the classic material that most universities offered, she earned degrees in developmental, social, cognitive, clinical, and personality psychology, as well as neuropsychology and psychophysics. Then she completed The Organization's internal courses and developed a curriculum for The Organization, such as the macro-cultural psychology of human development and psychoanalytic prediction.

By the time she turned eighteen, she was already in charge of The Organization's Personality and Psychopathology Division, which handled the profiling of targets and world leaders and predicted the future behavior of individuals and the masses. The army tried to recruit her for one its elite projects, but The Organization wouldn't hear of it. Following a bitter battle, both sides eventually decided to ask her what she preferred. She chose The Organization.

10483 fascinated her. She received his file after his death for the purpose of preparing a behavioral profile and submitted a detailed report to the European Operations Division, but she was still missing several pieces of the puzzle. The notebook now waiting for her was a treasure trove.

She soaped herself in the shower under the stream of cold water and broke into a loud and discordant rendition of the chorus to "The Scientist" by Coldplay.

February 7th 2006

"Emily!"

"What, Mom?"

"What did I ask you to do?"

"I'm doing my homework."

"No, what did I ask you to do before then?"

"Don't remember . . ."

"Something to do with your shoes, which are lying in the living room."

"Ugh."

"No ughs, please. Just put them away. And if you're on your way to the living room, check if my white wool hat is hanging by the front door."

"What, you're going away again?" Emily and Taylor both popped their heads out of the doors to their bedrooms.

"Yes, sweeties. But for a very short time only. I'll be back by the weekend."

"But, Mom. You know that tomorrow is the open lesson for parents at my jazz dance school! You promised you'd come!" Emily fixed her mother with an angry glare.

"Dad will go with you. He'll film it all and I'll watch when I get back. Don't worry."

"Dad will just sit there with his head buried in the emails on his phone."

"He promised me he wouldn't."

"Mom," Taylor tugged on the end of her shirt, "are you going to bring me a giraffe like last time?"

"Something even better! But it's a secret. You'll see when I get back."

"Yay!!!" he exclaimed as he started jumping up and down on the bed.

"I found the hat!" Emily returned to the bedroom. "It was behind the sofa in the living room."

"Thanks, sweetie."

Carmit threw her hat into her backpack and closed it. That's it. Everything's ready. Her flight will depart at night.

MORNING. FEBRUARY 2006

My plane lands in Frankfurt. I have a 3.5-hour layover before my connection to Buenos Aires. I buy a backpack and fill it with equipment I acquire at a duty-free travel gear store. A wool hat, jacket, gloves, hiking boots, a colorful sweater, a camera with a large lens, a scarf, eating utensils, and clothes.

I go into the disabled bathroom and change into the clothes I just bought. I put the clothes I was wearing into a bag and throw them in the trash.

This time I'm traveling with more than a small bag. I now have a large backpack, too, which I check for the flight to Buenos Aires. The stewardess informs me that my bag will go straight through to Bariloche and there's no need for me to collect it before the connecting flight.

During the flight I read through the material I saved on my laptop about Instituto Balseiro and Bariloche.

There's no train service to Bariloche. I rule out killing the target by means of a train crash. Too bad, as it's actually pretty simple to arrange one. You only have to hack into the train company's main control system and divert one of the tracks.

There's no subway either, so I rule out a plan to get into the subway tunnel with gas tanks and open them in the middle of the tunnel so that the gas explodes when the train passes through and sparks fly from its electrified tracks.

I'll have to study the target and think of something.

If my target doesn't have security detail, I can arrange an electrocution in the bath.

I board the plane to Bariloche. It's a 2-hour flight.

I land in Bariloche at night and retrieve my backpack from the baggage carousel. I don't take a random suitcase this time, so as not to carry too much. I take a cab to my hotel and go to bed.

It was three thirty in the morning and Carmit was sitting on the bed in the hotel room at the Hotel Premier in Bariloche. 10483 lay on the bed next to her, sound asleep and hooked up to her standard equipment. Headphones, glasses, electrodes, and an inhalator.

The blue lights flickered and Carmit put on her protective orange goggles. She was concerned they weren't offering her sufficient protection, but there was nothing she could do about it in the meantime. When she got home she'd conduct a little research and find a new protective measure. She didn't trust The Organization on such matters. Clenched tightly between her lips was an air regulator like that of a scuba diver. It was connected to a small filter. She made sure not to breathe through her nose.

Getting into the room posed no problem this time, too. The South Americans are much more open when it comes to providing information than their brothers are in the North. It took Carmit just a few minutes to get her target's room number and the name he was using.

This time she took the room adjacent to her target. She opened the cover of the air-conditioning duct in her room and slowly and carefully slid a thin flexible tube to the vent of the adjacent room. When she heard her target get into bed, she turned on the inhalator, which pumped an anesthetic gas into the room. That's why she's using the filter now. She needs to remain awake.

She recalled how surprised she had been when they summoned her to a meeting with the head of the Brain Engineering Department at The Organization after she returned from her studies. There had been no such department when she'd left. They'd set up an entire department based on her idea and hadn't even told her about it.

He showed her the brain mapping they'd been carrying out on sleeping subjects. The light-sensitive protein compound they'd developed was called the "sauce."

They hadn't concerned themselves with trying to repair blindness or deafness—instead they'd gone for altering behavioral patterns and personalities, the assimilation of precise traits.

"We call this transformation," he said. "As opposed to something simple like manipulation or playing with the senses, this requires actually programming areas of the brain. We had to incorporate pulses of blue light of various wavelengths together with text. It's a different league altogether than what you were studying."

He tried to talk her into joining him, but she'd already begun toying with the idea of quitting The Organization during the course of her studies abroad. At the same time, she already knew too much. She'd have to skip the country and start all over again. They wouldn't be able to risk her being out there with all that knowledge.

She told him she'd consider it favorably.

The softly spoken text continued to play through the headphones, and Carmit retrieved another energy bar from her backpack and started gnawing on it. She'd never tried listening to the text, which was always sent to her as an encrypted file along with the conversion file that controlled the blue lights.

It's easy to alter behavior. It's harder to instill insight. The client creates the methodology. She merely implements.

Still chewing on the snack, she flipped through the pages of a notebook she'd found in the room—a journal her target was writing. She carefully avoided mixing up the order of the pages attached to the notebook and returned it to the exact place it had been when she finished reading. She momentarily entertained the thought of copying the notebook and sending it to her client. That would undoubtedly shake him up a little. "Fuck 'em," she decided in the end.

Carmit stroked 10483's head, which was fixed in place between two rolled-up towels.

Sleep, sweetie.
It's okay.
Not long to go now.
Everything will pass.
It'll be all over and you'll feel wonderful.
It's okay.
They want you to live.

NIGHT. FEBRUARY 2006

I put the bags from the supermarket on the counter and turn on the light. He's sitting motionless on the sofa and pointing a gun at me. It's the first time anyone's pointed a weapon at me, aside from the machine gunner who released a burst of rounds above my head during a company drill in basic training, but that was unintentional because he didn't see me. Now, it's intentional.

I see a flash of light in front of me and feel the bullet pass through me and pierce a hole in my heart. It doesn't hurt. I look down at my shirt to see a hole on the left side and a bloodstain that starts to spread through the fabric.

I'm walking on the balcony 2 weeks after my son is born. I want to get a better grip on the bundle in my arms and he slips out of the blanket, head first. He falls from a height of just over 1 meter, but it all happens in slow motion and seems to take forever. I see his head approaching the floor. 30 centimeters, 20, 10.

I'm wading through a shallow pool. My feet are bare and I'm wearing shorts. Black clouds cover the sky; the pool is full of large orange fish. They're covered in black and white spots. They're swimming all around me, rubbing against my legs, splashing water with random movements. I stop in the middle of the pool, and the walls retreat until they disappear completely. I have no idea which direction to take.

I'm on the roof of my building. I have a key to the elevator control room. I stand next to the low fence around the roof and look down 8 floors to the ground. I climb onto the fence and try to maintain my balance. I start walking slowly along it. My palms are sweaty. I trip and fall in an endless descent. I'm lying on the asphalt. A snake approaches me. I'm unable to move. The snake climbs onto me and slithers up my body until it reaches my throat.

I'm walking through the streets of Geneva. I'm looking for the store where I once purchased equipment. Everyone's looking at me. Children are pointing at me. I notice that I'm not dressed. I run and look for a place to hide in one of the stores, but all the doors slam shut and I'm left on the street. People are gathering around me. Pointing at me.

"When did it start?"

"It's been several weeks now. I don't know what to do. I can't shake these dreams; I feel like I'm losing my mind completely. I'm exhausted when I wake in the morning."

"So about a month, let's say?"

"Yes, something like that. What can I do to make it stop?"

"Just a moment, I have something for you."

"What?"

"Here, take these, thirty-five pills at a time." The doctor gives me a box of pills. There's a picture of a black skull on the lid of the box.

I run out without closing the door behind me. The air is filled with the smell of something burning. I turn around and see the orange-red flames of a fire moving toward me. I try to run but I fall. One leg is simply no longer there. In its place is an old stump with suture markings around it. The fire is coming closer. I'm surrounded by black smoke. I remember the smell of gunpowder from the company drills during basic training, the smell left behind by a shell fired from a tank, the smell of a phosphorus grenade, the smell of charred flesh. The smell of war. Barbed-wire fences.

I crawl under the fence and it scratches me. The thing

chasing me is formless. The sand becomes increasingly boggy and I get stuck with my head between 2 wooden planks and cannot move. I look up and see the blade of a guillotine falling fast.

I sit up in bed.

The blanket covering me is drenched in sweat.

I cast it aside and go to the bathroom.

Darkness. Night.

I flush the toilet and the water fills the bowl and begins to spill over the sides. A stream of murky water rises up and begins to fill the bathroom. I turn toward the door and start to walk out. Glancing back for a moment I see that the floor is covered in a large pool of blood.

I sit up in bed.

I reach for the notebook that I placed on the nightstand.

The doctor told me to record the contents of my dreams the moment I wake up.

It's easier that way for me to remember what I went through during the night.

I can't take it anymore.

I write in the notebook: "Again it's the dream that begins with the man with the gun in the chair who shoots me."

I close the notebook.

Something doesn't feel right.

I reach for the notebook again and open it to last page.

The text I wrote a few seconds ago is gone.

"You will die tonight," it reads instead.

I throw the notebook aside.

A tooth falls out of my mouth.

I hear voices. There's someone else in the house.

The smell of something burning again.

I've lost something and I don't know what it is. I need to remember what I lost.

I'm in a cave.

I feel intense sorrow.

A loved one has died.

"No!"

"No!"

"Enough!"

The Lord is my shepherd; I shall not want.

He maketh me to lie down in green pastures: he leadeth me beside the still waters.

He restoreth my soul: he leadeth me in the paths of righteousness for his name's sake.

Yea, though I walk through the valley of the shadow of death, I will fear no evil: for thou art with me; thy rod and thy staff they comfort me.

"Wake up."

"Enough!"

"You're having nightmares again."

"I'm scared."

"Come, I'll make you something to drink."

She sits next to me and caresses my head.

The loud whistle of a kettle is coming from the kitchen.

And the smell of something burning.

I wake at −4:30. I'm lying on the bed at Hotel Premier. It's strange. I usually wake up earlier.

The bed is drenched in sweat.

I sense that there's someone else in the room.

I go to the shower.

There's no one there.

And there's no one in my room either.

My eyes hurt. I remove a can of 7 Up from the minibar, close my eyes and press the can to my face.

I write in my notebook and go back to sleep.

MORNING. FEBRUARY 2006

I go for a walk along Avenida Ezequiel Bustillo. The institution is at number 9500. A cool wind dispels the morning mist and the sun reflects off the blue waters of the lake, the banks of which are decked with trees. It's a good day to die.

The institution's students and faculty members begin to show up, getting out of their cars and hurrying inside. I recognize my target immediately. He's the only individual under armed guard. Heavy guard.

They may have heard about the first target I killed and they aren't taking any chances. The targets must be linked to one another. 4 armed bodyguards surround my target. They're alert. There's no getting close to him.

I take some pictures of the lake and go for a walk in the city. I pass by the institution's parking lot on the way. Sitting in the target's car is a bodyguard with his eyes peeled. I won't be able to booby-trap the car. His home, too, must be guarded.

I walk through the city. I'm carrying the backpack. I learn my way around the streets and buildings, take some scenic photographs and check out possible escape routes. After lunch I rent a closed van and park it at the side of the road at the bottom of Avenida Bustillo.

Cars pass by.

I wait for my target's car and see it leaving the institution as darkness begins to fall. I follow it at a safe distance.

My target lives in a single-family detached home surrounded by a high fence. There are cameras set up at all angles and alert guards surround the house. It looks like a military base.

The car drives in and a large iron gate slides back into place. It's impenetrable.

I monitor the target from afar for several days and reveal a point of weakness. My target goes for a 30-minute run in the park between the institution and the lake every afternoon. His bodyguards run with him, but they are vulnerable there. They're out in the open.

I walk through the park and check it out. The children's play facilities, the metal sprinklers, the walking trails, the lawns.

I draw up a shopping list. I don't send the list to The Organization so that the mole there won't get word of my plans. I already have the money to buy whatever I need.

I go into a large hardware store. I buy binoculars, several kinds of plastic pipes and pipe connectors, tools for fashioning screw joints for metal piping, pipe-cutting tools, and a small generator.

I buy the most powerful water pump they have in the store. I explain to the shop assistant that I want to build myself a big raft and sail on the lake, and that I'm putting together an engine that will draw water from the lake and spray it out behind the raft in order to propel the craft forward. The shop assistant looks at me and says in English, "The lake is very deep and the water is cold. Careful you don't drown." Addressing the shop assistant next to him in Spanish, he says, "This clown will find himself riding that pump at the bottom of the lake," and they both smile at me. I smile back at them.

I purchase yellow and blue overalls and black plastic boots from a different store.

I load all the equipment into the van.

I put on the overalls and a pair of work gloves and drive to the park. I park the van and walk through the open green expanse.

I adjust the sprinklers. Some I rotate 180 degrees so that they'll spray water onto the path and some I leave aimed at the grass and surrounding vegetation. I also adjust the rotation mechanism of the oscillating sprinklers to allow them full-circle coverage.

I follow the lines of sprinklers until I find the control mechanism for the irrigation system's main pipeline. It's in a large metal cabinet.

I break into the cabinet, close the main tap and then turn off the irrigation computer. No one will notice if the sprinklers don't turn on for a day. Several people walk past me and I wave to them and drink from the bottle of water I brought with me.

The main pipe has 2 taps. One before the irrigation computer's transmission and one after. It's built that way so that the water can be turned off while someone works on the computer.

I close the tap in front of the irrigation computer, saw through the thick metal pipe between the 2 taps, and remove a piece measuring half a meter or so. I screw on a standard 5-centimeter adaptor on the end of the pipe leading to the sprinklers. To the adaptor I attach a 2-meter-long flexible pipe with a connection that fits the discharge port of the pump I purchased.

I check to make sure that the pipe connects securely to the pump.

Then again.

One last time.

I roll up the length of flexible pipe, place it in the cabinet and shut the door.

I fit a standard connection for a domestic diesel oil storage tank and fit it to the suction port of the pump. I took measurements for the connector size at several homes I passed during my walks through the city.

I drive to a nearby fish restaurant for lunch. There I use my laptop to access the cameras in my apartment and check on my art exhibits. The aquarium is lit up in blue and the Last Supper is still underway. The food on the table has taken on a greenish shade and the 2 actors are still sitting across from one another, their heads sway.

After lunch I drive my van to the gas station. I fill the van with gas along with the tank of the small generator I bought. I leave the gas station and drive to a point from which I can observe it. I pull over.

I get out of the car and check to make sure the generator I bought works. It starts immediately. I turn it off and attach the pump to it. I turn it back on and check that the pump is working. The pump's motor quickly comes to life.

I turn off the pump and generator, put them back in the van and wait.

A tanker arrives later in the afternoon to refill the gas station's fuel tanks. I wait for the tanker to finish and then follow it to the fuel depot, 10 kilometers outside the city. Using the binoculars I watch the driver of the tanker refill his vehicle and speak to another driver next to him. They're smoking cigarettes. It's dangerous. You shouldn't smoke near fuel.

The driver gets into the tanker and parks it in a lot inside the depot. Then he gets into a private car and drives off.

I wait for nightfall and scale the back fence of the depot. There's only a guard at the entrance, and there aren't cameras.

He doesn't see me.

I walk over to a tanker parked outside the guard's field of vision. The door to the vehicle isn't locked. I get in and go to sleep in the cabin, behind the driver's seat.

I wake at 1:30. All is quiet. I go back to sleep.

February 14th 2006

"Kelly speaking, may I take a message?"

"Where are you??? I haven't been able to reach you for two days."

Carmit makes a point of turning on her cell phone only when she's at a safe distance from her home and children, so that no one can hone in on her address by monitoring the subway lines she takes or her location patterns.

"You know you're not my only client."

"But I'm your best one."

The last remark was met with silence.

"I need you in Montreal in three days."

"It'll cost you two hundred and fifty thousand."

"What???"

"Two hundred and fifty thousand pounds. Excluding flights. You're killing him, working at such a pace. This is the last time with him. It's already too much."

"You don't know him."

"I actually do. Two hundred and fifty thousand. I know you aren't authorized to lay out this kind of money without additional approval. If I get confirmation, at least I'll know it's not a personal vendetta. Two hundred and fifty thousand. And besides, I hate Montreal."

"I'll call you tomorrow. Just do me a favor and leave your phone on."

"Call tomorrow afternoon at two. The phone will be on."

"One of these days I'll get my hands on you."

"Careful you don't end up losing one."

"We'll talk tomorrow."

"Not before two."

"And one more thing."

"What?"

"This will be the final transformation."

"It better be. And I'd like you afterward to keep your distance from me for at least a year. You're pushing me too close to the fire; I can feel the heat."

The man on the other end of the line hung up.

I wake to the noise of the engine. The driver is in the seat in front of me. I lie quietly in the cabin behind him. The tanker exits the depot gates and heads off toward the city. It's very early in the morning. The roads are empty.

The driver accelerates to a speed of 100 kilometers per hour along a straight section of the road. I can see the speedometer. There are no other cars around us. I jump up, reach out, and open the driver's door. The driver isn't wearing his seatbelt. I push him out.

The tanker zigzags a little. I grab the wheel and pull off to the side of the road. I reverse back to the driver, who's lying on the road. His head is tilted back at an unnatural angle. His eyes are open. He isn't moving. I roll him off the asphalt into a clump of bushes at the side of the road. I remove the battery from his cell phone so they can't pinpoint his location. I return to the tanker and head off again.

I drive to where my van is parked and transfer my equipment to the tanker. I head from there to the park and park the tanker on a side street, behind a dense group of trees. The tanker can't be seen from the air or the road.

I sit in the tanker and wait. I use the time to prepare 3 glass bottles that I fill with gasoline and into which I stuff gasoline-soaked rags.

Shortly before 1 I start up the tanker and drive into the park. I pull up alongside the irrigation system's computer cabinet and connect the length of rubber hose I left there to my pump's discharge port; I connect the suction port to the tanker's 95-octane tank. The tank holds 30,000 liters of fuel. That'll do. I hook up the pump to the generator, which I turn on, but leave the pump off. For now.

Several Instituto Balseiro staff members are wandering through the park on their lunch break, and a number of families with children are walking along the paths and lawns.

My target jogs into the park with his bodyguards.

I wait for him to advance 200 meters along the path and then turn on the pump.

All the sprinklers in the park turn on and spray jets of 95-octane liquid fuel in all directions, drenching the paths and surrounding lawns.

The people in the park eventually realize this and start running.

I light 1 of the bottles I prepared and throw it as far as I can.

The park was peaceful that afternoon. The morning mist had disappeared and given way to wispy cirrus clouds. A warm summer sun shone down on the people in the park, workers on their lunch break, mothers and fathers with children, and joggers, out for an afternoon run.

The people in the park appeared somewhat amused at first when all the sprinklers came to life at once, spraying in every possible direction. *So typical of the Bariloche Municipality to screw things up with the direction of the jets ...* they must have thought.

The laughter, however, soon turned to cries of distress, as the park's visitors realized the sprinklers were spraying gasoline and not water. Mothers reached frantically for their soaked children, people rushed toward the park's exit and screams filled the air.

Then came the explosion.

The park ignited in a massive burst of flame as a huge ball of fire rose above the canopy of green trees with a thunderous *whooooshhh*.

Flaming people ran wildly in all directions, falling to the ground and rolling.

Baby carriages burned, abandoned on the walking paths.

The small group of joggers who were running along the center of the path didn't escape the fire. When the sprinklers started spraying, the bodyguards turned their heads to look at the individual running between them. He was a tall and thin man with short blond hair. He stopped jogging, realized what was happening and gestured for the bodyguards to make their escape. They broke into a mad dash out of the park. They didn't make it.

The tall man didn't run. He remained where he was and reached for a cell phone in his pocket. And while everyone ran screaming, he calmly placed a call.

A sea of fire swept toward him at a furious rate.

The phone emitted one call-waiting tone.

The ball of fire reached him.

The phone emitted another call-waiting tone.

His clothes caught fire.

One more tone.

December 4th 2016

Avner replaced the receiver.

He glanced at the open notebook on the table and sighed. There was nothing new here that they didn't already know. The Organization knew for sure that 10483 had carried out the massacre in Bariloche. It was depressing nevertheless to read how he'd prepared for and carried out the murder of over one hundred people with what seemed like no emotion whatsoever.

Grandpa was on his way.

He told Avner it was time to explain more about the Bernoulli Project, that it wasn't a matter for the phone.

Grandpa is one of the most brilliant minds to have ever worked for The Organization. He earned his nickname, thanks to the long white beard that adorns his face and his advanced age. He's always reminded Avner of Santa Claus— after a good diet. The running joke about him is that he received the order to set up The Organization from David Ben-Gurion himself, and that he was already then on the verge of retirement.

"I'll be with you in twenty minutes," he'd said on the phone to Avner. "Stay right where you are."

Avner got up to stretch and walked out of the small office to the branch's public space. He grabbed a stale biscuit from an open package on the counter in the kitchenette and washed one of the glass cups in the sink to make himself another cup of coffee, choosing to forgo Benny's espresso this time. He wasn't in the mood to talk to anyone right now.

His cell phone rang five minutes later and Grandpa was on the line again. "One more thing, Avner, go wash your hands and wear gloves before you touch that notebook again."

"Why? Are you worried about fingerprints?"

"The pages may be poisoned. He may have put something there."

"No way on earth I'm going to handle this notebook with rubber gloves. I'm not that paranoid. Besides, if that thing was poisoned I would be dead by now. I've been reading this thing for hours."

Avner put the cell phone back in his pocket.

The person outside the Ganei Yehuda satellite branch finished working under the white Mazda, put his tools back into a bag, checked the device now installed under the car, carefully looked around using a low-beam flashlight to make sure nothing was left behind, crawled out from under the car, and disappeared through the shrubbery and trees surrounding the villa.

I light the 2 remaining bottles, throw them into the cabin of the tanker and walk to the hotel. Ambulances, police vehicles and fire trucks speed by me on their way to the park. On my way to the hotel I call Aerolíneas Argentinas to book a flight to Buenos Aires, and then Lufthansa to reserve a ticket from Buenos Aires to Frankfurt and from Frankfurt to Montreal. That's where my final target is.

Back at the hotel I shower and wash off the smell of gasoline. Then I check out and take a cab to the airport. On the way there I ask the driver to stop at a post office and I mail the large backpack I bought, with all the clothes and equipment inside, to 406 East 32nd Street in Manhattan. There's no such address.

People at the airport are gathered in front of television screens watching the broadcast images of the fire. I sit at a café, order a hamburger and a Coke, and open my laptop. I read up on École Polytechnique de Montréal. It offers studies in chemical engineering, electronics, computer science, mechanics, mathematics, geology, biomedicine, physics, and nuclear research, and is located in the center of Montreal.

My flight's been delayed for an hour. The airport is operating in emergency/disaster mode and one runway has been set aside for airlifting casualties out of Bariloche. I use the time to go online and reserve a rental car that will wait for me at the airport in Montreal. I also book a hotel room near the school.

I save maps of Montreal and material from the school's website onto my laptop to study during the flight.

I land in Frankfurt and take off to Montreal. I retrieve a random suitcase from the baggage carousel at the airport in Montreal and take a cab to my hotel.

I open the suitcase at the hotel. It contains baby clothes.

I read up on the target. I browse through the list of faculty members at the school and cross-reference the names with photographs from the Internet. I recognize my target. His name is Bernard Strauss. He teaches molecular physics. He used to be in charge of the SLOWPOKE nuclear research project conducted at the school.

I read the SLOWPOKE project specification document I downloaded from the Internet. The SLOWPOKE is a small experimental nuclear reactor that uses 93-percent enriched uranium with aluminum cladding. The core, just 22 centimeters in diameter and 23 centimeters high, is an assembly of around 300 miniature fuel rods. Criticality is maintained as the fuel burns up by adding beryllium plates in a tray on top of the core, which sits in a pool of regular light-water measuring 2.5 meters in diameter and 6 meters deep. The reactor is mobile. It can be installed, for example, in a submarine, and the 20 kilowatts of power it generates could recharge the vessel's batteries for decades without the need for any additional fuel. Very interesting.

February 17th 2006

While Carmit hates hotels in general, she absolutely despises
freezing cold ones. Montreal was –23°Celsius. A cold that's
hard to describe to someone who has never experienced such
temperature. You wrap yourself in layers of clothing, scarf,
gloves, a thick coat, and you freeze your ass off every time
you step foot out the door. The residents of Montreal have
thus found a wonderful solution: They simply don't go outside. For the entire journey—from the airport to the central
train station, to the subway, to the mall in the city center, and
from the mall to the hotel—she never once goes aboveground.

Last night was the final transformation of her target. It
ended at five-thirty in the morning. She'd read in his notebook that he wakes every night at 1:30, so she waited for it to
happen and then waited for him to fall asleep again before
pumping four doses of anesthetic gas under the door to his
room. She began the work at 2:30. Three solid hours of headphones and glasses. It wasn't easy. She was forced for some
of the time to sit on him and hold down his arms and legs to
prevent him from throwing off the equipment when he was
struck by convulsions.

Luckily the jet lag from the flight and a thermos of coffee
kept her awake through the night, otherwise he would have
found her in his room in the morning, sleeping on the rug next
to his bed—and that certainly wouldn't have ended well at all.

Afterward Carmit slept all day and woke at five in the
evening. She was ravenous, but the thought of going out in
the freezing cold to look for a restaurant sent shivers through

her, so she slipped on a pair of jeans and a brightly colored sweater, donned her white woolen hat and went downstairs to eat something at the hotel restaurant. She'd be flying back home to London in just a few hours.

She sat down alone at a table for two, leaned back in her chair, and opened the menu. She decided to go for the salmon with a side of mashed potatoes and a bottle of red wine. As she lowered the menu, 10483 was sitting in front of her.

February 17th 2006

Keep your eyes closed.

Listen to my voice.

Breathe through your nose.

I want you to feel your body filling with air when you inhale.

I want you to feel your body emptying of air when you exhale.

Your breathing is becoming more relaxed.

Slower.

You're becoming more aware of the air flowing through your body.

Are you able to feel it?

Try to picture the volume of your thumb.

Can you picture it?

Now you try to picture the volume of your forefinger.

Can you picture it?

Now try to picture the volume of the space between your thumb and forefinger.

Can you picture it?

There is absolute silence all around.

Your breathing is calm.

You are now in an open and quiet place.

All you can hear is the soft sound of flowing water in the distance.

You're surrounded by green grass and trees with thick trunks and lush green canopies.

You can feel gravel beneath your bare feet.

You're standing on a trail.

The trail is straight and long.

It leads you forward.

Your feet walk over gravel. The sensation of gravel under your bare feet is a pleasant one. Not painful. You're in a safe place.

You look to the right and see a young boy walking by your side.

He's about fourteen years old.

You realize the boy is you.

He's you when you were that age.

Can you picture him?

You walk together and talk.

He asks you if you're happy.

He asks you if you regret some of the things you've done.

He asks you if you have any insights to share with him.

You talk.

The sun goes down and you walk together along the gravel trail.

Your breathing is calm.

You look to the right and see you are alone again.

You continue down the trail, which stretches into the woods.

You see a figure standing in front of you farther down the trail.

You approach it.

It's an old man.

The light is dimmer now and it's hard to recognize the figure from afar.

You reach him and see that it's you in another forty years.

You stop.

There's a stream alongside you. You can hear the sound of water trickling over pebbles.

You both sit on a large rock on the bank of the stream and dip your feet in the water.

The water is cool and pleasant and you can feel it running over your feet.

You ask the old man if he is happy.

He says he isn't. He tells you you've lived a meaningless life and that no one will remember you when you are dead.

The old man weeps.

You ask him what he would have done differently.

He says he would have killed himself on December 12, 2006.

You ask him why.

He says that's the date of the holy day on which the doors to heaven open once every one thousand years.

You promise him you will do so.

You won't allow yourself to end up like him.

Your old self looks at you with gratitude. He gets up off the stone you are sitting on and continues down the trail.

You remain seated on the stone. You know what you have to do.

The grass and woods around you disappear.

Your breathing quickens.

You won't remember this conversation.

You feel wonderful.

You won't dream anymore.

Never again.

You'll continue sleeping now until you are no longer tired and then you'll wake up.

This is your last dream.

– A blinding white flash –

I'm running and jumping on the sidewalk. My arms are stretched out to the sides.

– Flash –

I'm sitting on the train. My twin is sitting in front of me.

– Flash –

My car drives past the bodies on the road. The paramedic leaning against the side of the ambulance exhales a cloud of cigarette smoke and looks at me.

– Flash –

A note lands on the table next to me. "Remember not to sneeze again," I scribble on it.

– Flash –

Brown water is dripping from the room's ceiling. I lift my head and look up.

– Flash –

I pick up a knife and drive it into my heart.

– Flash –

I'm sitting at a café. The world around me is frozen.

– Flash –

It's dark outside. I stop my car at the side of the road and walk over to the pile of clothes lying on the road.

– Flash –

The large black ant moves closer to me under my blanket.

– Flash –

I'm in front of the refrigerator. Its door is open. The jar containing the kidney is resting on the shelf in front of me, illuminated from behind by the refrigerator's yellow lightbulb.

– Flash –

A hand reaches out and pulls me into the Metro tunnel.

– Flash –

2 shadows are moving across the floor outside the bathroom.

– Flash –

I'm standing in front of the large glass wall and pushing down relentlessly on the pedal.

– Flash –

I inhale cool air through my regulator, diving deep down along the endless wall of corals.

– Flash –

The elevator doors open. A torrent of brown water comes rushing out.

– Flash –

I look for the lighter in my shirt pocket. There is no pocket.

– Flash –

All of them must die.

She's sitting next to me and caressing my head. She gets up and leaves. She has a knapsack on her back and she's eating an energy bar. I think I know her but I can't see her face.

EVENING. FEBRUARY 2006

I get up very late. I've slept most of the day.

My eyes hurt and my head's a little dizzy. But I feel good. I have a sense of duty. A sense of purpose. I go over to the coffee corner in the room and boil water in a small plastic electric kettle. I then make myself a cup of tea without sugar. I don't like sugar in my tea.

I shower and go down to eat in the hotel dining room.

A woman is sitting alone at a table for 2. I don't recognize her but I feel as if I know her.

I sit down in front of her. She doesn't notice.

She puts the menu down on the table and sees me.

She smiles in surprise. "Do you have your tables mixed up?" she asks me in English.

"No," I respond. Her voice sounds familiar.

I ask her name.

She tells me her name is Kelly Grasso and that she's here on a business trip. She works for Cymedix. We talk about databases and operating systems. Her eyes smile. We eat dinner together. She tells me about her work. She lives in Boston.

I invite her to my room and she says that her flight is scheduled to depart soon. She says she needs to leave but would be happy to stay in touch. She gives me a business card. I hold on to it.

MORNING. FEBRUARY 2006

I no longer dream and no longer wake at 1:30 in the morning.

I've been following my target for several days now. He's completely inaccessible. His security detail is the tightest I've ever encountered and the members of the security team appear well trained. He goes to work at the university in the morning and returns home at night to sleep. He lives alone. The building is under guard around the clock. He doesn't go out at night, doesn't eat at restaurants and doesn't run. The only time he's vulnerable is on his drive home along the highway, but even then, he's protected by 3 vehicles with armed security personnel. He must know he's been targeted. Someone is guarding him closely. The university perhaps.

I rule out my first idea—to break one of the taillights of his car, fill it with a mixture of zinc and sulfur, and drill a hole from there into the fuel tank, thus causing the car to explode when the brake pedal is depressed, because it's impossible to get close to the car. It's well guarded even when not in use.

I draw up a shopping list.

1. MP3 player with microphone jack for recording
2. Sensitive external microphone with shirt clip
3. Several cables that connect to the player's earphone jack and allow the player to be hooked up to an external amplifier
4. Large toolbox
5. Blue overalls

6. Large iron pipe wrench
7. Webcam with cellular modem and a cellular Internet package
8. Electrical adaptor for a camera that can be plugged into a car's power supply
9. Cell phone with local SIM card and an Internet package

I use the Internet to find a quit-smoking hypnotherapy clinic and register for a course of treatment. I have an appointment in 2 days.

I continue to monitor my target from a distance. I notice I'm not the only one who has him under surveillance. 3 more people are keeping an eye on the target and his surroundings.

My target's drive home from work in the evening takes 35 minutes. 25 minutes at night, when there's less traffic.

I buy all the items on the list at a large shopping mall and check that all the electronic equipment works well. I get the logo of the Montreal cable company, Vidéotron, printed on the overalls.

MORNING. FEBRUARY 2006

I'm sitting in the clinic of Dr. Victor Sadovsky. He specializes in quit-smoking hypnotherapy. I pay him 500 Canadian dollars. He says I have to pay up front.

Before then, in the bathroom alongside the waiting room, I fit the microphone to my shirt, connect it to the MP3 device and press the record button.

The doctor starts up a metronome. "Close your eyes and listen to rhythm of the clicks," he says. I begin counting in my head all the prime numbers from 1 to 10,000. He speaks in a calm tone.

"In a moment I will count to three," he says. I'm already up to 151.

"Now I want your eyes to feel as if it's very late at night," he continues, "and you're sitting at home and watching an old black-and-white movie on TV. You should have gone to bed by now. You're so tired." I'm already up to 443.

"You feel your eyes closing," he says. "Your eyelids are heavy. They're closing." His voice remains very calm. My eyes are closed. I'm up to one 1,031.

"You're asleep now," he says.

I stop counting through the prime numbers and open my eyes. "Hypnosis doesn't work on me," I say to Dr. Sadovsky. "I'm sorry. You can keep the money."

I get up and leave. I stop the recording in the elevator. I transfer the file to my laptop back at the hotel and edit it, leaving only the hypnosis segment. I delete the rest.

I put on the blue overalls with the Vidéotron logo.

I drive to the parking lot where my target's car is parked and find a space several dozen meters away from it. There's a bodyguard standing next to the target's car. He doesn't notice me; I'm parked far enough away. I place a webcam on the dash above the steering wheel. I direct it at the target's car and turn it on.

I get out of my car, retrieve the toolbox from the trunk, walk out of the parking lot and hail a cab.

"Where to?" the driver asks.

"The CBC Radio One building," I tell him.

I enter the CBC building dressed in blue overalls and carrying the toolbox. I wave hello to the security guard. He responds with a tired gesture. I map the floors in my head as I walk up the stairs. Office floors, the computer room, the broadcasting studio.

It's almost 8 in the evening and the building is practically empty. Every now and then I open a communications cabinet on one of the floors and pretend to be checking something with the connections.

I leave the building and walk to a café farther down the street.

I eat dinner and keep an eye at the same time on the video feed on my laptop from the camera I left in the parked car. My target's car is still parked in its spot. I leave the laptop open and continue eating.

At around 8:30 I see my target get into his car and leave the parking lot escorted by his security team.

I place 50 Canadian dollars on the table and leave the restaurant. I have 15 minutes before my target will be halfway down the highway.

I wave hello to the guard again and he responds with a nod of his head. 2 minutes have gone by.

I take the elevator to the ninth floor. 3 minutes have gone by.

I signal to the technician in the studio to open the door for me. He sees the cable company's logo and presses a button on his desk that opens the door with a buzz. It's been 4 minutes.

"I need you to move your chair forward so I can get to the cabinet behind you," I say.

"What's happening? Is there a problem?" he asks.

"Yes," I say. "The transmission is down. I need to check the connections in the cabinet right now."

I stand behind the broadcast technician, open the toolbox, take out a large pipe wrench and smash it down onto the back of the technician's neck.

It's been 6 minutes.

I review the connections on the broadcast console. 2 CD players and a laptop are connected to the console. On air right now is a song by Beyoncé, from the laptop. While waiting for the song to end, I connect my player to the laptop's USB port and copy the Doctor.mp3 file to the studio's computer.

It's been 14 minutes.

When the song ends, I keep the broadcast running and play the edited recording of Dr. Sadovsky speaking. I return the pipe wrench to the toolbox, leave the studio and close the door, take the elevator down to the foyer, exit the building and start walking back to the hotel. Taking a cab now is too dangerous.

Dr. Victor Sadovsky was busy closing up his clinic for the day. It had been a particularly long day at work and it was already 8:45. He went over all the payments he had received during the day and made sure everything was correctly recorded in the accounting program on his computer.

A Beyoncé song on the radio came to an end and then someone started talking. It took a few seconds before he realized that the voice coming from the most popular radio station in Montreal was his voice.

A few more seconds went by before the potential danger struck him. His breath caught in his throat.

He grabbed for the office phone and called the police.

"Montreal Police."

"You need to get every available police officer out onto the streets! Quickly!!! There's no time!!!"

"Excuse me?"

"Someone made a recording of me performing hypnosis and he's broadcasting it now on the radio. Drivers are going to be falling asleep at the wheel all over the city within minutes! You need to switch all traffic lights to red right now and get all the officers you have out onto the streets, or thousands will die."

"Are you aware, sir, that filing a false report is a criminal offense?"

"Turn on CBC Radio."

The dispatcher at the police station turned on CBC Radio One. The broadcast was just ending with the words, "You're asleep now," and then the station went silent.

```
-   USERNAME

-   PASSWORD

-   KEYPHRASE

              WELCOME TO THE ORION SYSTEM,

              WAITING FOR INSTRUCTIONS

"SEARCH"

→ SEARCH FOR WHAT?

"MONTREAL 2006"

                        WAIT . . .

→ SEARCH RESULTS "MONTREAL 2006" DISPLAYING FIRST 5 RESULTS:

     1.  2006 – MONTREAL ROAD DISASTER

         ANALYSIS – INVOLVEMENT OF ISLAMIC ORGANIZATIONS

     2.  2006 – MONTREAL ROAD DISASTER

         CONCLUSIONS – ISSUES REQUIRING ATTENTION VIS-À-VIS SECURITY

         FOR LOCAL RADIO AND TELEVISION BROADCASTS

     3.  2006 – MONTREAL ROAD DISASTER

         AGENTS 6682, 7015, 6190

     4.  2006 – MONTREAL ROAD DISASTER

         CONCLUSIONS – AMENDMENT OF EMBASSY AND CONSULATE

         PROTOCOLS

     5.  2006 – MONTREAL ROAD DISASTER

         URGENT DISCUSSION AT COMMUNICATIONS MINISTRY

"OPEN DOCUMENT 3"

→ ACCESS TO THIS DOCUMENT REQUIRES REIDENTIFICATION
```

Avner swiped his finger over the reader again, entered his personal password, and the document opened in a new window:

DATE: 2/26/2006

CLASSIFICATION: BLACK

TO: ORGANIZATION – HEAD

FROM: CANADA BRANCH – HEAD

DISTRIBUTION: ORGANIZATION – SENIOR STAFF

                   DIVISION HEAD – OPERATORS EUROPE

                   CANADA BRANCH – INTELLIGENCE WING

SYSTEM: ORION / BASE: MTR / EXPIRY: __ / __ / ____

RE: DEATH OF AGENTS 6682, 7015, 6190

/

FURTHER TO EARLIER TRANSMISSIONS ON THE SUBJECT, I WISH TO UPDATE
THAT THREE OF OUR AGENTS WERE AMONG THE APPROXIMATELY ELEVEN
THOUSAND FATALITIES IN THE MONTREAL-AREA ROAD DISASTER.

THESE AGENTS WERE DEPLOYED THERE TO MONITOR THE MOVEMENTS OF
ONE OF THE TWELVE [XXX CENSORED XXX] PROJECT TARGETS WHO LIVED
AND WORKED IN MONTREAL.

THE PURPOSE OF THE SURVEILLANCE OPERATION WAS TO LOCATE AGENT
[XXX CENSORED XXX] AFTER LEARNING THAT HE HAD BEEN MISTAKENLY
DISPATCHED TO CARRY OUT THREE HITS, WITH DR. BERNARD STRAUSS OF
THE ÉCOLE POLYTECHNIQUE DE MONTRÉAL AS ONE OF THE TARGETS.

BERNARD STRAUSS WAS UNHARMED IN THE INCIDENT.

SINCERELY

/

Avner stared frozen-faced at the notebook and computer screen.

This notebook was a bombshell.

No wonder Amiram lost his cool. If this material gets out, it's the end of our relations with Canada. And half the rest of the world, too. No one outside the inner circle can get wind of this.

And if Bernard Strauss, target number eight on the Bernoulli list, wasn't killed in the Montreal road disaster, then who killed him? All the Bernoulli targets had disappeared off the face of the earth.

Avner added to his document:

> **9.** Agents 6682, 7015, and 6190 were killed by 10483 in Montreal. File can be closed.
>
> **10.** Convene a senior staff meeting tomorrow to discuss the implications of the new material found in the notebook.

MORNING. MARCH 2006

The roads by now have been cleared of mangled vehicles and the traffic lights are functioning again. I take a cab to the parking lot where my car is parked. I turn off the camera, put it in my bag, and see my target's car still parked there with the guard alongside it.

My target escaped unharmed.

I'll have to come up with something else. Something inside the school perhaps.

I start the car and drive back to the hotel.

The small piece of a staple from a paper stapler that I left on the door handle to my room is no longer on the round knob. I hung the DO NOT DISTURB sign on the door, so they weren't supposed to clean my room today.

Someone's entered my room and is probably in there now.

I've suspected over the past few days that my room had been bugged. So I make sure every night to conduct a number of fictitious phone calls in which I speak about my future plans.

My suspicions appear justified.

I turn away without entering and go back down to the lobby, exit the hotel through a back door, and never return.

I find a small hotel outside the city and reserve a room.

December 4th 2016

A knock at a quarter to five in the morning diverted Avner's eyes away from the notebook. He rose quickly to open the door.

Standing before him was Grandpa.

After a brief handshake and exchange of niceties they both sat at the round table in the kitchenette. Avner quickly brought Grandpa up to speed with what he'd learned from the notebook until now. He spoke in a soft tone and remained focused, trying not to leave out any important details.

Avner went over the principal details that shed additional light on the failures concerning the recruitment of 10483, the operation he carried out in the Netherlands, the killing of the agent in the subway, the operation involving the destruction of the building in Switzerland, his basement and murder of two agents there, the hit in Bariloche.

Grandpa's eyes grew ever darker as Avner continued, and when he got to the connection between The Organization and the incident in Montreal, Grandpa rested his chin on his right hand and sighed.

"I wasn't aware until now that he was behind the mega-attack in Canada. That we were behind it. I was sure it had nothing at all to do with our objective there—that the hypnosis broadcast in Montreal was the work of some local psychopath. We thought that all 10483 had done in Canada was push Bernard Strauss out the window of his room. This can never get out."

Grandpa fixed Avner with a tired stare.

"Twelve people were supposed to die, not eleven thousand. And of those twelve, eleven were innocent."

Grandpa went silent for a moment and then continued in a low voice.

"Eleven innocent individuals to save half a million."

February 28th 2006

The empty wine bottle fell off the table and shattered on the floor, and fragments of red glass flew everywhere.

Bernard Strauss rose wearily from his chair and walked over to the window, treading barefoot on the shards of glass on the floor and leaving behind a trail of blood. He appeared to be oblivious to the pain.

For months now his mind had been plagued and stifled by depression. He'd been functioning on automatic, lecturing at the university in the mornings, working apathetically on his research in the evenings, and sitting for hours in front of the TV at night.

Alone.

There was a time when he used to enjoy talking to people or going out and returning home with a woman he happened to meet at one of Montreal's numerous pubs and clubs; but he'd lost all interest. His senses dulled.

He found himself thinking more and more about the futility of it all.

He shouldn't have made that deal with the devil. Agree to help them just for greed. For money. Where will they detonate that bomb? How many innocent people will die because of him? He felt trapped.

That night, after downing far more glasses of alcohol than his body could absorb, he opened the large window and jumped.

December 4th 2016

"Eleven innocent individuals?"

"I'll tell you." Grandpa rested his coffee cup on the table. "Let's move to one of the rooms."

"When the Soviet Union fell apart, Kazakhstan was left in possession of one thousand four hundred nuclear warheads on missiles and armaments for aircraft. Kazakhstan made a decision to sign the Non-Proliferation Treaty and become a country free of nuclear arms. By the end of 1993, the Kazakhs had returned all this weaponry to Russia. According to intelligence assessments, ours and the Americans, several fifty-kiloton bombs 'disappeared' on the way and were hidden somewhere in Kazakhstan by military officials who planned to wait a few years and then sell them for a tidy sum. It had nothing to do with ideology; it was all about greed. You have to understand, fifty kilotons is about 1.8 grams of enriched Uranium-235—or put plainly, Hiroshima three times over for each of the bombs that were stolen.

"Intense yet quiet efforts to locate the bombs have been underway since 1993—on the part of the Russians in particular, but the Americans have also been involved and so have we. The Russians were afraid they'd fall into the hands of the Chechens or Georgia; the Americans were worried about them getting to Bin Laden; and Israel feared they could end up, with the help of Iranian funding, in the hands of a thousand different elements. I think it was the first time in history that agents from the three countries worked together on the same project. It hasn't happened again. We were under the impression that all the bombs were found and that all those involved were eliminated.

"Then, about twelve years ago, we received information from Military Intelligence Unit 8200 that opened everything up again. They picked up an encrypted online correspondence between Kazakhstan and Denmark that appeared to be part of an arms deal negotiation. It happens all the time—arms deal negotiations, that is—but the system highlighted this particular correspondence due to the unusually high sums of money involved and the fact that they were discussing 'one barrel of material.' "

"What kind of money are you talking about?"

"They were discussing a sum of two and a half billion dollars for this one 'barrel.' In other words, a state was clearly behind the efforts to make the purchase. This prompted immediate monitoring of the group in Kazakhstan that was trying to push the deal through. They weren't fools, however, and managed somehow to transfer the bomb to Mongolia, and that's where we lost track of the people who were holding it. And then they all disappeared as if the earth had swallowed them up. The Strategic Threats Department slaved over the matter for months before picking up another phone call from Kazakhstan to Brussels.

"Brussels at the time was hosting a scientific conference for physicists, and the call came in to one of the conference rooms in which the discussions were taking place. The conference was at the Hotel Metropole. We managed to catch the call in real time and immediately dispatched an agent to the scene; she opened the conference room door and peeked inside as though she had entered the wrong room but the call had ended by the time she got there. She did manage to take a look at everyone in the room though, so we could verify the faces with the list of participants in the discussion that was affixed to the door of that conference room. The agent photographed the list after she closed the door.

"There were twelve scientists. One of them took the call from Kazakhstan."

Grandpa logged into the Orion system and opened a document displaying the transcript of a phone call:

- THE DEVICE HAS ARRIVED AND IS IN A SECURE LOCATION, AS WE AGREED.

- IN THE CEMETERY?

- YES.

- THE REMAINDER OF THE SUM WILL BE TRANSFERRED TO YOU IN FULL THROUGH THE AGREED ACCOUNTS WITHIN A MONTH, FOLLOWING AN INSPECTION OF THE DEVICE.

- WE'RE PULLING OUT OF THERE. DOES ANYONE APART FROM YOU KNOW THE LOCATION?

- NO. I WILL INSPECT THE DEVICE PERSONALLY, AND I'M THE ONLY ONE WHO KNOWS THE LOCATION.

"And then they haggled over the timetable, and eventually came to an agreement."

"He or she? You said you were listening to the call, so why not simply use voice-recognition software to identify the person?"

"There were no voices. The entire conversation was conducted by means of the phones' touch-tone keypad buttons. A Morse code of sorts that they'd devised based on ten different tones. The phone at the hotel wasn't encrypted and they had no alternative. They must have been afraid of someone recognizing the person on the Brussels end of the line in the event the phone was tapped. We cracked the code in seconds. It was a pretty primitive one as it didn't involve any real encryption and was something performed manually, but we didn't know who in Brussels had taken the call and we came up with nothing from Kazakhstan, too."

"Fingerprints on the phone?"

"The agent checked for those too when everyone left the room. Nothing. It had been wiped clean. I made the decision. I gave the order to assassinate all twelve."

The room went quiet for a moment, and then Grandpa continued:

"I instructed the Operations Wing to kill them all, even though eleven had done nothing wrong. The plan was for twelve different agents to go after the targets and take them out one by one. One agent for each target. I didn't think we'd have any trouble with that madman we sent there. Based on the information you've just now given me, the price paid by the innocent has been high. Too high."

Grandpa sighed again. He sat slumped in his chair, as if a heavy load was resting on his shoulders. For a moment he looked very old.

"Look, if the bomb had fallen into the wrong hands, it would have made its way to Africa, to Egypt, and from there to Gaza through a tunnel; and they would have found a way to get it to Tel Aviv somehow. Half a million fatalities is a conservative estimate. And where would we seek retribution? It wouldn't be Iran; because they know all too well that they'd be sealing their own fate if they were to send a bomb here. I was left with no choice."

"You had no choice. I would have done the same."

"I read up on all twelve. Brilliant individuals. I tried in every way I could to find something that would point un-equivocally to one of them. Nothing. Did the possibility that the device in question was one of the missing bombs warrant killing all of them? None of the intelligence we had made mention of a bomb, but the evidence seemed to indicate that it was one. I guess we'll never know whether Bernoulli was justified or not. But the fact is that ten years have gone by since then and we're all still here.

"I thought I'd sleep well at night. I don't sleep well. And it's only going to get worse now. Everyone's blood is on my conscience. We made a horrendous mistake with that agent. I still don't understand how he came to be in possession of the details of three targets and not only one. I was sure he had obtained them himself, or that he was a double agent or a plant or any possible theory. And still now—are you sure that what it says in the notebook about how he received the envelopes is really true? It could simply be a ploy on his part, or on the part of whoever is behind him."

"What happened in the end with 10483 anyway?" Avner asked. "I recall reading a report that his body was found. I tried to find it now, but it's no longer in the system—just like the rest of the material on the Bernoulli Project—it seems to have disappeared from the computer."

"Yes, they upped the classification level of Bernoulli to include only the inner circle. That's why you'll only find details about it in partially censored indirectly related documents. In any event, his body was discovered in his apartment following his return from Canada. I gave the order for him to be followed from the moment he landed and not be allowed to disappear. The surveillance team saw smoke coming from his apartment that night and broke inside. He had poured a jerrycan of gasoline over himself and his bed, laid down and set himself on fire. He was already burned to the crisp by the time the agents called the fire department and rushed inside. Absolute madness."

"How did they know it was him?"

"Dental records—the fillings in his teeth. Fingerprints were out of the question and his DNA sample wasn't in the system. Another screw-up. The fire consumed almost the entire apartment. His parents were already elderly at the time. They sold the apartment after the fire. We searched it beforehand, but we overlooked the basement. Are you sending a team there this morning?"

"Yes," Avner replied, and then he remembered something else. "Tell me, did they find the tooth of a young girl on his body?"

"A girl's tooth?"

"Yes, he writes in the notebook that the tooth was in a plastic bottle around his neck."

"No, they found nothing of the kind. And they examined that body with a fine-tooth comb. What was left of it at least. Had they found such a tooth, it would certainly have appeared in the pathology report."

"Do you mind waiting here for a short while?" Avner said. "I have two pages of the notebook left to read; perhaps there's something interesting in them."

"No problem. I'll make some more coffee. You look like you could do with some too." Grandpa allowed himself a smile and headed to the kitchenette.

Avner picked up the notebook again.

MORNING. MARCH 2006

I make a list.

1. Rat poison—large package
2. Material for unclogging drains—3 cartons
3. Flexible air-conditioning pipe—20 meters
4. Large roll of cling wrap
5. 3 10-liter plastic buckets
6. Baking soda—1 carton
7. Vinegar—5 cartons

I buy the vinegar and baking soda at Walmart. The substance for unclogging drains and the rest of the equipment I pick up wholesale directly from the factory store. And I acquire the rat poison at the Great Farmer's Market about a half-hour drive from Montreal.

After loading all the materials into the car, I drive to the university.

When I get to the university my target's car isn't there. I drive to the target's residence. He isn't there. There's no guard outside either. I enter the building and take the elevator to my target's floor. Police crime-scene tape is stretched across the door to the target's apartment. Someone beat me to it. My target no longer exists. I can go home.

I dump the car and materials I purchased and buy a ticket back to Israel online. There's a tail on me from the moment I arrive at the airport in Montreal ahead of my departure. The tail stays with me in Tel Aviv, too.

I go home, walk inside, and open the windows to air out the apartment. I go down to the basement to check on my displays. I add more nutrient solution to the large container for the IVs. It's almost empty. The 2 people at the table watch me. Their eyes are wide open. Their breathing is heavy. There's a stench in the basement.

I remove the man from the aquarium. I shouldn't have to destroy my artwork like this, but I have no choice. I lay the body on the floor and open the man's mouth. I insert a teaspoon into his mouth so that it doesn't close.

Some of the oil in which he was suspended spills onto the floor around him, and I'm careful not to slip on it.

I have equipment I purchased from a dentist in the storage cupboard in the basement, along with my own dental X-rays. I get to work.

I carry the body upstairs to the bedroom when I'm done and lay it down on the bed. I wash the house thoroughly and remove all the oil that dripped on the floor.

I write a suicide note.

I write that I'm now a danger to The Organization because the enemy knows my identity, so it's best I kill myself. I leave the note in the refrigerator.

I glance out the window. The vehicle with the team sent to keep track of me is parked outside. This time there aren't just 2 of them. There are 4.

I pour a jerrycan of gasoline over the man in the bed, set him on fire and go back down to the basement. I shut the basement door well to prevent smoke from drifting in from above. The basement is well sealed and there's enough food and water down here for a 6-month stay, but I have no intentions of being here for that long. I'll leave in a few weeks with enough cash in hand to set myself up in a new apartment and make my plans.

I eat matzo with chocolate spread and begin my last entry in the notebook.

"Just as I suspected."

Avner closed the notebook.

"That wasn't his body they found there. He was hiding in the basement."

Grandpa tapped his fingers on the table.

"It's too simple, Avner. I don't buy it."

"I'm willing to bet you that three hours from now we'll be standing in that basement," Avner responded. "What's too simple about it? He hid down there while his bedroom burned upstairs, and our team didn't find the trapdoor leading down to the basement. He must have hidden it well. A few days or weeks later, after everything had blown over, he emerged and disappeared. He probably had enough food in there for months, just as he wrote. All I'm missing is the last page of the notebook. He says he's writing one, but there isn't another page."

"I agree with everything you say. But just think for a moment. Why would he want you to know that the body we found wasn't his? And why now? He's the one who wrote the story about the tooth. He's the one who sent the notebook to Amiram because he knew Amiram would run to you with it. He wanted you to know what you now know. That's not what bothers me. The damage is already done and there's nothing we can do about it. What bothers me is this: Why does he want you to know about it now? He knows you'll be sending a team to the basement this morning. He knows that after reading through just a few pages of the notebook, you must have gone to one of The Organization's branches to log in to the computer system. He's surely aware of it all. He may have followed Amiram and now he knows where you live, too. He may have followed you and is now waiting outside for you. And if so, why? You have no direct connection to him. You weren't his operator."

"And why wait ten years?" Avner added. "I don't get it."

"Everything in the notebook could be the absolute truth or simply dry facts mixed in with misleading information that he chose to insert. Don't take it all for granted. And Avner, do me a favor, warn the team that's going there today. The place could be rigged with an explosive device if that part of the notebook is true; they shouldn't take any chances and they mustn't touch a single thing there. Do you plan to send the Counter-Terrorism Unit, too?"

"No. I was thinking the police, firefighters, one of our teams and paramedics on standby."

"You should coordinate with the Counter-Terrorism Unit. One of their sappers should be on the team that goes in to the apartment."

Grandpa rose from his chair. "I'm going home, Avner, but first promise me that you won't leave here alone. I'll call in a security detail for you. Just to be on the safe side."

Standing in the doorway, Grandpa remembered something and turned around. "You have a visitor on her way over. Let her read the notebook when she gets here. She may find something you missed."

Grandpa left the room before Avner had a chance to inquire as to the identity of his guest.

He picked up the flash drive that came with the notebook and held it between his fingers. He looked closely at the label which displayed handwriting he was now quite familiar with. Avner plugged the flash drive into his laptop. It contained just a single file labeled Doctor.mp3 and Avner played it through the laptop's speakers.

- Click
- Click
- Click
- Click
- Click

- Close your eyes and listen to rhythm of the clicks.

- Click
- Click
- Click
- Click
- Click

- In a moment I will count to three.

- Click
- Click
- Click
- Click
- Click

Avner stopped the recording. He thought about Amiram.

Amiram was the one who had recruited 10483. Now he understood why Amiram was so agitated last night. Last night? An eternity seems to have gone by since eleven last night.

Avner clicked on Send and the Orion system, as efficient as ever, distributed the summary he had written during the course of the night to The Organization's headquarters.

10483 could be outside right now. The thought sent shivers down his spine. He hoped Grandpa's paranoia was overblown. He's been in The Organization for too long.

The door to the office flew open suddenly.

"Where is it?—Quickly, go wash your hands—Don't put your fingers in your mouth—I've got gloves—Call everyone who may have touched it and tell them to wash their hands, too—Who else has touched it?—Give it to me."

"Excuse me? Who are you?" A bewildered Avner stared at the young woman motioning frantically in front of him. She was dressed in jeans and a black T-shirt. Peering at him from under her crop of black hair was a pair of blazing green eyes.

"Grandpa called me. Didn't he tell you? I'm Rotem. I conducted a study of this agent ten years ago. I have to read it."

Avner handed her the notebook and the stack of pages that were in it and Rotem pulled a pair of latex gloves out of her pocket and slipped them over her hands. "Wash your hands with a lot of soap," she said. "I'm serious. You know who we're dealing with here. He may have coated the pages in something."

Avner went to the bathroom and Rotem picked up the notebook. "Amateurs," she muttered to herself. She sat at the desk and flipped through the pages of the notebook from left to right, at the pace of a photocopying machine. She then did the same with loose pages.

"Fucking hell. It's unreal!" Rotem placed the last page on the table.

She cast her eyes over the remaining items on the desk and spotted the handwriting on the label of the flash drive that was still connected to Avner's laptop. She grabbed for the laptop, unplugged its communication cable, turned it over, removed the battery and caused it to shut down. "Double amateurs," she muttered again.

"What are you doing?" Avner walked back into the room carrying two cups of coffee in his freshly washed hands.

"Do you have any idea what kind of viruses-worms-spyware and other devious things he's put on here for you? Who knows what kind of worm you've just put into The Organization's network!" She pulled out a cell phone and quickly typed a text message to the Computer Department's Control Center. **Check all the data transmissions from the Ganei Yehuda satellite and send someone from InfoSec here right now.**

"Give me a second to think," Rotem continued—and closed her eyes. The contents of the notebook flashed through her photographic memory; she arranged all the sentences, words and sketches on a large imaginary wall in her mind and began to draw lines between them, her fingers moving in the air in front of her face and closed eyes, mimicking her thought patterns that linked events on the imaginary map she pictured.

She continued for about two minutes and then opened her eyes and remained silent.

"Why don't I know about that?" Avner asked.

He got no response. Rotem appeared to be somewhere else. She was looking straight ahead but her eyes weren't focused on anything in particular.

"Why don't I know about that?" Avner asked again.

Rotem gathered herself. "Know about what?" she said.

"About the study you conducted on him."

"I did it for the European Ops division. They kept it to themselves. You know . . . the policy of keeping things separate. . . . What you don't know can't hurt you." Rotem remove her gloves. "What's on the flash drive?"

"Just the recording of the hypnosis—the one he used in Canada."

"How exactly did you get hold of the notebook?"

Avner told Rotem about the law firm and the delivery instructions they received with the notebook and about his meeting with Amiram.

Rotem stood and started pacing back and forth in the room. "He had ten years to plan things. God only knows what he managed to come up with in ten years."

Avner watched her as she moved agitatedly back and forth in the space between the desk and the door. *I wonder how she came to work for them,* he thought. The Operations Division had always had special privileges. Apparently some of their recruits don't go through his department.

"Look at what he managed to accomplish in just a few days with each of the hits he carried out. He's very creative. And now he's had ten years. It's a vendetta. There are no gray areas in his world; everything's either black or white, good or evil. He'll never forgive The Organization for what they did to him, for losing faith in him. From his perspective, going from good to evil in the eyes of The Organization is the end of the world."

"Why does he reveal everything in the notebook? He could have exacted his revenge without it too."

"It's pretty simple," Rotem sighed. "Everyone who's seen it during the course of the night is going to die. So he doesn't really care about all this exposure. To the contrary, he wants us to know that he's always been good, that we were all wrong. After he kills you, Amiram, Grandpa, me and anyone else in his sights, he'll destroy it. The material in the notebook is genuine; he hasn't fabricated anything. It fits the pattern to a degree that can't be faked. The basement's a trap. He's probably sitting there with night-vision goggles like Buffalo Bill in *Silence of the Lambs*, finger around the pin of a grenade. Or there's a motion sensor that will set off an explosive device to bring the whole building down the moment anyone steps foot on the ladder. Forget the basement; it'll only end badly down there. Evacuate the building and issue a demolition order. He's relishing this now. Don't give him the pleasure."

"The pleasure?"

"Yes. The pleasure. His plan was set into motion last night. After ten years of planning. He's loving every minute. He enjoys a good plan kicked off and running even more than the idea of hurting the organization that betrayed him. For him it's all about the planning and the execution."

"Amiram was his operator. I'm responsible for recruiting agents, Grandpa is part of the inner circle. Why kill you?"

"Because I know him better than anyone. I'm sure he's aware of that. He knew Grandpa would call me in, just like he knew Amiram would bring the notebook to your home, just like he knew that you'd come here within half an hour of starting to read it. He may be paranoid and a sociopath and suffer from crippling OCD, but he's not stupid. In fact, he's a genius of sorts in his own insane way."

"So why did he deposit the notebook a decade ago with instructions to send it now?" Avner continued. "If he's alive, he could have held on to it and sent it whenever he chose."

"He set himself a deadline. He knows himself and knows he could have devoted twenty years to planning this, too. He simply provided himself with a time constraint when he gave the notebook to the law firm. He WANTED to impose a time restriction on himself."

"You know, the three people on the Bernoulli list that he took out all had something in common. They were all nuclear scientists. Yasmin Li-Ang was a nuclear engineer who worked at the CERN particle accelerator, Professor Federico Lopez headed the Department of Nuclear Engineering at Instituto Balseiro and played a major role in Argentina's nuclear program, and Professor Bernard Strauss led the SLOWPOKE mini-reactor project in Canada. Doesn't it seem just a little too coincidental that all three nuclear scientists ended up as his targets? The remaining scientists on the list were physicists too, but none were involved in the nuclear field."

"I don't know how or why it turned out like that, but it certainly doesn't sound like a coincidence. I don't think he picked out the nuclear scientists on the Bernoulli list himself. Whoever arranged for him to receive the three envelopes had a definite agenda."

Rotem finally sat down again. She removed her shoes, rested her feet on the table and wiggled her toes. She sipped from the mug of coffee Avner had returned with. "I'm not leaving here until they show me his head on a platter. And we should call in more security."

A young man paced quickly down Tel Aviv's Ibn Gvirol Street. There was something different about today. He was sure. The sun warmed his short black hair and a pair of sunglasses shielded his eyes.

- You won't let yourself become him -

He was carrying two shopping bags from the Super-sol at 157 Ibn Gvirol in each hand. Had the supermarket been on the other side of the street, at 156, its street number would be divisible by three with no remainder. But it's not. That's why he doesn't really like shopping at that supermarket, but its business hours are more convenient.

- You won't let yourself become him -

He needs to get home to continue working on the basement. He moved into the new apartment some seven months ago and it would be another seven months before the new basement would be ready. He torched his previous apartment.

It struck him at once.

He knew exactly what he had to do today, the day on which the doors to heaven open once every one thousand years. He waited on the sidewalk for a bus to come speeding by. With the bus just two meters away, he jumped into the road in front of it and spread his arms, still holding the bags from the supermarket.

The bus driver stared at him, eyes wide, and didn't even have time to slam his foot down on the brake pedal. The look on the driver's face reminded him of the look on the face of someone he once pushed onto the tracks of the Metro in Amsterdam.

The bus and the man in front of it unite momentarily and then separate. Vegetables, bread, and bags of frozen food scatter over the road in front of the stunned onlookers. The bus comes to a stop.

The tall thin body of 10483 lies sprawled on the road. His jeans are ripped at the back, where his hip bones—displaced due to the two open fractures caused when the vehicle's bumper slammed into his pelvis—have pierced through the fabric. The pieces of bone are covered in shredded bits of muscle. One of his ribs is protruding from his side, too, through a tear in the black T-shirt he is wearing.

He tries to close his eyes but isn't able to. Fragments from his broken sunglasses are keeping them from closing.

10483 lies on the road, eyes open, smiling broadly. He can't remember the last time he'd smiled.

He can't remember ever smiling.

He feels light, as if a load has been lifted from his mind and disappeared.

He's free at last.

"I'll be your eyes"
I'm lying on my back, a blinding black light all around me.
The noise of a respirator.
"I'll be your eyes"
She repeats the words.
"Don't be afraid"

"Fifty-three to control, we have an attempted suicide with multiple-system injuries, sedated and on a respirator. We're on our way to Ichilov. Ready the ER. ETA two minutes."

"Got you. Relaying to Ichilov. Do you have an ID for him?"

"No. He's not carrying identification of any kind."

"What's the condition of his face?"

"It's a mess. He jumped off the sidewalk in front of a bus. He doesn't have a face. His mother wouldn't recognize him. I've given him twenty milligrams of morphine and he's on oxygen. They're going to need plenty of units of blood. He's lucky we were nearby in the ambulance when we got the call. Five more minutes of blood loss and he would have needed the coroner."

"Tali, are you coming by control after your shift?"

"Believe me; you don't want to see me now. I look like someone who works in a butcher shop. I'm covered in blood. All I need is that butcher's hat on my head and a meat cleaver in my hand. I have to take a shower. Let's catch up tomorrow."

"Cool."

The loud banging on the door startled Galia. She placed the sandwich she was preparing on the kitchen counter and went to the door.

"Who's there?"

"Police. Open up please."

Galia left the security chain in place and opened the door. She peered out through the opening and saw two uniformed police officers. One of them flashed his police ID.

"You need to leave the building," one of the officers said to her.

"What happened?" Galia asked alarmed.

"There's a gas leak. We don't know where it's coming from, but it appears to be from the building's main line. We're evacuating all tenants. Is there anyone else at home with you?"

"Yes. I have two children. I'll be out with them right away."

"Quickly. Don't turn on any electrical appliances and no open flames, of course."

Galia rushed back to the kitchen. Yonatan had left for work earlier that morning and Romi and Ido were finishing their breakfast of cornflakes with milk.

"Come, sweeties, we need to leave. Don't forget your bag, Romi."

"But I haven't finished eating!"

"There's no time, sweetie, we have to go right now. You can have some more cereal when you get back from kindergarten."

"Mom, was that a real policeman?"

"Yes, he came for a visit."

"Why?"

"To make sure that we're okay. The police look after us, and they came here to make sure that we leave the house right away because there's a gas leak and all the neighbors have to leave quickly until it's fixed."

They hurried out and Galia locked the door behind them. Parked across the rain-soaked street in front of the building were police cars and ambulances, a large fire truck and several additional unmarked vehicles with civilian license plates flashing blue lights.

"Wow! Did you see, Mom? Look how many of them are looking after us."

With Romi and Ido in tow, Galia quickly moved away from the building. She strapped the children in the car and got into the driver's seat. A policeman in a yellow raincoat pushed aside a barrier at the end of the street and allowed her to drive out.

Something was troubling Galia, and she couldn't quite put her finger on it.

It wasn't all the vehicles parked outside the building.

And it wasn't the dozens of emergency services personnel and various other official-looking individuals who were waiting downstairs as the tenants left the building.

Then she figured it out. It was simple, really. There was no smell of gas.

09:00

"No matter what, you're not to touch a thing down there. In one of the bedrooms there's a closet, something in its floor leads down to the basement. The light switches are booby-trapped; use only your flashlights. There's supposed to be a large steel cage down there in the middle of the basement, and a large aquarium, two bodies, and God knows what else. No matter what you find, you're not to touch a single thing; you're only scanning for explosives with the puffer machines and marking the walls. You're going to go through that basement little by little until everything's been marked, and then you're going to drill into the walls to locate the ignition fuse wire next to each block of explosives so they can be disconnected from the detonation mechanism. Scan the walls, the floor, the ceiling, the bodies, the aquarium, but don't touch a thing."

The man giving the briefing looked tired but he repeated the same instructions over and over again.

The leader of the team, Daniel, already had his gas mask on. He would go in accompanied by two agents from The Organization and two sappers from the Counter-Terrorism Unit. He nodded, then motioned slightly with his head in the direction of the building. They went in.

The door on the right on the ground floor was already open. The family had left in a hurry.

First, a quick scan of the apartment. It was an ordinary residential apartment with two children's bedrooms, a living room, a kitchen and a master bedroom with a large closet. They removed all the clothes from the closet and placed them on the bed. Then they disassembled the shelves and leaned them against the wall.

"There's no trapdoor here."

Their voices sounded mechanical through the gas mask filters. Like robots.

"Keep looking. Knock on the floor of the closet until you locate a hollow area."

"There's something here."

"Let me see."

Daniel knelt down in front of the open closet and examined the floor. It looked like the left side of the wood floor was covering something. Using a cordless screwdriver he inserted two large screws into the wood floor and then used them to grip and lift the wood. Underneath the flooring was a steel trapdoor with rubber sealing around its edges. Welded to its left side was a U-shaped steel handle.

Daniel pulled the handle to the right, and the steel covering slid along two rails across the closet floor to expose a small opening and a metal ladder leading down into darkness.

The team climbed down slowly, one rung at a time, taking care not to touch anything. Daniel, who went down first, aimed the beam of his head-mounted flashlight at the basement floor before stepping off the ladder to scan for possible tripwires or a switch that could detonate an explosive charge. The team then stood in the center of the basement and directed their flashlights around the dark expanse. Their gas masks emitted sounds of heavy breathing.

In the center of the basement stood a tall steel cage, which was empty. The cage door was open. One of the members of the team went in and looked around. There was something written on the floor of the cage, under a layer of dust. He retrieved a fine brush from one of the pouches in his vest and carefully brushed the dust aside to reveal words engraved into the concrete floor. Given the depth of the letters in the hard floor, someone had obviously gone to great lengths to scratch them into the concrete.

12/29/2005
The fucker got me
My name is ■■■■ ■■■■■■
I won't get out of here alive
Notify my family
03 - ■■■■■■■.

The name and number had been thoroughly erased using a powerful mechanical stone-cutting tool. Recovering the details would be impossible.

The agent from The Organization returned the brush to its pouch and pulled out a small digital camera. He photographed the writing, put the camera away again and continued to scan the cage centimeter by centimeter with the aid of his flashlight.

At the same time, the second agent from The Organization looked over a large table with dishes that contained something that once was food. The plates and eating utensils were covered in a thick layer of dust. Bound to chairs at either end of the table were two decomposing bodies draped in dust-covered robes, with empty and dusty tubes still attached to the loose skin that remained on the bones of their arms. The flashlight's beam followed the yellowing pipes leading from their arms to a large empty container, covered in dust too.

Their heads were slumped forward. Skulls with bits of dry skin still stuck to them. One scalp had the short hair of a man and the other, the long black hair of a woman, some of which remained attached to her head and some of which had dropped off into her lap and lay in a small pile on the robe she was wearing. Resting on the table, under a layer of dust, was an old piece of paper with writing on it. The agent cleaned it carefully with his brush and photographed it.

Up against the wall in front of the table stood a large aquarium filled with yellow liquid. Over time, some of the liquid had clearly evaporated, leaving bits of residue on the sides of the tank that were an indication of its original level. There was nothing in the liquid.

If the team members were not wearing their gas masks the unbearable stink of death in the basement would have made it impossible to focus on their mission. A mechanical-sounding voice interrupted the silence, which until then had been disturbed only by heavy breathing and the clicking of cameras. "Okay, guys, Rafi and I are going to scan the walls with the puffer machines; you check for trip-wires or other booby traps. Slow and easy. We're in no rush. Photograph everything."

The two members of the police's Counter-Terrorism Unit began charting the explosive devices while the two organization agents continued to document the basement, photographing the remains of the food and water and the ventilation and electrical systems. Now and then, one of the puffer machines would emit a series of short beeps, and its operator would carefully draw a circle with a black marker on one of the walls or the floor.

A sudden mechanical buzzing sound caused them to freeze and they all directed their flashlight beams at the ceiling, in the direction of the source of the noise.

A camera.

It was rotating slowly and scanning the basement from side to side in a one-hundred-and-eighty degree arc.

"Move it! Get upstairs now!"

The four of them dropped the equipment they were carrying and made a dash for the ladder, the beams of their head-mounted flashlights flickering frenetically through the dark interior of the basement.

09:40

Despite the drizzle, a crowd had gathered under umbrellas behind the police barricades. The tenants who had been evacuated from their apartments, together with curious onlookers from nearby buildings, were trying to figure out what was going on.

"Why did they close the street?"

"They say there's a gas leak in that building over there."

"A gas leak?"

"Yes."

"Twenty police cars for a gas leak? It looks more like a police orgy."

"Too true. And what are the CTU vehicles doing here?"

"Since when have you been such an expert? How do you know which ones are CTU vehicles?"

"Can't you see the . . . ?"

The conversation was cut short by an explosion.

The four-story building rose a centimeter or two off the ground for a moment and then caved in on itself like a house of cards. The powerful blast sprayed chunks of concrete and broken glass in every direction, injuring onlookers who were standing too close to the police barriers and shattering the windows of cars parked in the vicinity of the building. The structure disappeared in a large cloud of dust; and when the dust cleared, there was nothing left but a pile of concrete and brick, with twisted pieces of metal protruding from the rubble. Flames were coming from a burst gas pipe, ignited by the blast, and a fountain of water gushed from another pipe torn apart by the shockwave.

Everything went silent for a few seconds.

And then chaos broke out. The screams of the injured, ambulance and police sirens, and instructions to clear a path for the emergency vehicles blared through loudspeakers.

Covered from head to toe in a fine white powder, Avner stood across the street with his hands over his ears. Everything around him appeared for a while to be moving in slow motion, and then suddenly, as if someone had released the Pause button, the world began moving again.

"You have to keep this under wraps," he shouted to The Organization official standing next to him. "The media will be here any minute. Sell them a gas-leak story. This has to be covered up. Get everyone in the picture as quickly as possible."

"Did the team get out?"

"No," Avner sighed. "No one must be allowed to see the rescue teams bringing the bodies out from the basement when they get to them. Erect a large canvas tent over all this shit and make sure our teams handle the evacuation."

Avner sipped from a bottle of water someone handed to him. "I'm going to the main base. Make sure they retrieve the memory cards from the cameras and recording equipment—when they eventually get to the bodies." Avner glanced at the smoking pile of rubble that was once a building. "It'll take some time," he added.

09:53

Efrat woke and stretched in bed.

By the look of the sheets and blankets on Avner's side of the bed, she could tell he hadn't come to bed at all during the night.

He must have fallen asleep in the living room again, she thought.

She got up, went to the bathroom, washed her hands, and brushed her teeth.

Then she went downstairs. She glanced at the living room and vacant couch and realized Avner wasn't there. He'd left a message for her on the magnetic board on the refrigerator. He'd gone to The Organization once again.

It really is getting a bit much, she thought to herself. She resolved for the thousandth time to persuade him to find a job in human resource management and quit selling his soul to the ungrateful organization he currently worked for. He'd earn twice as much and work half the amount of time. *That's it.* She'd speak to him about it this evening.

She went into the kitchen, took out a bottle of orange juice from the refrigerator and was pouring herself a glass when the doorbell rang. *Perhaps it's Avner*, she thought. *But why would he ring the bell if he has a key?*

She opened the door.

Standing in a brown rain-soaked uniform was a UPS messenger.

"Hello," he said.

"Good morning."

"I have a package for Avner Moyal. Are you his wife?"

"Yes."

"I'll leave it here with you then. It's important. You should call him and tell him to come and get it."

Efrat's first instinct was to tell him to go to hell, she doesn't like being told what to do. On second thought, the messenger seemed a bit off, so she decide not to mess with him.

"Do I need to sign something?"

"Yes, here's a pen. Sign here, please."

Efrat signed the form and the messenger turned around and left.

She turned her attention to the package.

10:05

"Hi, sweetie!"

"Hi, honey. You bailed on me last night. Work again? You're crazy."

"Sorry, sweetie. I had to. Someone brought me something very urgent last night. I had to check a few things at work. I'll make it up to you."

"A package just arrived here for you. I was about to open it."

Avner could feel his heart start to race. He broke into a cold sweat. "Put it down right now!!!" The scream tore from his throat.

Startled by his reaction, Efrat placed the package on the table. "What's up?"

"It could be a bomb. Get out of the house. There's a psycho on the loose who has it out for me. Go to Rona's place. Now. I'm on my way. Place the package gently on the floor and don't touch it. Keep an eye out on your way to Rona's and let me know if anyone's following you."

"Avner! You're scaring me!"

"Just do as I say. I'm on my way to Rona's place now. I'll meet you there. What did the messenger look like?"

"I dunno . . . thirty-five, forty, or so. With cropped hair and a short beard. And a strange voice. Like a robot."

Avner screeched into a U-turn and began heading toward home.

Messengers are usually young guys.

It must have been him.

Avner floored it. He was completely unaware that there was a black device, the size of a thick book, which had been fitted into that very spot under the floor of his car while it was parked outside the satellite office where he had spent the night.

10:15

The large glass wall enclosing the den offered a view of well-manicured stretches of lawn. The room's walls were lined with bookshelves and the floor was dark hardwood. Several logs ablaze in a fireplace in the corner of the room dispelled the chill of the winter morning. The lights in the room were off; the early morning sunshine filtering through the glass wall was enough to illuminate the expanse.

Breakfast was laid out on a table on one side of the room—bowls of salad, fresh bread, several types of cheese, smoked salmon, omelets, hard-boiled eggs, fresh orange juice in a pitcher, and a selection of breakfast cereals. Neatly arranged next to an espresso machine at one end of the table were plates, glasses, mugs, and sets of cutlery.

The person who had arranged the spread left the room, closing two large doors behind him.

In the center of the room was a heavy wooden table, four corners adorned with black metalwork. There were eight people seated at the table—five men and three women.

"Good morning everyone," the host began.

"This meeting will be held entirely off the record and is not a part of The Organization's ongoing activities. I've called this urgent session because the agent who carried out the operation in Canada in 2006 has surfaced."

Drops of rain trickled down the large glass wall.

"Are you certain? It's been ten years since then," one of the men said.

"Yes. He's alive. He managed to slip under our radar for ten years. He surfaced in Israel yesterday. I'm guessing he's kicked off a plan of action against The Organization. He knows he was played. He's known it for ten years."

"That the notion of a mass killing was planted in his mind?"

"No, I don't believe he's onto that yet. No one outside this room knows that we assumed control of Bernoulli and used Canada to divert the United States off the bad road it was on. The U.S. was the primary objective; Canada was secondary; and the Bernoulli project was merely the facilitator. The bottom line is it worked."

Everyone around the table nodded in agreement.

"The mass killing factor was there in his personality. We strengthened it in the transformations he received causing him to do bigger and more extensive collateral damage without his being aware of it. To him it was just plans he made and carried out. We needed someone who was screwed up to begin with so I personally neutralized the screening mechanisms during his recruitment. He failed his polygraph test and half his CV was fabricated, but we needed someone with his profile. As you are all well aware, no agent would have agreed to carry out the operations he did."

"How many transformations did he undergo?"

"In addition to the four infrastructure transformations he underwent during the basic agents' course, we also had to carry out three operational transformations in the field, of varying intensity and over a relatively short period of time, in order to steer him in the direction we wanted."

"Is that why he was given three targets?"

"That's one of the reasons."

One of the individuals at the table, a large man, scratched his chin. "Are we certain about the effectiveness of the transformations? If I'm not mistaken, we've been using an outside contractor to perform them for us—a woman who used to work for us and then quit. It's costly, and doesn't always work that well. His last transformation involved the implanting of a self-termination date. He was supposed to commit suicide at some point, wasn't he? What went wrong?"

"Let me fill you in a little. Look, the brain of a fly is slightly smaller than a grain of sand. It contains approximately two hundred thousand neurons. Relative to its size, it's an amazing brain. It controls the fly's motor functions, survival and reproduction, and does it all with a minimalistic learning mechanism of just twelve neurons in total. Researchers at the Department of Molecular Neurobiology of Behavior at Georg-August University in Göttingen, Germany, successfully caused flies to smell light. I guess you could say they 'reprogrammed' the flies' sensory system. We were quick to recognize the potential it held for us. We came across the study completely by chance. In fact, the contractor you're referring to is the one who stumbled across the information when she was studying abroad, while she was still a part of The Organization. It's safe to say that the world's leading experts in the field are sitting today in our offices in Ramat Hasharon, only no one knows about them because they don't publish articles in scientific journals. They apply their trade in the field."

"A fly's brain is not a human brain."

"Remarkably, the basic learning mechanisms, the building blocks, are not so different. What we do with the transformation is simply on a larger scale. The difficulties and high cost are related to the creation of precise transformation files, rather than the cost of the outside contractor who applies them to the subject. A transformation file for a person has to be tailored to his or her specific brain. The wavelengths, the illumination, and the sound synchronization have to be combined perfectly, and the creation of each transformation file, based on its level of complexity, costs anywhere from tens of thousands to millions of shekels in computing expenses. But it's effective. Very effective. Don't forget that half of those released in the Gilad Shalit prisoner-exchange deal were subjected to transformations of intense paranoia and anxiety during their time in prison, and are just waiting for a trigger to activate them remotely. We've already tried remote activation on some of them, and the results were excellent. This is more than just planting an idea. This is programming. This is making someone act and do very precise things without being aware that they've been manipulated. That's the beauty of this method, we are not making the patient more psychotic than he already is, we just channel this behavior to specific activities we want him to do. But there is a price. We have seen that undergoing transformations eventually may speed up Alzheimer's, raise the chance of a brain tumor, speed up dementia. It's not a free ride."

"And what's the story with this agent, specifically?"

"As for the agent in question, he certainly knows all the particulars of the Bernoulli Project and he's aware of the fact that he received three targets, not just one. I assume he dug through The Organization's network and found all the Bernoulli material and the addresses of our doubles who are supposed to absorb any attempted hits on members of this inner circle. He did the math and realized that there was no mistake and that he received the three targets intentionally. That's the least of my concerns. More troubling to me are his exceptional analytical skills and the fact that he's had more than enough time to prepare something big for us now. He can do a lot of damage to The Organization's outer layer. The last transformation did indeed include the implanting of a self-termination date. He was supposed to commit suicide on December 12, 2006. For some reason, however, he didn't and we'll have to figure out why, but that's less of an issue right now."

An elderly woman, gray hair tied up in a bun, stubbed out a cigarette in an ashtray on the table in front of her. "I'm assuming you've deployed a clean-up team to locate him?" she said.

"Yes, the same team that was assigned to him for the three Bernoulli hits that he carried out. They know him well. We have several decoys that he's bound to go after. They're all under surveillance."

"Are you going to allow him to get to them?"

"I don't think we have a choice. We need to limit the collateral damage."

Everyone around the table nodded in agreement.

"Yasmin Li-Ang, Federico Lopez, and Bernard Strauss all worked for the same Iranian intelligence cell. We learned of this only in 2010, from Majid Shariri, the nuclear scientist who was taken out with a car bomb in Tehran but is alive and well today in Holon with a wife and three sons. Before interrogating him, we could only surmise why out of the twelve physicists, only the three nuclear scientists were under guard. Shariri confirmed our suspicions; he knew the names of all three. They were part of just one of six Iranian cells that were trying to get their hands on an old bomb from the former Soviet Union. A lot quicker than trying to develop a bomb yourself.

"The bomb slipped out the Iranians' hands at the very last minute thanks to our nutcase, who was dispatched to take out the three scientists. We were forced, of course, to eliminate all the other scientists who were in the room, too, because we didn't know which of them was involved. The remaining nine scientists died as a result of accidents of some kind or from 'natural' medical causes over a period of several years up until 2009. Each was handled by a different agent. We assigned the three nuclear scientists to the psycho because they were all heavily guarded and we knew that his extreme methods, with the addition of the transformations he underwent, would be our only chance of getting to them. And besides, it fit with our overriding objective. Had we managed to get our hands on Shariri a few years earlier, we wouldn't have had to take out the other nine. It was all about the timing. Tough luck."

"What about the bomb?" One of the men at the table, with gray hair and thick-rimmed glasses, looked at the raindrops trickling down the glass wall.

"We tried to locate it. Based on the call we intercepted at the conference in Brussels, the bomb was supposed to be in a cemetery somewhere. We dispatched more than a hundred agents with Geiger counters to sweep all the cemeteries in all the countries of origin of the scientists. It took years and they didn't come back with anything other than a reading from one grave in Buenos Aires that we opened, only to discover that the body itself was the source of the radiation. Someone who had moved to Argentina from Chernobyl."

The room went silent.

The woman with the gray hair lit another cigarette, inhaled deeply and spewed out a cloud of smoke as she started talking.

"I'd like to remind you all that I was opposed to this plan of action ten years ago—due to the high level of uncertainty and the huge risk involved. I'm not here to say, 'I told you so,' but I'd like to make sure that we never adopt such extreme measures again."

The host poured himself a glass of cold water from the pitcher next to him and remained silent. A man with curly gray hair, which showed clear signs of once being red, spoke up.

"We have to bear in mind that we were concerned with maintaining a constant defensive mode," he said.

The others around the table listened.

"I am aware not all of us were in the loop of that activity ten years ago. Those who were in the loop—please excuse me for dumping all this information. From our perspective, the United States functions well in the global arena when faced with a specific threat. Terror. The Cold War. The threat of a Saudi oil embargo. The Gulf War was a clear demonstration of this. That same year, a quarter of a million people died in civil wars in Africa, and no American aircraft dropped a single bomb there. But the moment Iraq invaded Kuwait—that spelled the end for Saddam. As far as NATO and the United States are concerned, the Syrians can pulverize each other to death until not a single one is left standing; but look at what happened the moment oil production in Libya came under threat.

"Because we don't have large oil reserves, our strategic value in the international arena isn't fixed. It's a linear function that is related directly to the threat level felt by the Pentagon. We can amuse ourselves with the thought that the enlightened world actually cares about us because we contribute to humanity. Bullshit, my friends. Bullshit. If the map of interest doesn't place us in the role of a watchdog loyal to the values of its masters, a watchdog that maintains order in a problematic neighborhood and bites sometimes whenever necessary, then we are worthless. All of a sudden, we're no longer a shining light of democracy in the Middle East but a pain in the ass that the entire world would be more than happy to see disappear in a flash. Let's not fool ourselves."

No one around the table said a word. The wind played with the raindrops sliding down the glass wall of the large room. The redhead continued:

"Following the end of World War II, the balance between the Soviets and the Americans preserved their defensive mode. '49—the Communist revolution in China. '50—the division of Korea. '53—Laos. '60—Congo. '61—the Bay of Pigs. '62—the Cuban Missile Crisis. '65—the war in Vietnam. '70—Cambodian invasion. '79—Afghanistan and the Soviets. '83—the Grenada invasion. '46 to '91—the nuclear arms race. There was an ongoing sequence of external incidents between two superpowers that boosted our strategic worth to the United States; but this worth gradually diminished following the break-up of the Soviet Union. For an entire decade, since 1991, we have witnessed a steady decline in American interest and behind-the-scenes assistance. I'm not talking about the numbers they publish every year in the framework of their "so-called" aid budget, but the real numbers, the sharing of technology and satellite intelligence, the integration of control systems.

"The slide came to an abrupt halt on September 11, 2001, when al-Qaeda brought down the Twin Towers along with the three thousand Americans who were in them at the time. Washington went berserk and invested six trillion dollars to set things straight in the region. I'll say that number again. Six trillion dollars. Strategic threats we had no idea how to cope with disappeared within two weeks.

"From then on, the defensive mode again fell into a state of decline. We had to wait for radical Islam to do something, or take action ourselves. Operating on U.S. soil was certainly out of the question. There are enough conspiracy theories going around without us actually having to do anything; and from the perspective of security as well—every foreigner who enters through a border crossing is monitored by the NSA until the moment he leaves the country. We decided to go for their neighbors. Much less security, and pretty much the exact same effect."

"I have to cut in," said the gray-haired woman. "Nothing is worth the risk of this operation coming to light. It would completely destroy our relationship with the United States, not to mention Canada. You all know what happened in the summer of '54 with Operation Susannah. It changed the entire political-historical course and overturned the political map—and all over a few incendiary devices the size of a wallet that didn't even injure anyone aside from one of our own agents. Do you have any idea what would happen if someone were to link us to Canada?"

The redhead fidgeted with the cap of his pen and went on:

"Of course Canada shouldn't have been hit on such a large scale. No one thought a lone agent without special equipment could cause such extensive damage; but if we look at the effective impact it had on preserving our interests, we saw the Americans ended up spending eight hundred and fifty billion dollars on security to protect *their* interests in the Middle East after the incident in Canada—and we can't ignore that."

Another one of the previously silent participants joined the discussion "And why did we think that doing this kind of operation in Canada would alert the Americans? After all, everyone thought this was the single act of an insane person."

The redhead placed the pen back on the table and replied "Right after this happened in Canada two agents we had planted deep in al-Qaeda made a phone call from Iraq.

One of them called the other and congratulated him on the successful operation in Canada and asked him if they were going to publish a tape about it before continuing with the U.S. operation. The other replied that this one would remain unannounced. That's all it took. ECHELON SIGINT collection did the rest. As a part of the 'Five Eyes' the U.S. is collecting every bit of digital data that moves in the Middle East—Satellite transmissions, fiber optics, radio stations, cell carrier channels, all sent back to NSA HQ at Fort Meade, Maryland, for decryption and processing. We do not know why the U.S. did not share this one with the rest of the ECHELON partners who are in the UK, New Zealand, Australia, and Canada. For some reason they kept it to themselves."

The host folded his arms and rested them on the table. He took charge of the discussion again.

"Friends, let's get back on track and talk about the matter at hand. Whether or not we should have carried out the operation is a subject for another time, and I'll arrange a separate meeting for such a discussion in the near future. For the operation in Canada, we needed someone who didn't know why he was carrying it out or what exactly he was doing. Someone who couldn't even explain it to himself. Someone who even if caught, in the worst-case scenario, would reveal at most that he was sent to assassinate someone and that the extensive damage he caused was at his own initiative. At that point, the interrogators would stop. They'd have no reason to think there was still another layer to peel off after extracting such a confession from him. Sure, it would have caused quite an uproar, but no one would have known the real reason.

"I'll make sure that in the end, when he's done with the little performance he's currently busy with, he will also disappear. For good this time. Does everyone agree with this course of action?"

Seven hands went up in silence, along with the raised hand of the man who called the meeting.

The rain was coming down harder outside. Water streamed down the glass wall. Thunder boomed overhead. The logs in the fireplace crackled.

"Okay then, ladies and gentlemen, the meeting is adjourned. Please, help yourself to breakfast," Grandpa said. He unfolded his arms, gulped down the remainder of the water in his glass, and placed the empty glass on the table.

The members of the inner circle stood up and went to fill their plates, and Grandpa used the time to go over to a corner of the room, sit down on a large leather sofa and enter a ten-digit number into his phone. After three rings, someone picked up.

"Rachel speaking, at your service."

"It's been ten years," Grandpa said. "We need you."

10:25

Efrat could feel her heart pounding in her chest. She bent down slowly, gently placed the package she was holding on the floor, stood back up, and left the house. But before she had a chance to lock the door, a blow to the back of her head dropped her to the floor.

She tried to look up and raise her arms to protect her head, but a second blow rendered her unconsciousness. A man in a brown UPS messenger's uniform leaned over her with something that looked like an oxygen mask in his hand. He reached into his pocket and took out a syringe and attached a sterile needle to the tip.

The needle slid into Efrat's arm and a few drops of blood were drawn into the syringe, creating a small red whirlpool within the clear liquid in the plastic tube. The mixture was then injected back into her vein.

The man in the uniform lifted her onto his shoulder and placed her in the back of a large van with the words MASHANI—CARPET CLEANING painted on both sides.

Fixed to the ceiling of the van were several powerful lights. The man turned them on before tying Efrat's hands and feet to the four metal rings soldered to the floor of the vehicle. He then removed his brown uniform, along with his shoes and socks, and stuffed all the items into a trash bag.

Two wooden cabinets stood on either side of the van's cargo space, blocking the vehicle's windows. The man reached into a drawer and retrieved a set of blue overalls bearing the same slogan and logo as displayed on the sides of the van. He sung cheerfully to himself as he dressed:

> *Twinkle, twinkle little star,*
> *How I wonder what you are.*

10:39

Avner pulled up outside Rona's home and dashed out of his car without bothering to close the door. He left the engine running.

Rona and Yigal's front door was locked. No one was home.

Avner banged his fist on the door. "Efrat!" he shouted. No response.

The homes where he lives are only a minute's walk from one another. Avner stood still for a moment to catch his breath. He had to remain focused.

He looked around and began walking slowly from his neighbors' front door toward his own home, looking for the signs of an abduction or a physical struggle.

On reaching the entrance to his home, he found the front door wide open.

"Efrat!"

No one answered. Avner noticed a few drops of blood by the front door. He went inside.

The house was empty. Avner looked around the entrance hall. He didn't see the package.

"Efrat!"

He went into the kitchen. There was a full glass of orange juice on the table. Next to it was a white sheet of lined paper.

Avner recognized it at once—both the type of paper and the handwriting on it.

He felt the blood drain from his face.

He sat down on the same chair he'd occupied last night during his brief meeting with Amiram and picked up the sheet of paper.

NIGHT, MARCH 2006

I'll tear this page out of the notebook and leave it in the basement when I'm done writing. I'll return to the basement at some point to retrieve it. But not now.

The bedroom upstairs is ablaze and I'm sitting in the basement at the Last Supper table eating dinner together with the 2 people on either side of me. They're still alive, but their heads are unstable and keep flopping from side to side. I add more liquid to the container to which their IV feeds are connected and throw in some antibiotics to prevent their pressure sores from becoming infected. They've lost weight and the zip ties holding them to their chairs are a little loose. I tighten them.

I wait for 3 o'clock and leave via the back balcony.

The surveillance team tracking me is still parked outside on the other side of the building.

Perhaps they think I have an accomplice.

I recognize the license plate.

It's an Organization vehicle. The middle 3 digits on the license number are 171, which is a number divisible by 3. I remember seeing the same car parked at the main base when I last met with Amiram.

I realize that the people trying to kill me are members of The Organization. I realize that they've decided to eliminate me so as not to leave behind any evidence of the missions I carried out with such success. This is how they want to repay me for all I did for them.

I walk away from the building and take a cab to the satellite branch in Ra'anana. The branch is located in a building marked

THE ISRAEL ELECTRIC CORPORATION LTD. Several large transformers on the roof of the building are hooked up to cables coming from a nearby pylon, but they're inactive.

I go inside, pass through the security check and leave my cell phone with the guard with the battery removed.

I get myself a glass of water and a few cookies from the kitchenette and go into one of the private offices with a desktop computer. I close the door and lock it. I log into the system using a system admin password.

I do a search for each of my 3 targets. I learn more about the Bernoulli Project. I now know the truth. The people in The Organization are the real enemy. I operated on their behalf and they betrayed me. They followed me. They sent people to my home.

I compile all the information I can about the Bernoulli Project and the members of The Organization's inner circle. They are the ones who gave the order to kill me. You can't connect a flash drive to The Organization's desktop computers, so I write down all the details on several sheets of paper, which I then fold and slip into the pocket of my pants.

I delete all traces of my searches from the system, along with any record of my having entered the branch.

I'll get them all. Amiram. His boss. All those who tried to kill me. And all the members of the inner circle. I'll make sure they all die, together with their families.

Professor Federico Lopez stopped in his tracks in the middle of his afternoon run. There was a strong smell of gasoline in the air. It took him a moment to connect the smell to the sprinklers that had suddenly come to life.

He saw a fuel tanker parked at the edge of the park. The air was thick with fuel vapor. Then he caught sight of a figure crouching beside the tanker. The figure threw a small ball of fire at the park. He knew he wasn't going to get out of there alive.

He reached into his pocket for his phone and started dialing.

The sea of fire rushed toward him, threatening to engulf him. The heat was overwhelming.

The phone sounded a single call-waiting tone.

He had to pass on the location. He's the only one who knows it.

His clothes caught fire. He could smell his own burning flesh and hair.

The phone sounded a second call-waiting tone.

The skin on the hand holding the phone was melting. His eyes were burning.

He had to pass on the location, or it would be lost forever.

Someone picked up.

"Hello, Herr Schmidt speaking."

The burning phone went dead.

Federico Lopez's burning lips kept repeating the same two words that nobody ever heard.

Then he dropped the blackened phone and fell to his knees, engulfed in flames.

He sat in the dimly lit den. A small reading lamp cast a small circle of light on a dark wooden table; outside the window, snowflakes fell softly in a slow swirling dance.

> *Majid Shariri is living in Israel under the name*
> *of Sharon Tuvian.*
> *He resides at 7 HaNarkisim Street in Holon.*

Those were the words on the piece of paper he'd removed from the envelope that was waiting for him under the door to his office. The envelope gave no indication of who sent it. All it showed was a date and the name of the intended recipient.

The envelope also contained a photograph of Sharon Tuvian. The man didn't look exactly like Shariri, but he wasn't different enough to completely rule out the possibility. Who delivered the envelope? None of the office employees had seen anything.

Shariri is the common thread that connects everything.

Perhaps he knows the location.

Perhaps he held it back during his interrogation.

Perhaps they never asked him at all.

He pressed on the Speak button of the intercom at the table. "Set up a meeting in Toronto for the entire group for the day after tomorrow. I want them all here in person."

He leaned back in his black leather chair and cast his eyes over the rows of books along the walls of his room and the snow swirling in the freezing cold outside. "*Es gibt noch Hoffnung,*" he said to himself. "There is still hope."

His personal assistant entered the room, her shoes clicking across the hardwood floor.

"Your tea, Herr Schmidt."

She woke up and stretched, letting out a loud sigh. It was one of those days. She felt like just staying in bed and not going anywhere. A strange sense of déjà vu overcame her, a tickling sensation at the back of her head, something inexplicable.

She got out of bed. It was Wednesday. There was no way she was going to miss another cognitive psychology lecture—not if she ever wanted to complete her degree.

A quick shower got her going; and after a few spoons of rice from a pot in the refrigerator and a cup of strong coffee, she was behind the wheel of her Fiat and on her way to the Mount Scopus campus. The roads were relatively traffic free, and she arrived at the university a little over an hour before the start of the lecture—an excellent opportunity to review the list of available student experiments and possibly earn a little money.

She'd participated two weeks earlier in an experiment in which not only did she earn thirty shekels for participation, but she also received an additional fifty shekels as a reward for exhibiting a certain behavior during the experiment itself. With any luck, she'd find something interesting and profitable today, too.

This time, the board only listed two active experiments. "No need for additional subjects today (Wednesday)," said a hand-written note in red ink over one item on the list, which left only one relevant option. It read: "The Physics Department in collaboration with the Computer Science Faculty needs subjects for an experiment relating to the discovery of a segment of the source code of the universe." Strange, she thought to herself, the geeks from the Givat Ram campus don't usually come to Mount Scopus to conduct experiments. The title of the experiment sounded odd, too. But it also read: "Fifty shekels for a fifteen-minute session."

She found the office noted in the ad and knocked on the door.

"Who's there?"

"A volunteer for the experiment."

"Come in, please."

She entered the room. There was a young man with red hair and a smile on his face.

"Hi, I'm Michael. Did you see our ad?"

"Yes. What's this about? The source code of the Universe?"

Michael smiled. "It sounds a little weird but it's exactly that. Are you familiar with CERN?"

"No."

"Okay, so CERN is the international research institute in Geneva that houses the world's largest particle accelerator. Our team is working with them and we have access to the computer database with the results of all the collisions that have taken place in the particle accelerator. We've been running mathematical models not on the mass or direction of the particles but on their derivatives. We thought initially that nothing would come of it, but we suddenly realized that we were coming up with segments of binary code—machine language that wasn't written by a human hand and is actually the engine behind all the laws of physics that we currently know."

"What?"

"Yes, we didn't believe it either at first, but we started playing with it and now we've discovered all kinds of interesting things. We're now running a test on a segment of code that we believe is responsible for the time dimension. We're actually quite similar to neuroscientists—we don't understand how it all works, but we're trying to touch on random things and see the results."

"So what's the experiment all about?"

"We'll try to send you two and a half hours back in time."

"Are you kidding me?"

"No. And it's not all that complicated either. There's no need for a time machine or any of that crap you see in the movies because we work on the source code directly. All that will happen is that I'll read out a series of one hundred and twenty-eight numbers to you, in groups of eight, and you'll repeat them after me. I won't read the last group out aloud and will only show you the last eight numbers on a note, but you will speak them out loud. That's it."

"Okay."

"Great. Let's begin then. Zero, zero, one, zero, one, zero, one, one."

She repeated the numbers in groups of eight, one group after the next, and finally read out the last eight from the note Michael handed to her.

She woke up and stretched, letting out a loud sigh. It was one of those days. She felt like just staying in bed and not going anywhere. A strange sense of déjà vu overcame her, a tickling sensation at the back of her head, something inexplicable.

She got out of bed. It was Wednesday. There was no way she was going to miss another cognitive psychology lecture—not if she ever wanted to complete her degree.

#Loud ring#

A quick shower got her going; and after a few spoons of rice from a pot in the refrigerator and a cup of strong coffee, she was behind the wheel of her Fiat and on her way to the Mount Scopus campus.

#Loud ring#

The roads were relatively traffic free, and she arrived at the university a little over an hour before the start of the lecture—an excellent opportunity to review the list of available student experiments and possibly earn a little money.

#Loud ring#

Carmit woke. She could still picture the corkboard displaying the list of experiments, but it began to fade gradually. She could remember every detail of the dream and the fact that it had repeated itself in a loop a few dozen times during the night. She glanced at the bedside clock. The glowing green digits indicated that it was already 11:20 in the morning. Nice of Guy to get the kids organized and off to kindergarten and school and let her sleep in.

These transformations are killing her. She slept for sixteen hours yet still felt tired, as if she'd been up all night. It could be frequency interference from the headphones, or maybe the orange filter on the sunglasses only offers partial protection, but she was fully aware of the fact that content from the transformation was seeping into her brain, too. The Japanese from the last two subjects she'd worked on for the Chinese government, information about the CERN institute that must have spilled over during the treatments she carried out on that agent in Geneva ten years ago, corporate transformations she'd conducted in Europe in recent years—they were all mixing together and creating a mess in her brain.

She turned off the alarm that Guy must have set to prevent her from sleeping the entire day away. And she resolved to quit. From now on, she was only going to sell books. She'd dismantle the lab and use the space to enlarge the bookstore's warehouse. She'd release the mice in Hyde Park, where they could compete for food with the squirrels.

She showered, feeling completely satisfied with the decision she'd just made. Then she got dressed, left the house, and rode the Underground to Westminster. As she left the station, she retrieved a battery from her purse, inserted it into her cell phone and turned on the device. The phone rang five minutes later.

"Rachel speaking, at your service," Carmit said into phone.

"It's been ten years," said a familiar voice on the other end of the line. "We need you."

"Forget it."

Carmit hung up, threw the cell phone into a small trash can and continued walking.

Without realizing she was talking to herself out loud, she repeated two sentences over and over again as she walked:

"A big wave is approaching."

"It'll get here soon."

11:08

Still at the Ganei Yehuda satellite branch, Rotem was sitting at the computer and compiling a Word document entitled

"Study Unit 6: Spheres of interest, with an emphasis on two dimensions—the individual versus society, and legal versus illegal/criminal." She needed a bit of a break from thinking about the material she had read that night.

"Benny, you're the man!" she gratefully exclaimed when the branch's guard showed up with two cups of espresso. "Is the team of reinforcements on the way?"

"They're already here. That's why I'm allowing myself a break. Someone's replaced me at the camera station. Look, I found you a packet of cookies too."

"You're the best!" Rotem was starving. She opened the packet of butter cookies. "Got anything to spread on them?"

"Don't get carried away. Do you know what the fuss is all about? This branch is usually dead."

"Yes. But you know . . ."

"Okay, I figured no one would tell me. Are you going to be here for much longer? If so, I can order you a pizza."

"Sounds like a plan. Looks like I'm going to be stuck here all day. Thanks, Benny."

They sat together for a minute or so in silence, drinking their coffee. The phone in the room rang and Rotem lifted the receiver.

"Rotem?"

Rotem signaled to Benny that she was sorry but that he had to leave the room. He turned to her, bowed slightly, smiled, and left the room with his coffee, closing the door behind him.

"Avner? What's going on? I heard about the explosion in the building. Are you okay?"

"He got her. That piece of shit took Efrat!"

"Are you sure?"

"He left me a page he tore from the notebook on the kitchen table. It's him."

"Take a picture and send it to me."

Rotem waited a few seconds and then opened the image Avner sent to her phone.

"Come here," she said. "There's no point in you hanging around there. He's gone. I don't know where he's taken her but he's had ten years to plan things, Avner. Come here and we'll sit down together and figure out what to do. He's a whole lot of steps ahead of us. We need to sit down and think about this. As much as I hate saying this to you, you've read the notebook, too. You also know that he's not going to kill her now. He likes to take his time. Come back here."

"On my way."

"And one more thing. There is no way on earth that this guy passed the tests. No matter what he writes in this notebook. Someone wanted him in and by 'him' I mean someone with his qualities, with his personality. We need to think. We need to understand why someone ignored his recruiting tests and let him into The Organization. I won't even bother to trace those tests in the Orion HR files. I'm sure that I will find a copy of a perfect test result that is not the original. I want to catch this son of a bitch. I want him sitting hand-cuffed in a chair in front of me while I inject sodium pentothal into his blood and then have a lovely honest conversation about everything that he neglected to write in his notebook."

"Rotem, we have to catch him."

"We will."

Rotem hung up and continued to devour the packet of cookies in front of her as she arranged the thoughts running through her head. First she would need to catch him, but this is clearly just the beginning of something bigger. He's the tail of the dragon and when she pulled that tail the dragon would wake up angry. Someone sought him out and recruited him, tested his ability in Holland and then gave him those three missions from the Bernoulli project ON PURPOSE. Why? She feels like this is a two-thousand-piece puzzle and she's been able to put together just a few sections. She loves puzzles. When she was just three years old, she was playing at her room and then came back to the living room to see what her parents were doing. Toys and kid's games were getting her bored so quickly. Her parents were sitting on the living room floor, building a picture from many small pieces of different shapes. That's when it happened to her for the first time. She looked at the picture on the puzzle box. Three kittens playing in a back yard full of flowers. So many details! It was beautiful. Then she looked at the floor where all the pieces of the puzzle were spread. The small picture on the box was broken to a thousand small pieces on the floor. At first, it was almost painful for her to look at. Her mind worked so hard that her head started aching. So she closed her eyes and then it started. She could see the links. She could see how each part connects to the next. In front of her closed eyes the 2D matrix on the floor rose in the air and she started moving her hands quickly in the air placing in her mind the right pieces in the right place, her mother signaled her father to look at their kid sitting eyes shut rapidly moving her hands in the air in front of her face. They were worried but they did not touch her and waited. It took a minute till she opened her eyes and when she looked down the puzzle below her was solved in her head. Now she just needed to put the pieces in the right place. She went at it connecting the pieces together at an unbelievable speed. Five minutes and the puzzle was done and the pain in her head stopped and turned into bliss. She started laughing "This is fun!" That minute they understood she was way more than just a smart kid that could read the ABC when she was two. For her parents, this puzzle was a wake-up call. That puzzle changed her life course.

Tomorrow she would speak with Grandpa and try to squeeze some more information out of him.

She turned back to the open Word document and continued typing:

> Before starting to analyze spheres of influence and spheres of control we should have a look first at the foundation, which is spheres of interests. If we sum it up in a few simple words before drilling down to equations and graphs, the question we should ask is, "what is the interest of an individual or a group to perform or not to perform a specific action." Note that eventually this is ALWAYS a choice between action and nonaction.

19:45

Amiram woke. His lips were dry. He sat up on the concrete floor and tried to figure out where he was. The room was dark except for a few small lights on the ceiling that cast a yellowish glow on the iron cage in which he was enclosed. A shiver went down his spine. He remembered vividly what he had read in the notebook just the day before, along with the sketches he'd seen in it before passing it on to Avner. It was an almost exact replica of the cage 10483 had built in his basement ten years before. He realized immediately what was going on. He had ten years, Amiram thought to himself. It's not going to end well.

The cage looked to be about 3×3 meters in width, depth and height. Thick iron bars, welded together, ran both vertically and horizontally on all sides. *There's no way to break out of this thing,* Amiram thought, though he did notice something different about the cage he was in. First, this cage contained a metal toilet fixed to the floor. Agent 10483 must have tired of cleaning the original cage all the time. In addition, half of one of the sides of the cage was made instead of a smooth sheet of metal at the bottom of which, about half a meter up off the floor, was a small rectangular opening, and under that a metal bowl was welded to the large sheet of metal.

A buzzing sound and series of clicks from the direction of the sheet of metal startled Amiram. He stood up and backed away from the source of the noise, which was coming from somewhere behind the metal sheet.

Something fell through the opening into the metal bowl, followed by two one-and-a-half liter bottles of mineral water. The buzzing stopped and the basement fell dead quiet again.

Amiram approached the metal bowl, which was now illuminated by a spotlight fixed to the concrete ceiling above the cage. He removed the two bottles of water, opened one and took a few sips. He wasn't afraid to drink the water. Truthfully, he was even hoping that the bottle contained crushed sleeping tablets—it would go faster that way. He examined the hard chunks that had fallen into the bottom of the bowl just moments before, picking one up and sniffing it. He immediately recognized the smell. It was dry dog food. He spotted a pile of familiar looking bags against one of the basement walls. The writing on the bags read: Bonzo Meat—Adults. 20kg.

Amiram looked again at the sheet of metal in front of him and noticed a short piece of neatly engraved text at its center:

> Welcome. You will each
> receive a kilo of food and 1 1/2 liters
> of water every evening at 8. Please
> make sure to eat well and keep the
> cage clean.

A movement on the floor on the far side of the cage caused Amiram to jump. Something he hadn't noticed before in the darkness was moving and groaning on the floor.

"Where am I? What's going on here?"

Amiram recognized the voice and his shoulders slumped in despair.

"Efrat?"

Lunch. 2015. 1 year ago.

The icy wind blew up dust clouds of fine white salt, and the seemingly endless salt flats shimmered in the sun like a huge mirror. Clouds swirled in a harmonious dance above the entire expanse of the dry lake.

Close to the salt flats, on the outskirts of the city of Uyuni in Bolivia, there's an ancient train cemetery.

The trains were used in the past primarily by the mining companies that worked in the area. In the 1940s the mining industry collapsed, and many engines and coaches were abandoned there to rust and crumble.

The train cemetery is quiet and peaceful, aside from lone tourists who show up every now and then to survey the surrealistic scene—the abandoned trains slowly fall apart from the effects of the dry climate and frequent salt storms.

If someone were to wander around there with a Geiger counter, he'd be surprised by the radiation levels beneath the disintegrating train skeletons; levels way higher than humans can safely be exposed to.

Buried under a pile of salt on one of the ancient train cars is a black barrel. Only its tip can be seen peeking out from under the pile of salt that has amassed atop it over time.

Lying in this barrel is death itself. Waiting.

The only person who knew its location died nine years ago.

No one else knows the location of the barrel.

Except for one person.

One person who watched Federico Lopez's lips closely as he dropped to his knees, engulfed in flames, and tried to shout something into a charred phone. The noise of the raging fire made it impossible to hear a thing, but Lopez repeated the same two words with his burning lips. Again. And Again. One more time.

"Bolivia, Uyuni."

"Bolivia, Uyuni."

"Bolivia, Uyuni."

One person who spent the last nine years in the Loewenstein Hospital Rehabilitation Center.

One person who opened his eyes today.

1 YEAR AGO

The room in which I'm imprisoned is painted in a smooth, white acrylic paint. 2 white fluorescent lights cast a white glow around the space. The room's floor isn't white. It's made of some kind of pale green rubbery plastic and my white bed is fixed to it with 8 large bolts, 2 bolts for each of the bed's iron legs. If the bed wasn't bolted to the floor, I'd be able to drag it under the fluorescent lights, reach up, dismantle the steel mesh protecting them, break one and be able to use the sharp glass.

I don't make a sound when I walk barefoot across the rubbery green floor.

It seems like I've always been here.

I have no recollection of what happened before I got here.

The room's heavy metal door is also painted white. At head height there's a small opening in the shape of a square measuring around 20×20 centimeters and fitted with 3 thick bars. Visible through the opening is a corridor that stretches to the edge of my field of vision. The room in which I'm imprisoned is at the end of the corridor.

I sit on the bed, bare feet resting lightly on the cool and rubbery green floor, and listen to the echo of the footsteps clicking in the corridor, amplified by the confined and lengthy expanse. I hear the heavy shoes of one of the caregivers and the light and more rapid steps of a patient. They're approaching the room in which I'm imprisoned. Any moment now a key will turn in the lock of the white door, the tumbler will click twice, the door will open, and they will appear in front of me.

I close my eyes and massage my temples with my fingers in wide circular movements.

The door opens. I open my eyes. There is a caregiver dressed in blue overalls, with a girl in a light blue dress by his side. The caregiver ushers the girl in. He doesn't budge from his position at the open door. He's scared of me. 2 beads of sweat are trickling down his cheeks. The girl enters with quiet steps. The rubbery floor of the room absorbs the clicking of her shoes. She appears to be about 6 years old.

The caregiver steps back and closes and locks the door. He remains outside the room and peers in through the barred opening.

The girl has no hair.

She tucks her elbows into her sides, the palms of her hands are facing up, and she walks toward me. I look into the roots of the light hair she once had before the radiation and I see her damaged DNA.

When the human body is subjected to radiation, the gamma rays that are released bombard the water surrounding the DNA molecules within the cells. DNA is a molecule surrounded by water. It loves water. And the gamma rays strike the water around the DNA, releasing electrons. A water molecule is 2 atoms of hydrogen combined with 1 atom of oxygen; but the moment the gamma rays slam full force into these water molecules and send the electrons flying, the water molecules become free radicals—and they don't like that. They want to revert back to their original configuration and become water again, and that means having to steal electrons. And they steal them from the nearest molecule around—the DNA. They ravage the DNA like a pack of ravenous hounds on a piece of flesh. The DNA of the girl in front of me, with the palms of her hands facing the ceiling, was broken as the result of a rather unsuccessful dose of radiation that missed its target—a grade 4 astrocytoma.

I look at the girl and sense her cell division process.

"*What grade are you in?*" I think.

She thinks back to me: "*Second grade. Our teacher's name is Tamar.*"

She smiles at me.

"*I'll fix you,*" I think.

"*I know,*" she thinks back and walks toward me.

I place the palms of my hands on hers and close my eyes.

I'm standing in the middle of the room. Barefoot on the cool plastic floor. If he sees me here, he'll approach. He won't be scared. I'm not close to him here. He'll think he's safe.

I'm facing the door. My 2 hands are behind my back, my blood pooling into and filling the bowl I form with my interlocked palms. I bit into them just a few minutes ago, on the insides of my wrists, tearing through fine veins with my canines. If I had a small razor blade it would have made things a lot easier.

2 seconds. That's all I need. Even less. The moment he steps in, I'll swivel quickly and empty the contents of my hands into his eyes. 2 seconds of confusion and I'll have the keys. After that, everything will be simpler.

The bowl I've formed with my hands is overflowing now and blood is dripping behind my back into a small puddle on the floor behind me.

I don't have much time left.

I fill my lungs with air and scream.

"Guard!!"

He's lying on the floor. I force his head back until a cracking sound is heard and his body goes limp. I exit my white cell and lock the door behind me, leaving the guard stretched out on the green floor—dotted with dark red spots of blood.

My clothes have no pockets, so I hold the bunch of keys I took in my left hand and walk down to the end of the corridor, dotting the floor with drops of blood from my hands as I go. I have no idea of the time. I think it's night, but I'm not sure. The fluorescent lighting is always the same. I'm looking for the medical clinic so I can bandage my wrists. I'm not supposed to be familiar with the building—but I am. I turn right at the end of the corridor, walk past 2 doors and turn right into the third room that serves as the clinic. I retrieve pads and bandages from a large shallow drawer and a tube of Polydine from a small cabinet on the opposite wall.

There's a large round object covered with a white dusty sheet in the center of the room. After dressing my wrists, I lift the sheet to reveal a spherical container filled with a clear liquid. The glow coming from a white light at the bottom of the tank illuminates the preserved body inside. The body is curled up. I can't see the face—only the hairless skull and the line of the back with its strangely protruding vertebrae. The creature doesn't appear to be human. Swimming slowly around it in the clear liquid are purple jellyfish. I stand in front of the tank and the creature suddenly raises its head and opens 2 black eyes without irises. I stumble backward and my hand strikes a metal tray containing a number of medical instruments that fall noisily to the floor. I quickly cover the glass again and hurry out of the room.

I continue down the corridor. Several children are dreaming in one of the rooms to my left. I shake my head to rid it of their dreams and turn left into another white corridor with 2 red stripes painted along its length. At the end of this corridor there's a heavy metal door with a large metal strip across its width. I know that when I push the metal strip and open the door everything will change. A big wave is approaching; it will be here soon. I start running faster and faster down the corridor. The whispers of the patients and caregivers are burning in my head.

I reach a large door. Above it is a white sign lit with red letters—EMERGENCY EXIT. I push against the big strip of metal across the width of the door and it opens onto the cold and rainy street.

I'm standing on wet asphalt.

I'm free.

I open my eyes.

I have no idea who I am.

I'm lying on a bed that's covered in a white sheet bearing the words Loewenstein Hospital in pale blue.

Next to my bed is a small white cabinet on which I see a binder filled with papers and a pencil resting by its side. I want to record this dream before I forget it. It's important. My hands don't move. They ignore the instructions from my brain to take hold of the binder, tear out a page, pick up the pencil, and record the dream.

I go over the dream in my head several times, memorizing it. I'll put it all down on paper when my hands are working again. And when I get out of here, I'll buy a big notebook and record everything in an orderly fashion. Until then, I'll have to remember it all by heart.

In the meantime, I close my eyes. And open them again. It's the only movement I can make right now.

MORNING. I DON'T KNOW WHEN.

2 white coats are standing over me. One is a doctor and the other a nurse. They are speaking and I hear them. They don't know I'm awake. I don't open my eyes.

"You probably won't have much work with this one."

"Who is he?"

"A John Doe. He's been here for almost nine years. He was admitted on January 12, 2006, Spent a month in ER after a suicide attempt then transferred here. No one knows who he is and no family member has ever come looking for him. He requires the regular treatment—turning, washing and nourishment through a feeding tube. He's breathing independently. His face was an absolute mess when he got here. We have no idea who he is. He's already undergone eight reconstructive plastic surgery procedures."

"Is there brain activity?"

"Yes. Otherwise they'd have switched him off a long time ago. He undergoes an ECG every month and the findings are normal. There's brain activity but he's locked in his own head."

I again try in vain to remember who I am and how I got here. But it's not my first priority. First I need to regain control of my body. I keep practicing whenever the doctors and nurses aren't around. I can already move the fingers on my right hand a little. I've been working on it now for several days.

They're keeping me alive without knowing who I am. It's nice of them but there'll surely be budget cuts soon and they'll stop feeding me. No one will know. I have to get the hell out of here.

The doctor leaves the room and the nurse stays behind to take care of me. When she bends over to adjust my catheter, I peer down her shirt. I can move my eyes now, too. At this rate, I'll be able to stand up in just a few weeks.

NIGHT. 3 WEEKS SINCE WAKING.

Sometimes the doctors and nurses on the ward mention the date and then I know how long it's been since I woke up. Today marks exactly 3 weeks. I can now move both hands and my range of motion is gradually increasing. I work on it mostly at night when the rest of the ward is asleep—and by that I mean the duty nurses. The patients on the ward are asleep all the time. Some wake, but anyone who does soon leaves the ward and moves to the rehabilitation department. I remain here with the living dead. I refer to them as "zombies" in my thoughts.

In the meantime, I recount to myself when I wake up every day everything that has happened since I woke for the first time.

When I wake up tomorrow, I'll work on moving my feet and flexing my stomach muscles.

MORNING. 5 WEEKS SINCE WAKING.

I don't have much time left here. I heard the duty nurse speaking to the shift manager. She tells her that something doesn't add up with my muscles, which should have atrophied like those of someone in a coma but haven't. She thinks I should be examined by a doctor. Both approach my bed and the head nurse uses a hypodermic needle to prick my arms and legs. I remain motionless.

"He's full of life," the head nurse says, and they both laugh.

"Could they be involuntary movements that occur while he's dreaming?" the duty nurse asks.

"Maybe. But any conscious person would jump up screaming when jabbed like that."

They both laugh again.

I remember the conditioning I did with hypodermic needles when I was a kid. It hurts the most when inserting the needle into one's belly button or jabbing the tip against an eardrum. The rest is nonsense. I remain lying there motionless while the head nurse uses a piece of gauze dipped in rubbing alcohol to wipe away the droplets of blood caused by her jabs. The smell reminds me of something. I recall the image of a preserved body suspended in an aquarium filled with yellow liquid. I can't place it but the fact that I've regained 2 memories pleases me. Others will surely follow. I try not to smile until the 2 women return to the nurses' station on the ward.

Left alone again, I work on my legs and flex my stomach muscles for several hours. In the evening I retrieve a pile of pages and a Pilot pen from under my mattress. I've collected the pages over time from the various reports left next to my bed, and a doctor once left the pen on the shelf by my bed. The pages contain a record of all the dreams I've had that I remember, some even from before I woke up. I also write down everything that happens to me every day.

NIGHT. 5 WEEKS AND 4 DAYS SINCE WAKING.

I sit up in bed and put my feet on the floor. The dressing gown wrapped around me is open at the back. It flaps at my sides. I remove it and place it on the bed. Naked, I step quietly, dropping down on all fours as I approach the nurses' station.

I go into the doctors' room and quietly open the doors to the lockers there. In one I find a pair of pants and a shirt and I put them on. Another locker contains a pair of sneakers. I put them on. I'm not wearing socks or underwear—there were none in any of the lockers.

While scouring the room for other useful items, I see a stranger looking back at me from the mirror. It takes me a second to realize it's me. I don't recognize myself. I'm unshaven. When I get out of here I'll find a place to shave. As long as I'm still here, there's no way I'll remember who I was before I came to this place.

I get down on all fours again and go back to get the pages from under my mattress. I fold the pages, slip them into one of the pockets in the pants, and then crawl back the same way on all fours toward the exit.

I leave the 4th-floor ward and take the emergency stairs so as not to meet anyone in the elevator. At the ground floor, the doors open and I walk through the lobby. I wave to the guard and wish him a good night. I don't recognize my own voice. It's a little hoarse.

There's a big stretch of lawn outside. I look back at the large building. Fixed on the roof above the 8th floor is a large steel menorah alongside a large sign reading, LOEWENSTEIN HOSPITAL—FROM THE CLALIT GROUP. I follow the path next to the grass and then onto a small and quiet street with private homes. I may break into one of them later to find something to eat. I'm hungry. I haven't ingested any food by mouth for almost 9 years. I keep walking until I get to Jerusalem Street. I stop before crossing the road. A bus drives by. The trail of wind in its wake causes me to move a little.

Boom

A series of images hit me all at once: I'm lying on the road, my shopping bags scattered across the tarmac next to me. The basement I once built and my creations down there, The Organization, the missions I carried out for them, their betrayal, my home. The table of the Last Supper in my basement. Federico Lopez ablaze, speaking into his burning phone with burning lips.

Bolivia, Uyuni.

Bolivia, Uyuni.

Bolivia, Uyuni.

I know exactly who I am. I know exactly where I need to go right now.

I break into a run.

EARLY MORNING. 5 WEEKS AND 5 DAYS SINCE WAKING.

I'm standing in the basement of the residence I left 9 years ago. My Last Supper creation is still there. Resting on the table among the dishes is the last page from the journal I once kept and then handed over to the law firm. I tore out that last page. I'll use it in a year's time when my plan is put into action. I slip the page into an empty binder, which I then place in my backpack. It's a shame I had to destroy *The Man in the Aquarium*. My apartment above me is empty. A family is living there now but no one is home. It's Friday and they're probably away somewhere. I wipe away the sweat that has accumulated on my forehead and arms on my walk here from Ra'anana. I ran initially, but my body couldn't take the pace after 5 kilometers. I drank water from a faucet at a gas station and walked the rest of the way, getting to know the reduced capabilities of my body. I have a lot of work to do to get back into the shape I was in 9 years ago, when I jumped into the road in front of that bus on Ibn Gvirol Street. Getting into the apartment wasn't a problem. I know that the locking mechanism on one of the windows works only if you slam it shut. They hadn't slammed it shut.

I went straight down into the basement through the trapdoor in the floor of the closet. I passed through the area of the basement where the storage cabinets and bathroom are and went into the control room. The rooms are dusty but I don't clean them right away. Despite the pitch-black darkness of the basement, I remember the way by heart. Once in the control room, I flip the power switches and the basement comes to life with a buzz.

Fresh air starts to flow through a ventilator, the batteries begin charging, lights go on, and there's water pressure in the faucet in the bathroom again. I'm pleased with the way in which I built the basement. 9 years have passed and everything still functions well. I go over to the basin, open the faucet and allow the murky water to flow into the bowl until it clears. I piss and flush the toilet.

I undress and place the clothes I took from Lowenstein Hospital in a trash bag. I stand in front of the mirror and examine my body, going over the scars caused by my encounter with the bus 9 years ago.

I walk over to the basin. The water pouring from the faucet is clear now. I drink and then collect water in my hands and wash down my body with soap and water a number of times. Water collects on the bathroom floor and I use a squeegee to drag it to the drain.

I turn on the backup computer in the control room and hope it connects to the Internet router in the apartment above me. It doesn't. They must have disconnected the cable in the utility cabinet or switched service providers. I need to find out what's happening with my bank account but I'll do so from elsewhere. I guess there've been numerous technological changes during the 9 years in which I slept. I have a lot of catching up to do. I'll acclimatize here in the basement for a few weeks until I'm fully fit and then I'll leave.

I go into the storage cupboards and retrieve some clean clothes that were washed 9 years ago. I put on a shirt and shorts and go over to the cupboard with the dry food and canned goods. Everything is years past its expiry date but I don't want to risk going up into the apartment above. I open cans of tuna, corn and pickles. The tuna is off. I throw it into the trash. The corn and pickles taste fine. I eat a little of each. My stomach is still not accustomed to solid food. Tomorrow I'll begin training to get back into shape. I'm tired now after the run and walk from Ra'anana to Tel Aviv. I spread a blanket on the floor of the cage in the basement. Before I lie down on it, I place a carton of mineral water alongside the cage's open door to prevent it from slamming shut and locking me in while I sleep.

I check again to make sure the carton is blocking the door.

And again.

One last time.

I write in the notebook, place it beside me, and go to sleep.

"Decrease thrust to zero"

- Thrust zero

"Turn automatic choke to off"

- Automatic choke off

"Activate de-icing of wings and engine"

- Wing de-icing and engine activated

"Fire up secondary power unit"

- Secondary power unit fired

"Oxygen in cockpit to 100"

- Oxygen in cockpit at 100

"Activate continuous ignition in engines one, three, and four"

- Activating continuous ignition in engines 1, 3, and 4

No response again, with only engine 2 still running at half its thrust capacity. Without any engines at all, the 747-200 can glide a distance of 15 kilometers for every kilometer of altitude it loses. Engine 2 buys us a little more time but we continue to lose altitude.

"Decrease thrust to zero"

- Thrust zero

"Turn automatic choke to off"

- Automatic choke off

"Activate de-icing of wings and engine"

- Wing de-icing and engine activated

"Fire up secondary power unit"

- Secondary power unit fired

"Oxygen in cockpit to 100"

- Oxygen in cockpit at 100

"Activate continuous ignition in engines one, three, and four"

- Activating continuous ignition in engines 1, 3, and 4
  Nothing happens.

Fear paralyzes you at first. All the drills in the simulators are erased from your mind and replaced by self-pity and deep and despairing sorrow, but your mind quickly begins to recite the drill.

"Decrease thrust to zero"

- Thrust zero

"Turn automatic choke to off"

- Automatic choke off

"Activate de-icing of wings and engine"

- Wing de-icing and engine activated

"Fire up secondary power unit"

- Secondary power unit fired

"Oxygen in cockpit to 100"

- Oxygen in cockpit at 100

"Activate continuous ignition in engines one, three, and four"

- Activating continuous ignition in engines 1, 3, and 4

And nothing again.

From a cruising altitude of 11 kilometers, we've already fallen to 5—and we continue to lose height above the black water of the ocean. A bright moon illuminates the layer of clouds spread out like a woolen blanket beneath us. We'll be among them soon; and when we are, the shaking of the airplane's fuselage will illustrate to all the passengers that something is wrong. Most are fast asleep right now.

"Decrease thrust to zero"

- Thrust zero

"Turn automatic choke to off"

- Automatic choke off

"Activate de-icing of wings and engine"

- Wing de-icing and engine activated

"Fire up secondary power unit"

- Secondary power unit fired

"Oxygen in cockpit to 100"

- Oxygen in cockpit at 100

"Activate continuous ignition in engines one, three, and four"

- Activating continuous ignition in engines 1, 3, and 4

  Nothing.

At our current rate of descent, we have 22 minutes left before we crash into the ocean. Did I remember to turn off the electrical system in the basement? I need to get everything done. It can't all end now before I manage to put my plan into action. Where did I put the notebook? I have to write down everything that is happening here.

"Decrease thrust to zero"

- Thrust zero

"Turn automatic choke to off"

- Automatic choke off

"Activate de-icing of wings and engine"

- Wing de-icing and engine activated

"Fire up secondary power unit"

- Secondary power unit fired

"Oxygen in cockpit to 100"

- Oxygen in cockpit at 100

"Activate continuous ignition in engines one, three, and four"

- Activating continuous ignition in engines 1, 3, and 4

  Engines 1, 3, and 4 fire up one after the other.

  The Boeing accelerates gently and begins to gain altitude again.

"Dear passengers, this is your captain speaking. We'll be touching down in Tel Aviv in about two hours. The cabin crew will serve you breakfast shortly and we will then begin the preparations for landing. The weather at our destination is partly cloudy with a temperature of eighteen degrees Celsius. We'll be landing at five-thirty in the morning Israel time. We hope you enjoyed the flight and we look forward to seeing you again in the near future."

I wake up.

It's still night.

I record in my journal that this is my first dream outside Lowenstein Hospital. There's no refrigerator in the basement so there's no need to check any bottles of water. I allow the water from the faucet to run for a few minutes to discount the possibility that someone may have mixed something into the building's water system, and then drink from the faucet and go back to sleep.

MORNING. 6 WEEKS AND 1 DAY SINCE WAKING.

The family living above me has sent their children to school and left for work. It annoys me to have to sneak into the apartment each time they are there so I consider killing them when they return in the afternoon, keeping them inside the bathtub, wrapping them in cling film to prevent them from smelling, and taking their place in my old apartment, but decide it would only arouse suspicion if they don't show up to wherever they need to be and that it's best to leave them alone up there. They offer good cover. I recall the words, "human shields," from the army. In general, I can remember everything now—even things that happened when I was a kid.

In a drawer in the basement's storage room I have €60,000 in cash left over from my last trip, along with 30,000 shekels. It'll be enough for me to rent a house with a basement and begin purchasing everything I need for my plan. I only have a little less than a year left before the notebook I deposited with the law firm comes to light. I decided not to go to the firm and retrieve it but to stick instead to my original timetable. It doesn't leave me much time and I'll settle for renting a secluded house with a basement that I'll be able to alter at will the moment I move in. I have to get out of here as quickly as possible. I have a lot of work to do. I also need to buy a car.

I undress and train for 3 hours—muscle-building work and cardiovascular exercise, and then I eat a little more canned food.

I look through the pile of passports next to the wad of euros in the drawer. I no longer look like the old photograph of me they all display. I'll have to change the picture in the passports. They'll be fine for entering less sophisticated countries but not for traveling to Europe or the United States. That's okay, because I need to get to Bolivia. I need to check out this Uyuni thing. I'll do so as soon as I find a computer with an Internet connection and check what's happening with my bank account. I think it's a place. If what I read over and over again in the Bernoulli Project files before jumping in front of that bus 9 years ago is true, there's an interesting surprise waiting there for me in a barrel. "Remember to buy a Geiger counter," I jot down on a Post-it note that I stick to the wall alongside the others:

"Remember to change the photographs on all documents"

"Remember to check your investment portfolio"

"Obtain a yacht skipper's license"

"Retrieve Avner's address from the file of names you took off The Organization's ERP server and take a cab there to check out the area"

"Remember to be outside Amiram's house when he receives the package"

"Learn Russian"

"Re-read all the Bernoulli reports"

"It's important to eat liver and legumes. Eggs, too."

"Run a check on Kelly Grasso from Cymedix"

9 years ago, using money left over from the missions I carried out, I invested 30,000 Swiss francs, 102,000 Canadian dollars, and 30,000 Argentine pesos in Apple stock. I'm sure they've turned a good profit from 2006 until now. I noticed while lying in bed at the Loewenstein Hospital that almost every doctor there walked around with an Apple device.

It's going to take a great deal of money to implement my plan. I'm going to bring down The Organization.

I'll detonate the bomb where it'll hurt them most. Where it'll bring The Organization to its knees. I'll tie it to them.

It won't be in Israel.

ACKNOWLEDGMENTS

Parts of this story are inspired by a scientific study held by Klemens F. Störtkuhl and André Fiala titled "The Smell of Blue Light."

I would like to thank both scientists for allowing me to quote from their study.

ABOUT THE AUTHOR

Nir Hezroni was born in Jerusalem. After studying physics in high school and completing several years of military service in intelligence, Hezroni retired to study economics and business management. He then proceeded to build a career in high tech. *Three Envelopes* is his first novel. He lives with his family near Tel Aviv.

ABOUT THE TRANSLATOR

Steven Cohen attended the Hebrew University in Jerusalem. He is a freelance writer, copyeditor, editor and translator. He lives in Ra'anana, Israel.

The story continues in

LAST
INSTRUCTIONS

"Why didn't he close his eyes?"

Dr. Weinberg removed fragments of glass from the eyeball of the attempted suicide victim using a pair of tweezers, placing each piece in a small aluminum basin. The blood that clung to the pieces of glass created circular patterns as it came in contact with the sterile substance in the metal bowl. This wasn't the first time that Dr. Weinberg had encountered a road accident in which the victim's glasses had shattered into his eyes, but usually the shards penetrated the eyelids first, which closed instinctively to protect the eyeball. This victim's eyes had remained wide open.

"I've never seen anything like it." The nurse standing beside him handed him an even smaller pair of tweezers. Several doctors were working simultaneously in the operating room on this nameless suicide-attempt. He wasn't carrying any documents, and his face had been smashed beyond recognition. The plastic surgeon next to them was busy trying to piece together bits of his shattered cheekbones.

"How did he manage to do this to himself again?"

"Jumped in front of a bus on Ibn Gvirol Street. Lucky for him an ambulance was in the area. Otherwise he'd be downstairs on the slab by now."

"I'm not sure if you can call it luck. He may have been better off dead," said the orthopedic surgeon on the other side of the table. He was cleaning denim thread from two open fractures in the victim's thighs.

"We still have a good few more hours of work on him. We need to bring in a psychologist for when he wakes up. Make a note of that. I don't want him jumping again the moment he wakes up."

"The last thing he's going to be able to do when he wakes up is jump."

"If he wakes up."

Dr. Weinberg made a note in the records and then went back to removing fragments of glass. "We'll keep him under for at least two weeks; there's no point in waking him yet." He started humming the words to the song "Ten Little Fingers" from his young son's favorite CD.

"Are you familiar with the definition of anxiety?" he asked the nurse beside him.

December 5, 2016

An incessant drizzle had been falling on London since early in the morning. The city's residents went about their business. It was a Monday and Oxford Street was packed with umbrella-carrying pedestrians. One of them held a white plastic box with a black handle, crossed the busy road coming from the Marble Arch tube station and turned toward the entrance to Hyde Park. She wore a yellow hoodie and black sneakers, walked at a brisk pace, and glanced occasionally to the side. The park was quiet. Squirrels scampered among the trees, and a small group of giggling girls strolled leisurely along an adjacent walkway. She stopped beside one of the trees and placed the box on the ground and looked around. The park was quiet and peaceful. The weather had left most of the tourists on the streets of London themselves, with the option of fleeing from one store to the next rather than getting soaked in the city's parks. She lifted the lid off the box and tipped the container over. Dozens of white mice poured out onto the ground.

They froze momentarily in a white pile on the green grass, before scurrying off in all directions, some even hopping with delight. They were free.

Carmit closed the box and walked over to a green garbage can. She placed the box on the ground and left it there.

She then continued walking, breathing in the scent of freshly cut grass. Two people on horseback trotted past and she waved to them. If not for the dreams that plagued her nights, she was almost happy with her husband Guy and their children. She'd thought the dreams would disappear once she stopped doing transformations, but they hadn't.

She'd even tried exhausting herself by going for a run every night before bed.

They continued.

Carmit made her way back to the Underground station. She decided to take the Central Line to Notting Hill Gate and then switch to the Circle line to Gloucester Road. The Piccadilly line would take her from there to Hammersmith. She'd arranged to meet Elliot at the Starbucks there. Besides her clients, he's the only other person who's aware of her work outside the bookstore. Actually, the bookstore is her only job now. She'd thought that dismantling the laboratory in the back of her store and releasing the mice in Hyde Park, would make her free, just like the mice; but she only felt emptiness. She'd speak to Elliott about her recurring dream.

Maybe he could help.

A hawk hovered above the trees in the park, following the movement of the mice in the grass below.

```
DATE:              12/05/2016 [08:31]
CLASSIFICATION:    BLACK
REFERENCE NO.:     623846635
TO:                INNER CIRCLE
FROM:              OPERATIONS DEPARTMENT HEAD
DISTRIBUTION:      RECRUITMENT DEPARTMENT HEAD
                   PERSONALITY AND PSYCHOPATHOLOGY RESEARCH
                   DEPARTMENT HEAD
SYSTEM:            ORION / BASE: OTR / EXPIRY DATE: 12/13/2016


RE.: REAPPEARANCE OF AGENT 10483
/
I WISH TO SUM UP THE EVENTS OF THE PAST 24 HOURS DURING
WHICH WE HAVE LEARNED THAT AGENT 10483, BELIEVED DEAD,
APPEARS IN FACT TO BE ALIVE AND OPERATING AGAINST US ON
ISRAELI SOIL.
```

BACKGROUND:

IN 2006, IN LIGHT OF INFORMATION RECEIVED FROM MILITARY
INTELLIGENCE'S UNIT 8200, WE LEARNED OF EFFORTS BY AN
UNKNOWN PARTY, POSSIBLY IRAN, TO GET ITS HANDS ON A
RUSSIAN NUCLEAR DEVICE FROM AMONG THE ARSENAL OF 1,400
NUCLEAR WARHEADS RETURNED TO RUSSIA BY KAZAKHSTAN
DURING THE LATTER'S VOLUNTARY NUCLEAR DISARMAMENT
PROGRAM FROM 1991–1995. (IN ALL LIKELIHOOD, THE DEVICE IN
QUESTION IS A 42-KILOTON RDS-3 MODEL, A 62-KILOTON
RDS-3I MODEL, OR A MORE MODERN WARHEAD FROM THE EARLY
1960S)
WE KNOW THAT THE INDIVIDUAL WHO SERVED AS THE GO-BETWEEN
FOR THE TRANSACTION WAS ONE OF 12 SCIENTISTS WHO
PARTICIPATED IN A CLOSED CONFERENCE IN SWITZERLAND DURING
WHICH THE DEAL WAS FINALIZED BY MEANS OF AN ENCRYPTED
TELEPHONE MESSAGE. SINCE WE WERE UNAWARE OF THE IDENTITY
OF THE DEALMAKER FROM AMONG THE GROUP, WE DECIDED TO
ELIMINATE ALL 12 OF THEM (PROJECT CODENAMED "BERNOULLI").
ONE OF THE AGENTS (10483) ASSIGNED TO THE MISSION
RECEIVED (APPARENTLY ERRONEOUSLY) THREE TARGETS OUT OF
THE 12, INSTEAD OF JUST ONE. THE COLLATERAL DAMAGE HE
CAUSED IN CARRYING OUT THE THREE ASSASSINATIONS WAS
EXTENSIVE:

1. 40 INCIDENTAL FATALITIES IN THE FRAMEWORK OF THE
ASSASSINATION OF YASMIN LI-ANG IN GENEVA (YASMIN
LI-ANG'S TWO DAUGHTERS, PLUS 38 RESIDENTS OF A BUILDING
AT 21 RUE DE DELICES THAT COLLAPSED AFTER 10483 SEALED
ONE OF THE APARTMENTS ON THE TOP FLOOR AND FILLED IT
WITH WATER, THE RESULTING PRESSURE BROUGHT DOWN THE
ENTIRE STRUCTURE)

2. 128 INCIDENTAL FATALITIES IN BARILOCHE IN THE
FRAMEWORK OF THE ASSASSINATION OF FEDERICO LOPEZ IN A
PARK NEAR THE INSTITUTO BALSEIRO (FEDERICO LOPEZ'S
THREE BODYGUARDS, PLUS 125 INNOCENT BYSTANDERS IN THE
PARK, WHICH 10483 SET ABLAZE USING A GAS TANKER THAT HE
HOOKED UP TO THE PARK'S SPRINKLER SYSTEM)
3. [**NEW INFORMATION**] SOME 11,000 INCIDENTAL FATALITIES
IN MONTREAL IN THE FRAMEWORK OF THE ASSASSINATION OF
BERNARD STRAUSS (APPROXIMATELY 11,000 PEOPLE—INCLUDING
53 ISRAELI CITIZENS, THREE OF WHOM WERE OUR AGENTS—DIED
IN A STRING OF ROAD ACCIDENTS CAUSED BY THOUSANDS OF
DRIVERS SIMULTANEOUSLY FALLING ASLEEP AT THE WHEEL OF
THEIR VEHICLES AFTER HEARING A HYPNOSIS-INDUCING AUDIO
TRACK BROADCAST OVER A LOCAL RADIO STATION, CBC RADIO
ONE)

FOLLOWING THE ASSASSINATION OF BERNARD STRAUSS IN
MONTREAL, 10483 RETURNED TO ISRAEL. MEMBERS OF A
SURVEILLANCE TEAM ASSIGNED TO HIM FROM THE MOMENT HE
LANDED SUBSEQUENTLY FOUND WHAT THEY THOUGHT TO BE HIS BODY
IN HIS COMPLETELY TORCHED APARTMENT. DENTAL RECORDS SERVED
TO IDENTIFY THE BODY AT THE TIME AND A SUICIDE NOTE WAS
FOUND IN THE REFRIGERATOR.
IN LIGHT OF THE ABOVE, THE CASE WAS CLOSED. THE 12 BERNOULLI
SCIENTISTS WERE ELIMINATED, 10483 PRESUMED DEAD, AND THE
IRANIAN CELLS THAT WERE TRYING TO FIND THE WARHEAD LOST
TRACK OF ITS LOCATION.

NEW INFORMATION:
TWO DAYS AGO (12/03/2016), AMIRAM HADDAD, 10483'S FORMER
HANDLER, RECEIVED A PACKAGE THAT 10483 HAD DEPOSITED WITH

A LAW FIRM WITH INSTRUCTIONS FOR IT TO BE SENT OUT ON THAT
SPECIFIC DATE. AFTER READING THE NOTEBOOK HE RECEIVED,
AMIRAM WENT TO THE HOME OF AVNER MOYAL, THE HEAD OF THE
RECRUITMENT DEPARTMENT, TO DISCUSS THE IMPLICATIONS OF
THE MATERIAL IT CONTAINED. THE PACKAGE INCLUDED A LARGE
LINED NOTEBOOK ALONG WITH NUMEROUS ADDITIONAL DOCUMENTS—
SKETCHES, CALCULATIONS, MATERIAL FROM THE ORGANIZATION AND
MORE. FROM A REVIEW OF THE CONTENTS OF THE NOTEBOOK, THE
MAIN FINDINGS ARE AS FOLLOWS:

1. 10483 IS ALIVE. HE STAGED HIS OWN DEATH 10 YEARS AGO
USING A BODY HE'D BEEN KEEPING IN HIS BASEMENT ON WHICH
HE'D CARRIED OUT THE APPROPRIATE DENTAL WORK TO MATCH
HIS OWN (FILLINGS, EXTRACTIONS, ETC.) WHEN HE TORCHED
THE APARTMENT, HE KNEW THAT WE WOULD IDENTIFY THE
REMAINS BASED ON DENTAL RECORDS BECAUSE HIS DNA IS NOT
IN THE SYSTEM (HE MUST HAVE DELETED THIS DATA FROM THE
ORGANIZATION'S SYSTEM AT SOME POINT.)
2. 10483 IS PERSONALLY RESPONSIBLE FOR KILLING THREE
OF OUR AGENTS WHO WERE SENT TO LOCATE HIM DURING THE
COURSE OF HIS MISSIONS. ONE IN THE NETHERLANDS (AGENT
6844—PUSHED ONTO THE TRACKS IN FRONT OF A METRO
TRAIN) AND TWO IN TEL AVIV (AGENTS 6452 AND 7274)
IN THE BASEMENT OF HIS APARTMENT.
3. THE HYPNOSIS INCIDENT IN MONTREAL—BELIEVED UNTIL
NOW TO BE A NONNATIONALISTIC ATTACK CARRIED OUT BY
A PSYCHOPATH—WAS ORGANIZED BY 10483. THE NOTEBOOK
CONTAINS MATERIAL THAT INCRIMINATES BOTH HIM
AND US.
4. 10483 ACQUIRED ADMINISTRATOR ACCESS TO ORION. HE
KNOWS ABOUT THE BERNOULLI PROJECT AND HIS ROLE IN THE

ASSASSINATIONS. HE SUFFERS FROM PARANOIA AND BELIEVES
THAT THE ORGANIZATION BETRAYED HIM. HE ALSO MANAGED
TO GET ACCEPTED TO THE ORGANIZATION DESPITE THE
VARIOUS PSYCHOLOGICAL DISORDERS HE SUFFERS FROM BY
HACKING INTO OUR SYSTEMS.
5. 10483 HAS EMBARKED ON A REVENGE MISSION AGAINST THE
ORGANIZATION THAT BEGAN TWO NIGHTS AGO.

EVENTS OF THE PAST 24 HOURS:
AVNER SPENT THE NIGHT READING THROUGH THE NOTEBOOK, THEN
BROUGHT GRANDPA UP TO SPEED. GRANDPA CALLED IN ROTEM
ROLNIK, HEAD OF THE PERSONALITY AND PSYCHOPATHOLOGY
RESEARCH DEPARTMENT, WHO ALSO REVIEWED THE MATERIAL.
AT 09:00 THIS MORNING, A TEAM OF OUR AGENTS—ACCOMPANIED BY
POLICE, FIREFIGHTERS AND A SWAT TEAM—WAS SENT TO THE
BASEMENT TO FIND OUT WHAT WAS THERE AND TO RETRIEVE THE
REMAINS OF THE TWO AGENTS THAT HAD BEEN THERE FOR
10 YEARS. BECAUSE 10483'S NOTEBOOK DESCRIBES HOW THE
BASEMENT WAS BOOBY-TRAPPED, ALL THE BUILDING'S
RESIDENTS WERE EVACUATED, AND THE STREET WAS CLOSED TO
TRAFFIC.
FOLLOWING A BRIEFING THAT INCLUDED WARNINGS NOT TO TOUCH
ANY LIGHT SWITCHES, THE TEAMS ENTERED THE LOCATION. AT
09:40 THE BASEMENT AND THE BUILDING ABOVE IT WAS BLOWN UP.
EVERYONE IN THE BASEMENT—THE SECURITY AND RESCUE TEAMS AND
OUR AGENTS—WAS KILLED IN THE BLAST, AND THE BUILDING
COLLAPSED. THE AREA HAS BEEN CORDONED OFF AND TEAMS FROM
THE ORGANIZATION, THE FIRE DEPARTMENT, POLICE AND THE HOME
FRONT COMMAND, ARE CURRENTLY SIFTING THROUGH THE RUBBLE IN
AN EFFORT TO RETRIEVE THE BODIES AND ANY OTHER MATERIAL
THAT 10483 MAY HAVE LEFT IN THE BASEMENT THAT COULD ASSIST
IN HIS CAPTURE.

AT 10:05 THIS MORNING A MESSENGER DELIVERED A PACKAGE TO EFRAT MOYAL, AVNER'S WIFE. HER DESCRIPTION OF THE MESSENGER HAS LED US TO SUSPECT THAT IT MAY HAVE BEEN 10483 HIMSELF. SHE WAS INSTRUCTED NOT TO OPEN THE PACKAGE AND TO GO IMMEDIATELY TO THEIR NEIGHBORS' HOUSE. AVNER RETURNED HOME AT 10:39. RESTING ON THE KITCHEN TABLE WAS A PAGE THAT HAD BEEN TORN OUT OF 10483'S NOTEBOOK. ON THE PAGE, 10483 OUTLINES HOW HE "DEALT WITH" THE TEETH OF THE BODY LEFT IN HIS TORCHED APARTMENT SOME 10 YEARS AGO; HE ALSO DESCRIBES HOW HE SPOTTED THE SURVEILLANCE TEAM OUTSIDE THE APARTMENT AND ASSUMED (MISTAKENLY) THEY WERE A CELL SENT BY THE ORGANIZATION TO ASSASSINATE HIM, HOW HE SET FIRE TO THE APARTMENT AND HOW HE THEN WENT TO THE ORGANIZATION'S NEAREST BRANCH WHERE HE RETRIEVED INFORMATION ABOUT THE BERNOULLI PROJECT AND THE MEMBERS OF THE INNER CIRCLE.

THE PAGE ALSO NOTES THAT HE PLANS TO TAKE ACTION AGAINST EVERYONE INVOLVED IN HIS RECRUITMENT AND HANDLING, AND AGAINST THE ORGANIZATION'S MANAGEMENT—THE INNER CIRCLE. PRESUMABLY, THE BLOWING UP OF HIS BASEMENT AND EFRAT'S DISAPPEARANCE WERE THE INITIAL STAGES OF HIS PLAN. ATTEMPTS IN THE PAST FEW HOURS TO CONTACT AMIRAM HAVE COME TO NAUGHT. IT SEEMS LIKE 10483 HAS GOTTEN HIS HANDS ON HIM, TOO.

WE CLEARLY MADE A MAJOR MISTAKE AND RECRUITED A PSYCHOPATH WHO SUFFERS FROM AN ENTIRE RANGE OF MENTAL DISORDERS. HE MANAGED TO PREPARE HIMSELF VERY WELL FOR ALL OUR TESTS (INCLUDING A POLYGRAPH) AND WAS ACCEPTED INTO THE ORGANIZATION. THEREFORE, IN ADDITION TO THE IMMEDIATE ACTIONS WE NEED TO TAKE IN ORDER TO APPREHEND 10483 AND LOCATE EFRAT AND AMIRAM, THERE ARE ALSO THINGS WE NEED TO PUT IN PLACE TO SERVE US IN THE LONG TERM:

9

• A REVIEW AND ADJUSTMENT OF OUR RECRUITMENT SYSTEM IN
ORDER TO PREVENT THE HIRING OF INELIGIBLE CANDIDATES IN
THE FUTURE (LESS DEPENDENCE ON FORMAL TESTS AND MORE
WEIGHT ON PERSONAL INTERVIEWS, GROUP BEHAVIOR UNDER
PRESSURE, AND INTERVIEWS WITH FRIENDS, FAMILY MEMBERS,
TEACHERS AND NEIGHBORS.)
• CLOSER COLLABORATION WITH THE ARMY WHEN IT COMES TO
ITS SCREENING PROCESS FOR CANDIDATES FOR SENSITIVE
POSITIONS.
• MAINTAINING CONTACT WITH THE DISTRICT HEALTH OFFICES IN
ORDER TO GAIN ACCESS TO INFORMATION ON PSYCHOLOGICAL
PROFILES / PSYCHIATRIC TREATMENTS CONCERNING FUTURE
RECRUITS, ALONG WITH A REVIEW OF OUR ENTIRE NETWORK OF
EXISTING AGENTS+RETIREES. (DOCTOR—PATIENT CONFIDENTIALITY
DOES NOT APPLY IN THIS REGARD.)
• THE MECHANISMS IN PLACE TO RESTRICT ACCESS TO THE
ORGANIZATION'S SYSTEMS ARE SORELY LACKING—WE NEED TO
IMPLEMENT INTERNAL ENCRYPTION MECHANISMS AND AUDIT
SYSTEMS THAT CAN IDENTIFY SYSTEM ADMINISTRATOR ACCESS.
IMPLEMENTATION MUST BE CARRIED OUT EXTERNALLY BY A
DATA SECURITY GROUP, WITHOUT THE INVOLVEMENT OF OUR
INFORMATION SYSTEMS UNIT.

IN CONSULTATION WITH ROTEM AND AVNER, WE MUST PUT TOGETHER
A TEAM CHARGED WITH APPREHENDING 10483. I REQUEST YOUR
AUTHORIZATION TO APPROACH THE SHIN BET FOR ASSISTANCE TO
THIS END.
SINCERELY,
MOTTI KEIDAR
OPERATIONS DIVISION CHIEF

/

Avner reviewed the document circulated via the Orion system. It looked a lot better than the version he'd written during the night.

After spending part of the morning looking for Efrat, Rotem asked him to return to the Ganei Yehuda Base, where she'd spent the night. Unaware of the device that had been attached to the underside of his car during the night, he drove back to Ganei Yehuda and contacted his connection at the police on the way, asking him to arrange for a forensics team to examine his home in an effort to find something that 10483 may have left behind and could assist in his capture. The man asked Avner if he wanted to blow up another one of his teams because the last one he'd requested was still buried under a building that had been blown to bits. Avner asked him what he would do if a psychopathic killer had abducted his wife.

Even though Avner knew his body needed sleep, his state of mind wouldn't allow it. His head was filled with thoughts of Efrat in the clutches of that psychopath. Where could he have taken her? What had he done to her? He couldn't bear the thought of Efrat in his clutches. The shock she must have felt when he abducted her.

He assumed Grandpa would try to take him off the case. But he wasn't going to let that happen. He had to be there when they close in on him. He had to make sure that they go in carefully so as not to harm her.

Avner listened to the sounds at the satellite base—Rotem speaking to the guard, the rattle of an air-conditioner compressor, soft and muffled music coming from the house upstairs that served as a cover for the activities taking place below, someone flushing a toilet. His weariness was fading. He would find her and rescue her even if it's the last thing he does.

```
DATE:              12/05/2016 [09:14]
CLASSIFICATION:    BLACK
REFERENCE NO.:     623846649
TO:                SENIOR DIRECTOR — 9
FROM:              PERSONALITY AND PSYCHOPATHOLOGY
                   RESEARCH DEPARTMENT HEAD
DISTRIBUTION:
SYSTEM:            ORION / BASE: OTR / EXPIRY DATE: 12/06/2016
```

RE.: REAPPEARANCE OF AGENT 10483

/

HI GRANDPA!

FURTHER TO MOTTI KEIDAR'S REPORT FROM EARLIER TODAY: THERE
IS NO WAY THAT AGENT 10483 WAS ABLE TO PASS THE ORGAN-
IZATION'S TESTS. IT'S SIMPLY IMPOSSIBLE. REGARDLESS OF HOW
WELL HE MAY HAVE PREPARED HIMSELF, AFTER READING THE
NOTEBOOK, I AM ABSOLUTELY CERTAIN THAT SUCH AN INDIVIDUAL
WOULD NEVER HAVE MADE IT THROUGH A COMBINATION OF
MINNESOTA, MYERS-BRIGGS, DSM-5, AND VARIOUS OTHER SUCH
DELICACIES, AND THEN A POLYGRAPH FOR DESSERT.
SOMEONE WANTED TO HIM IN THE ORGANIZATION.
THAT SAME SOMEONE WAS ALSO THE ONE WHO MADE SURE HE WAS
GIVEN THREE TARGETS AS PART OF THE BERNOULLI PROJECT, AND
NOT JUST ONE LIKE THE OTHER ASSASSINS.
HIS THREE TARGETS WERE ALL NUCLEAR SCIENTISTS. THAT, TOO,
IS NO COINCIDENCE.
WE NEED TO TALK.

Rotem sent the mail to Grandpa, locked the computer screen and
went to find the satellite base's security guard, who was reading a
thick book.

"Is there a shower here? I stink like a skunk," she said.

"No, we're all about the bare necessities here," the guard responded. "And the aboveground areas of the building are off limits."

"Okay then, I'm off to the home base. When you see Avner, send him there, too. I'll shower there and take a nap in my office. Tell him to wake me when he arrives. I need to get hold of Grandpa in the morning."

```
DATE:              12/06/2016 [11:30]
CLASSIFICATION:    BLACK
REFERENCE NO.:     623846762
TO:                INNER CIRCLE
FROM:              SENIOR DIRECTOR - 9
DISTRIBUTION:
SYSTEM:            ORION / BASE: OTR / EXPIRY DATE: 12/07/2016


RE.: REAPPEARANCE OF AGENT 10483
/
GOOD MORNING,
FURTHER TO OUR MEETING YESTERDAY, AND IN THE WAKE OF
EFFORTS BY THE HEAD OF THE PERSONALITY AND PSYCHOPATHOLOGY
RESEARCH DEPARTMENT TO GET TO THE BOTTOM OF OUR REASONS
FOR USING 10483, I INTEND TO FILL HER IN TO A CERTAIN
EXTENT IN ORDER TO ALLOW HER TO BEGIN SEARCHING FOR HIM.
FURTHERMORE, AN ADDITIONAL TEAM FROM THE OPERATIONS
DIVISION HAS ALSO BEEN ASSIGNED TO HUNT FOR 10483. ITS
MEMBERS ARE WORKING WITH THE SEARCH AND RESCUE PERSONNEL
AT THE SCENE OF THE EXPLOSION IN TEL AVIV, THEY'RE LOOKING
FOR CLUES FROM THE VIDEO FOOTAGE CAPTURED BY THE TEAM THAT
WAS IN THE BASEMENT AT THE TIME OF THE BLAST. THE CAMERAS
WERE DESTROYED BUT A DATA FORENSICS TEAM IS TRYING TO
RECONSTRUCT THE MATERIAL FROM THE MEMORY CARDS.
```

APPREHENDING 10483 IS A MATTER OF THE UTMOST URGENCY. WE
NEED TO ASSUME THE WORST—THAT HE IS IN POSSESSION OF THE
NUCLEAR DEVICE THAT DISAPPEARED DURING THE COURSE OF HIS
ACTIVITIES SOME 10 YEARS AGO, AND THAT HE INTENDS TO USE
IT. ALL NECESSARY RESOURCES FOR THE PURPOSE OF LOCATING AND
CAPTURING HIM WILL BE AT OUR DISPOSAL. IN DEALINGS WITH
OUTSIDE ENTITIES (THE SHIN BET, IDF, PRIME MINISTER'S
OFFICE,) OUR COVER STORY IS THAT THERE'S A TERRORIST /
ISLAMIC STATE CELL. PLEASE INFORM YOUR RESPECTIVE TEAMS.
I BELIEVE THAT THE HEAD OF THE PERSONALITY AND
PSYCHOPATHOLOGY RESEARCH DEPARTMENT CAN OFFER ADDITIONAL
INSIGHTS THAT MAY HELP US TO LOCATE 10483. I PLAN TO TELL
HER IN GENERAL TERMS ABOUT THE TRANSFORMATIONS AND THE
TRANSFORMATION CONTENT (THE FINAL ONE ONLY) THAT 10483
UNDERWENT, INCLUDING THE IMPRINTED EXPIRY DATE, SO AS TO
GIVE HER A LEAD TO WORK ON. I ALSO INTEND TO SHARE THIS
INFORMATION WITH THE HEAD OF THE TEAM THAT IS CURRENTLY AT
THE BLAST SITE.
I WILL ALSO INFORM THE AFOREMENTIONED ABOUT THE SECONDARY
OBJECTIVE (ONLY) OF THE BERNOULLI PROJECT—THE ELIMINATION OF
THE SCIENTISTS. THE PRIMARY OBJECTIVE OF THE BERNOULLI
PROJECT WILL OF COURSE REMAIN CONFIDENTIAL.
YOU SHOULD BE AWARE, TOO, THAT THE SUBCONTRACTOR WHO
CARRIED OUT THE TRANSFORMATIONS ON 10483 DURING THE COURSE
OF HIS BERNOULLI PROJECT ACTIVITIES HAS SEVERED TIES WITH
US AND WE HAVE NO WAY OF LOCATING HER.
I WILL ARRANGE A FOLLOW—UP DISCUSSION ON THE SUBJECT IN
KEEPING WITH THE DEVELOPMENTS IN THE INVESTIGATION.
REGARDS,
GRANDPA

The parched orange earth appears to stretch on forever in every direction. Cracks cut through the ground and a fine orange dust rises up with my every step. Fossilized crustaceans are scattered about, red and pinkish hollowed-out crab legs and black and empty sea urchin shells with long spines.

I tread carefully to avoid them.

I don't know which way I'm supposed to go, so I head in the direction of the sun that's casting a bright orange light over everything. A smaller white sun is rising on my right and my shadow is split into 2—1 behind me and 1 to my left. Once every 16 days the 2 suns are aligned and then I have just a single shadow for a few minutes.

I retrieve a somewhat battered metal water flask from my backpack, unscrew the top and take a sip of warm water that tastes like sand. I screw the top back on, return the flask to my backpack, and continue walking.

In the distance, I see a black dot. I walk toward it. My steps kick up orange clouds of dust. That's where I need to go.

As I move closer, I can see that the black dot is a large black rock, like the dome of a mosque buried in the ground with only the very top protruding from the earth. The portion of the rock protruding from the earth looks about 3 meters in diameter and it's dotted with small holes the size of a coin on all sides. Scattered around the rock are the remains of those who got here before me. I refrain from stepping into the kill radius and slowly circle what's left of those who were here before me at a safe distance. Some of them are nothing more than whitened skeletons, while some are still partially covered with bits of clothing, their dried-out skin still stretched over their bones. It's extremely dry. It never rains here. They've probably been here for a very long time. I sense something I haven't felt in years.

Fear.